PRIME

A NOVEL OF POST-APOCALYPTIC HOPE

BOB MAYER

LET US NOW PRAISE PRIME NUMBERS

In the beginning where Chaos
Ends and zero resolves,
With our fathers who begat us:
The power, the peculiar glory of prime numbers
Is that nothing begat them,
No ancestors, no factors,
Helen Spalding

BEGINNING OF THE 21ST CENTURY, BEFORE THE CHAOS

"'S urely some revelation is hand; Surely the Second Coming is at hand'."

"You were never religious," Ryker paused his typing and looked over his shoulder. "Or into poetry."

"Of course you would recognize it," Michael said as he walked over from the freight elevator. He had a polished wooden box in one hand and a bag with a bottle inside in the other. He grabbed a chair next to his brother and sat down, took at look at the dozen large displays in front of the desk, covered in code, and shook his head. "I don't know how you can work multiple screens. I have to focus on one at a time."

"Remember Bobby Fischer?" Ryker asked. They were inside a large but dreary place, surrounded by pitted concrete walls, floor and ceiling. It was a large space though, with twenty feet of reinforced concrete above their heads. It was the ammunition magazine for the abandoned turn-of-the-20th-century coastal fort above. Built just before airplanes made such structures obsolete.

"Chess player?"

"That's the one. A Grandmaster and World Chess Champion. At one time, as a publicity stunt, he played fifty opponents simultaneously. I only have twelve screens."

"Mind if I take one?" Without waiting for a response, Michael typed into the keyboard in front of him. The display directly in front of him flickered.

"Knock yourself out," Ryker said. "I'm almost done."

"Fischer played fifty," Michael said. "But he didn't win them all."

Ryker laughed. He stopped typing and leaned back in the chair, stretching his muscles. "You Googled that."

Michael was offended. "I don't Google. I asked Dealer. It's got more data than Google will ever have." Michael indicated the two-dozen rectangular cargo containers crowded into the open space in front of them, taking up almost all the magazine. There was only eighteen inches between each one. Large vents were above, humming loudly as they pulled air up, keeping the Spin-Q server inside each one from over-heating.

"I was using a term," Ryker said.

"If you worked for me, I'd fire you for using the name of one of my former competitors."

"I don't work for you," Ryker said, "and why do you say former?"

"We're far beyond Google's capabilities. Everyone's as a matter of fact. You know that. You helped design Dealer." Michael was reading the screen. "Fischer won 47, drew 2, and lost 1."

Ryker shrugged. "Not a bad record considering he was playing them at the same time. Of course, he had a big advantage. He had white, which meant he had the first move. Thus setting up the strategy for the entire game. All fifty of his opponents were reacting to him. He could present a gambit, where he's offering to sacrifice one of his pieces for an advantageous position. It put the onus on his opponent whether to take the bait or lose the advantage."

"I know what a gambit is," Michael said. "We played often enough. And you rarely opened with one."

"There is more to everything than just the opening advantage," Ryker said. "After just four moves, there are millions of possibilities. The thing about chess is that while strategies and patterns often repeat, there is always a way to create a unique game." But his brain had already moved on. "I did some checking on the system since I last visited. I see the CNS is on-line. How's it working?"

Michael was like a kid with a new toy. He typed briefly and a schematic came up on the screen in front of him. Ryker scooted over.

"I still don't like it," Ryker said. He pointed. "If that containment field around the core metal sphere gives?" He shook his head. "Then it's a bomb."

"It's not a bomb," Michael said. "You always expect the worst. CNS is exactly what is stands for: Contained Nuclear Sphere."

"But it will implode if the field fails, and it's generating the field."

"That's why it's self-sustaining."

"That's a paradox."

Michael rolled his eyes. "It's a power source. A small nuclear reactor, very small, the size of a basketball, that will be able to use its own power to contain the reaction and keep it stable. When it works, it will revolutionize the entire power industry. Get rid of so many sources of pollutants. I'd think you'd be happy about it considering you've accused me of not caring about my fellow man. Only caring about money. Power. Myself."

"Well, you have tended to be, what was it the shrink we saw called it? Narcissistic. Hey. Apparently I was wrong." Ryker gestured to the large service elevator that Michael had come down in. "So what was with the poetry? That was different too. The Second Coming. Yeats."

Michael swiveled his seat to face his brother. "Centre. Spelled c.e.n.t.r.e.. That's what I decided to name this place."

"An odd choice," Ryker said. "'Things fall apart; the centre cannot hold; Mere anarchy is loosed upon the world'. The context—"

"I know the context," Michael said. "Of course you would know the damn poem. I was focused more on the Second Coming part. Forget it." He turned his attention to the screens, which had gone dark. "Done?"

"We're done. It's fully loaded and programmed. I'm sure there will be a glitch or two and some fine-tuning, but you now own the most powerful computer in the world."

"So any problem can be solved if we input it."

"That's a bit of a stretch," Ryker said. "Any problem can be analyzed. A solution is a different matter."

"How so?" Michael put the wooden box on the desk next to the keyboard. "Enter enough data to be analyzed, let Dealer crunch it, and it *will deal out the answer. That's the term we're to use, by the way. Deal. Not Google. Not wiki. Not Bing. Deal."*

"There's a problem with that," Ryker said.

Michael flipped open the top of the box, revealing two champagne flutes. "And that is?"

"A machine can't factor in the human element."

"It's got every text, every paper, every speech on psychology and psychiatry uploaded," Michael said. "Every piece of literature, every image of art, everything man has ever done or produced in its database. I think it can figure humans out." He pulled a magnum of champagne out of the bag. "Rather tacky to carry this down here in a paper bag," Michael said. "Considering it cost slightly over two million."

Ryker was used to his brother's extravagant ways. "How many cases for that price?"

"Just this bottle."

"You're kidding."

"Do I ever kid?" He held the bottle up. "Gout de Diamants, known as a Taste of Diamonds. It's not just the champagne; it's also the bottle. Exquisitely handcrafted. It's a work of art by itself. Only five are sold every year." He put the bottle down, reached into the velvet-lined box and removed a flute. "These are—"

"I don't want to know how much they cost," Ryker said. "I can't even think about drinking something that costs so much. Do you know how many—"

Michael cut him off. "Starving kids in wherever that this would feed? Yes. Yes. But indulge me this, brother. This is the last time I'll ever ask for a favor." He poured some into each glass and held one out to Ryker.

"You know I'm a beer guy."

"The last favor."

Ryker reluctantly accepted it.

"To Dealer!" Michael said.

"To Dealer." Ryker gingerly clinked his glass with Michael's. Then sipped.

"Drink it!" Michael ordered.

ON THE EDGE OF HEAVEN, where land met water, Haydn slowly waded out into the chill dark swell. To his right was a white wall, over fifty feet high, the surface smooth as glass. It extended out into the water fifteen feet, far enough that even at low tide, the water was deep enough one couldn't walk around it; a person had to swim.

burners were never taught how to swim.

Haydn went deeper, water coming up to his waist, recoiling as the cold soaked through his clothes and goose-bumped his skin. He continued, water climbing up until he was as far as he could go and still have feet touching the bottom.

So close.

He felt the wall, the absolute smoothness of it, nothing to grip onto.

He could hear the chanting from those escorting the burners being gathered on their Deathday, but still couldn't make the words out.

A swell spilled water into his mouth and he gagged.

So close.

Haydn took a deep breath and threw himself into the water, flailing, arms splashing, feet kicking. His world was dark.

He reached, felt the wall, and kept flailing.

Then his hand felt an edge. The end of the wall. Desperate, lungs screaming for air, he grabbed and pulled.

To the edge, then grabbed with both hands, pulling himself upward. Broke surface, sputtering, spitting out salt water. Taking deep breaths, clinging to the edge of the wall.

He was surprised for a moment that his view was blocked by a large tree, growing up against the wall and extending out over the water.

He shoved off toward the tree. Not quite swimming, but a deep, primal memory causing his arms and legs to push him forward.

His feet scrambled for a hold as his arms pulled at water. A toe touched, and then the other.

And then he was on the shore, next to the old tree. He lay on the pebbly beach, cold wet, gasping. Haydn's sparkling green eyes reflected the stars shining overhead. His blond hair, unruly and barely combed, lay soaked and flat against his skull. What had been blond stubble on his chin at the beginning of the journey out of hive with Millay, was now just slightly thicker and really not any longer. His nose was the most distinctive feature, broken long ago and poorly set.

He got to his knees, then to his feet. He panicked as he saw another, lower wall about two hundred yards ahead, blocking his view. A large gray ship with a flat deck, floated just off shore to the left. Almost as long as the building in the Wasteland, which he and Millay had run past. It was dark except for a green glow where a gangplank sloped up to an opening in the side of the ship.

Haydn looked up. Reached, grabbed a branch. Climbed. Branch to branch.

Higher. Higher.

He made his way around the trunk as he did so. Until he was high enough to see over the wall in front of him. He stopped, feet on a thick branch, arms clinging to a smaller one across his chest, sick from salt water, exhausted.

He could see down. The Deathday burners were channeling in between two walls, ten feet apart.

Haydn scanned left, following their path.

They went straight for about fifty feet, but the walls gradually narrowed, until they were barely three feet apart, forcing the burners into a single file. At that point, the walls began a gentle curve, almost back toward the white wall, then curved back again toward the ship.

There were people on a ledge on the outside of the wall, chanting the same thing the ones on the other side had been and now he could make it out:

"Second Room.

"Second Room.

"Second Room."

The vague promise made to Haydn, and the other burners, upon arriving here. That there was something beyond Heaven, a way of living longer.

Ingenious, to keep hope burning. It the fuel on which burners survived.

For the first six years, the hope of a white, green or blue card. When that was crushed on Dealing Day, then the promise of Heaven. And once in Heaven, another dangling of hope in the form of Second Room and the Spice of Life.

The burners filed between the walls. The first one began to walk up the gangplank toward the ship. A figure waited, silhouetted against the green glow. When the first burner arrived, that figure took the burner in arm and led her into the ship. The figure was immediately replaced by another escort.

In the light from spotlights on the inside of the wall, Haydn finally made out the dark silhouettes and saw details. The escorts at the top of the gangway had flowers in hand, which they gave to each burner as they arrived, one by one.

Haydn leaned over the branch he was holding and vomited, not from the salt water, or the strange food he'd eaten in hall.

The chanters and the greeters all had shaved skulls, except for two-inch-thick lines of hair, one centered front to back, and the other side to side.

Renderers.

The same as those he'd watched slaughter and butcher over seventy-five cattle in fifteen minutes in a rendering hive out in the Wasteland, beyond sight, sound, and most importantly smell of other hives.

Haydn took several deep breaths.

A lie. It was a lie.

He looked at the ship. It was over a thousand feet long and at its widest over two-hundred-and-fifty feet wide. A flat deck. Near the far end, he could barely make out the top of a building poking up from the deck

The long ramp from the shore entered about two-thirds of the way up the landward side. Even in the dark, the flickering torches held by the escorts showed that it was painted gray, time having faded the color and there were rust streaks down the sides. Squinting,

Haydn could make out a name in large, dim black letters on the side: *USS JOHN F. KENNEDY.*

Facts. Facts outside of Code. Like the large building in the Wasteland where there were rows and rows of Soldiers and Lifts and other vehicles.

Lies. Sound was full of lies. Which meant Dealer was full of lies.

The last of the burners entered the ship.

Followed by the renderers that had called them forth and formed the cordon leading the burners here.

The last renderer slammed the hatch shut behind her, the sound echoing off the curved white wall.

Haydn looked to the east. No sign of dawn.

He climbed down, turned to the water. No longer afraid of it, because now he knew there were much worse things here in Heaven.

He waded out, then did his burner approximation of swimming, got to the edge of the wall, held on, took several breaths, pulled himself around, and pushed off for shore. When his feet finally scratched the bottom, he took a few steps, lungs heaving, then collapsed forward, face plant into the water. Lifted his head. Got to his hands and knees and crawled out of the water.

Once on land, he rolled over and stared up at the stars.

Nothing is as it was.

"What are you doing?" A head intruded on Haydn's view of the heavens above.

A head with the crisscross hair of a renderer.

"Enjoying the beach," Haydn said.

"What were you doing in the water?" the renderer demanded. "Why are you near the Wall? The Wall is off-limits. Everyone's told that. It's Code."

Haydn sat up. The renderer shook his head. "I'll have to report you."

"You don't have to," Haydn said reasonably, as he gripped a large stone from the beach in his hand.

"It's Code."

Haydn stood up. "I went for a swim. So what?"

"burners don't swim."

"I know. That's why I tried." He smiled, the effort lost in the dark. "As you can see, I didn't do well."

"It's Code and—"

Haydn smashed the stone into the top of the renderer's head. *X marks the spot* he thought as it thudded home.

The renderer dropped to the beach.

Haydn looked about. He couldn't see anyone else, although he could hear the sounds of partying come from the halls inland; a mixture of drunken shouts, arguing, sexing and all around burner excess, free of the shackle of having to go to work for the next shift. There were no shifts here in Heaven.

Haydn nudged the renderer. Out cold. Dark blood flowed, forming a red rivulet that seeped into the pebbles, rocks and sand of the beach.

Haydn knelt and checked for a pulse.

With a deep breath, Haydn pulled his hand back. He'd killed before. Jokers in the Void that were attacking him and the others. When it was kill or be killed. And then eaten. Which jarred him, realizing this was a renderer. Whose job in hive had been to slaughter and butcher cattle. What was his job here in Heaven was?

Haydn reached down and grabbed the straps on the man's coveralls, dragging him off the beach and into the water. Haydn went neck deep, the body half submerged next to him.

He paused before shoving the renderer out into the deep water of the Sound. Grace had spoken of the death ritual she'd done for Mrs. Marash. Burying her. The time and the effort to do such an odd thing, that it reflected an honor to the dead.

Haydn doubted this man deserved such honor. But he was still human. But one who betrayed other humans.

Haydn pushed the body away. Dead was dead.

"How can burners give time to People?" Ryker asked.

"They don't give it," Ruth said. "It's reaped from them."

"How?" Grace asked.

"That's one of many things I don't know," Ruth said.

"Then how do you know it's reaped?" Grace pressed.

"I don't know the details," Ruth said. But her attention was on Ryker. "There's something familiar about you. From the first moment I saw you in Deep Void. All the time I was following you north. As if we'd met before."

"I can't tell you whether we've met," Ryker said. "I don't remember my past."

"But you're a cyborg," Ruth said. "Better made than I am. The skin, the apparent breathing, the--" She stopped talking. "Oh."

"What?" Grace said.

"There was only facility pre-Chaos that worked on cyborg technology that had succeeded in producing a working model. Here. The Russians and Chinese were undoubtedly also working on it. But up until Chaos, the scientists here were very confident that no one had succeeded in the most critical aspects: transplanting the brain into the machine, with a bio-tech support system that could keep it functioning. And integrating an onboard computing cache with the brain. And you're better made than the best model this place produced. But we're all pre-Chaos." Ruth jabbed a metal finger at Ryker. "He's post-Chaos."

"That still doesn't explain—" Grace began, but Ryker was one step ahead.

"I'm from here. I was made here."

"Yes. But I don't remember you. And it's more accurate to say you were reborn here," Ruth said. "That's the term we prefer. 'Made' sounds so mechanical. Dealers are made. Soldiers are made. Dark Angels are made."

"I'm confused," Ryker said. "Who was I before I was—" he hesitated—"'reborn'?"

"You were Ryker," Ruth said. "Just like I was Ruth."

"How did I get here?" Ryker demanded. "What happened to my human body? And what of this reaping? Stealing time?"

"One thing at a time," Ruth stepped back and sighed, if machines could sigh; more a noise programmed into her interface. No movement of the chest, although the mouth did imitate enough to match the sound. "If you were made here, but our system doesn't have a record of you, and I don't remember you, then we're all blocked regarding you. Yet I had a cache directive to track you once you came into Deep Void."

"Blocked?" Grace asked.

"Just like he's blocked from his own past," Ruth said. "It's for security reasons. But there are keys to blocks. And if—"

Ryker had already jumped ahead. "I must have the key to your memory of me. But do you have the key to my own memory?"

"I don't think I would. A block of an entire personal past? That's unprecedented. A block of a specific memory is the norm. Like me not remembering you. That's to keep you safe." She looked over at a table covered in tools and equipment. "That's why there are things there that we don't use. We thought they were all experimental. And they are. Except you were the experiment.

"Come. I think I can fix your arm."

Ryker went the table with her. He was lean, like the burner he'd thought he'd been until arriving here. His black hair hadn't seen a comb in a while, and was slicked back from sweat and dirt. He had a narrow face, with piercing gray eyes. His stubble had grown out to a short beard.

Ryker extended the arm, but rubbed his chin with the other hand. "How can I be a machine when my hair still grows? My nails?"

"You're a cyborg," Ruth said as she searched through the pile of stuff, then picked up a metal tube, reading some tiny writing on the side of it. "As I said, you're obviously the most advanced model ever developed. You pass for human on the exterior. Everything else about you mimics human, including appearing to breath. As you can see, I don't have that."

"Do you have any others like me here?" Ryker asked.

"No." She corrected herself. "Not that I can remember."

Ryker glanced over at Grace. She had one hand on top of Ace's head, absently scratching behind the dog's ear. "Then where do I come from?"

Ruth smeared something greasy from the tube onto the slice she'd made on his arm, which had revealed metal, artificial ligaments and tendons, strands of carbon nanotube 'muscle'. The machine part of him, underneath the human exterior. Done, Ruth capped the tube and put it back on the table. "Let's see."

Grace came over and they all watched as the skin on either side of the slash grew together. In less than a minute, the only sign of the cut was the greasy smear.

"Interesting. Much more efficient than what would have to be done to repair my cover." Ruth wiped the smear off with a rag.

Ryker held his arm out, flexing it, twisting it.

"Wait a second," Grace said. "How can you fix him if he's more advanced than any cyborg you have here? How you can mend his skin when you say none of you have it?"

Ruth indicated the table. "This is material that's been here since Chaos. For the next generation. What he is."

"We're wasting *time*," Grace said, a natural enough thing for a burner to say, since their red card counted down every day, closer and closer the end. The day of their birth was insignificant in the face of that harsh reality. Median Deathday for a burner: twenty-five. There was very little variance from that; at most a year.

Except Grace's Deathday had passed by two days ago.

Ruth glanced at the flickering green lights on top of the closest rows of pods, indicating that the cyborgs inside were activating.

"Information is never a waste of time," Ruth said. "Unfortunately, as we used to say in the military before the Chaos, information is not intelligence. Our greatest weakness right now is the lack of intelligence. Our capability extends only as far as the limits of what we know."

Grace was exasperated. "How about telling us what you *do* know."

"That's not much," Ruth said. "All we know of reaping is that it happens in Heaven. There's a ship there, what was called an aircraft carrier in my day." She shook her head. "I flew off it many times.

Before I was—" she hesitated—"reborn. The *USS John F. Kennedy.* Ford class. The most modern ship in the fleet."

Grace opened her mouth to say something, but Ryker shook his head, very slightly, but she caught the gesture and remained silent.

"It was also your friend's," Ruth said, turning toward Grace. "Mrs. Marash. Hanan. She was my wife. But that story is for a later time. You are correct, you do need the essentials up front. Now on that ship, beached just offshore of Heaven, something is done to burners on their Deathday. We don't know the procedure or why it is done. We've speculated it might be something that occurs at the moment of death. Something that allows humans to counteract the life span phage imposed on them."

"'Phage'?" Ryker repeated. "What is that?"

"The virus that infected everyone. We were all the same before the phage. Born, lived. No one knew when they were going to die. But a death at twenty-five was considered unusually young. Most people lived into their seventies or eighties. Then the phage struck. It cut ninety-eight-point-seven percent of the population down to burner life span, and that initiated the Chaos."

Both Grace and Ryker took a moment to absorb that.

Ruth continued. "The best and brightest were put to work to try to destroy the phage or find a cure once it started spreading, but there wasn't enough time. Humans were dying off quickly, starting from the oldest down, so the most experienced, the leaders, the elders, the generals, the most knowledgeable scientists; they were gone fast. And then the Chaos happened and . . ."

"Back to the reaping," Ryker said. "How do they get life from burners on that ship?"

Ruth frowned, at least that part of her face that still had synthetic skins and twitch fibers in it. "There's something more about the reaping that I should know. More about you," she indicated Ryker.

"What about me?" Grace asked. "And Millay. What about the Prime?"

"We were told about the Prime." Ruth was frustrated. "I hate not being able to remember."

"It was hard for Mrs. Marash," Grace said. "But she gave me a key. It helped Ryker remember something."

"What was that?" Ruth asked. "What did she tell you?"

"'*Things fall apart; the centre cannot hold*'," Grace said. "I don't know—"

"The Second Coming," Ruth said. "Oh, yes. That's it. It's my key too! Centre. Oh yes. Now I remember. The Prime. The Backdoor. It's all happening now. Just as was foretold."

"Foretold by who?" Ryker asked.

Ruth lifted her 'skin'-covered hand and pointed at him. "*You* did."

EARLY IN THE 20TH CENTURY,
BEFORE THE CHAOS

T hey were called meruta. Logs.
 Because that is what they looked like when the bodies, what
 was left of them, were stacked and then bulldozed under.

Today, as often happened, 42 naked prisoners were marched out into a wide, empty field. Nothing grew in that field. There were just poles set in the ground, in concentric circles from the center out. Each ring of poles was separated by approximately ten meters. In the very center, there was a white X, made from staked down sheets. Bolted onto each pole was a thick, rusty iron chain. Each pole had a letter and number designation, indicating its position.

The prisoners would be known by that letter and number in the reports that followed.

The guards wore protective clothing and gas masks. They prodded the prisoners forward with bayonets. Their hands were securely tied behind their backs. They were secured in place with handcuffs to the iron chains. The letter and number designation of the pole was painted onto each prisoner's body.

It was all very efficient, indeed scientific.

The meruta were an eclectic mixture of ethnic groups: mostly Chinese, but there were also Koreans, and a smattering of Australian, American and

British prisoners of war. They were also a cross-section of people: men, women, children. There were even three infants, with special cuffs to the secure them, even though they weren't even capable of crawling. These were carried out in small reed baskets and left on the ground. One of the infants was in a red basket, different from the other two. It was place on the innermost circle.

Nothing could be left to chance. Three of the women were clearly pregnant; deliberately impregnated by Japanese surgeons stationed at the camp, supposedly in the name of science.

Once all were secured, the guards quickly withdrew.

Some of the prisoners cried out for mercy. But most had been here long enough to know better. There was no such thing here.

The camp was located in the Pingfang District of the city of Harbin, in Mancukuo, a puppet state of the Japanese Empire since 1932, a year after being over-run. The rest of the world called the area Manchuria. The camp was run by Unit 731. Originally it had been named more blatantly, although still misdirection: The Epidemic and Water Purification Department of the Kwangtun Army. It was supervised by the Kempeitai, the Japanese version of the Gestapo. In 1941, General Ishii took command and the designation was changed to Unit 731, in an attempt to further hide the camps true purpose, since the original name gave too much of a hint.

Some of the meruta looked up at the sound of an approaching plane. They could only hope it would be fast.

The navigator/bombardier in the nose of the plane had the site set on the X, offsetting the speed of the plane and wind readings recorded from the ground before take off. The bomb bay doors opened and at the right moment, the single bomb was released.

The pilots immediately banked hard, gaining altitude at the same time. They had no idea what the payload was, but they were taking no chances. The bomb detonated at two hundred feet altitude, releasing a fine mist, which slowly drifted down.

None of the prisoners were looking up any more. Except for the three babies on their back, who didn't know any better. Many tried not to breath, but one can only do that for so long. As the mist settled on the people and field, there was no apparent reaction.

Minutes passed.

It wasn't going to be fast.

Two hours after the bombing, the first meruta began to vomit uncontrollably. Others followed suit. In addition, some lost control of their bowels. Most became feverish. Cramps caused spasms. Blood seeped from the eyes, the mouth, the ears, the nose.

One prisoner tried to get ahead of whatever was occurring to him by smashing his head against the wood pole in a vain attempt at suicide, but only succeeded in knocking himself out.

Which was a small blessing, as long as it lasted. Not long.

After twelve hours, six prisoners were dangling, hands held up behind their backs by the chains, bodies slumped forward.

Large searchlights flashed on. Soldiers in protective gear and masks rolled wheelbarrows into the field. They collected the dead, but also one living prisoner from each ring, including one of the pregnant women.

They checked the three babies, even though their wailing indicated they were very much alive. They set up cameras and took pictures of some of those still tied to the stakes and also quite a few of the baby in the red basket.

The guards withdrew with their grisly load, living and dead, in the wheelbarrows. They were taken to a windowless block building on the edge of the compound. Two doors unsealed and the prisoners were wheeled in, the dead to one side, the living to the other.

Autopsy tables were set up on both sides. The guards hoisted the dead onto the tables. The living took a little more work, but all were quickly secured with straps, thus making the table a vivisection table, rather than dissection.

The guards quickly exited and the doors closed.

A cluster of scientists waited. At each table, those assigned checked the letter and number designation painted on the body. Double-checked.

Then the cutting, and the screaming, began.

The purpose of the vivisection was to study the progress of the virus in the various organs while they were still functioning, often a much more valuable source of data than the dead.

In a glass enclosure, set ten feet higher than the floor of the building,

General Ishii observed. The room was over-pressured by an air pump, allowing him to be in uniform and not use protective gear. There was a man with him, a Westerner dressed in a suit that showed the wrinkles and dust of a long hard journey.

A muscle rippled on man's jaw as he watched, but other than that, he showed no reaction to what was occurring.

"Is there a reason you are showing me this, General?" the Westerner finally asked.

Ishii waved a dismissive hand. "Please, call me Doctor. The General title will soon no longer apply, Colonel Langston."

"No, it won't. That's why I'm here."

"Indeed."

"Admiral Yamamoto knew the war with the United States was lost before it even began. I spent—"

"Two years in the United States," Langston said. "Studying biological and chemical warfare in the aftermath of World War I. We have a very detailed file on you."

Ishii nodded. "I am sure you do. And you killed Admiral Yamamoto."

"We did."

"And you secretly met Prince Chichibu, the Emperor's younger brother, before traveling here."

"I did."

"The Prince will profess ignorance of what you are seeing, but he has stood exactly where you are. And he gave you the information on Yamamoto's flight over two years ago to gain your organization's good will. The Admiral was a problem, especially as it became clear the tide of the war was changing, just as he predicted. He was a liability to the Emperor and a coup for your military. I believe you call that a win-win situation."

Langston didn't respond.

Ishii sighed, obviously tired of having to explain, obviously knew he had to, especially to this guest. "We did not sign the Geneva Protocol ban on biological weapons. Of course, we were not alone in that among the Great Powers after the First World War. Your country also did not sign it. One wonders what nefarious things your scientists are up to?"

Langston's response was terse. "Not this."

"*Of course not. Or else you wouldn't be here. Honestly, and we must be honest with each other over matters of such importance, the Geneva Protocol had the opposite effect. We realized it was a way for our country to gain an advantage. To pursue research in an area where others were forbidden. Many of our generals and admirals believed that if some weapons were so terrible that they were outlawed, then they must be something that could be very effective. And, of course, was the awareness your country also was not abiding by the Protocol.*

"*Do not act as if you speak from a moral pedestal. Compared to what your country did to Hiroshima three days ago—*" he shook his head— "*what we have been doing here pales in comparison.*"

"*You started the war.*"

"*Let us not descend to schoolyard arguments, Colonel. We are both pragmatists. That is why you are here. We must—*" he paused as there was a commotion on the floor below. The scientists stopped cutting, weighing, inspecting and gathered round a man who had just rushed in. He'd put on protective gear but it was obvious he was breathing hard, trying to catch his breath through the limits of the mask.

"*What's going on?*" Langston asked.

Ishii didn't answer. He turned and pulled a lever near the outer door. The pressure equalized and he was able to open it. Langston followed and they descended the metal stairs. The camp was in an uproar. A lieutenant ran up to the General, leaned close and whispered something in his ear, while glaring at Langston.

Ishii waved the junior officer away, but then another officer burst out of a building, sword in hand, screaming something and charging right at Langston.

Ishii pulled his pistol and shouted an order. Such was the discipline that the officer actually stopped, sword poised for a strike.

"*What is happening?*" Langston demanded.

"*Another atomic weapon,*" Ishii said. "*Dropped on Nagasaki.*"

"*Your Emperor should have acted faster after Hiroshima,*" Langston said.

Ishii stared at the American for several seconds, then gave a slight nod. "*Yes. Should have. Ought to have. Many things, many things out to be different. There is no doubt the war will be over very soon now. The Emperor cannot allow any more cities to be destroyed."*

"As you said," Langston replied, "let us not get caught in a squabble."

"Did you know this was coming today?"

"Of course not," Langston said. "How many in your country know of this place? The atomic project was highly compartmentalized."

Ishii gestured. "Come." He led the way across the compound.

Langston found it odd that soldiers and scientists were gathered in small groups, some crying, others consoling, yet screams had started up against in the autopsy building. The selectivity of the human mind and heart.

Ishii spoke as they walked: "Your country already owes me a debt of gratitude."

"How is that?"

"As you country has just used the weapons it has, we have used poison gas against the Chinese. We have used bacteria to initiate plague. We have some very effective chemical and biological weapons. But we have not used them against your troops. Even on Okinawa, which is Japanese territory. And there were plans for worse. I sabotaged all those."

"Why?"

"Look what you have done to us since Pearl Harbor. Another attack on your homeland and we would not be standing here negotiating. You would use more of your bombs and there would be no more Japan."

"Are we negotiating?"

"We will give you all our files in exchange for amnesty. You will have all of us," he indicated the compound, "at your disposal. We recognize we must be tried. A show must be put on. Some even sentenced to death if need be. If you have to execute some of my men for appeasement, I will give you a list of those who are expendable. But the core of 731; we will all be pardoned after the war. Perhaps a year or two, once everyone forgets."

Langston still remained silent.

"The Russians will over-run this facility," Ishii said. "If you do not get the files, they will."

"We'll level this place," Langston said, "before that happens."

"Then you get nothing." Ishii cast a sidelong glance. "And what did the

Prince promise you for the pardoning of the Royals?" When Langston didn't respond, Ishii answered hi own questions. "The fortune from Golden Lily, perhaps?"

The tic on the side of Langston's jaw grew worse.

"I offer something more," Ishii said.

"What?" Langston said. "What can you possibly offer?"

"Come with me," Ishii said and they walked across the compound.

A scream, muted by concrete walls indicated the work was still in progress.

General Ishii didn't bother to salute the two guards at the entrance to his office. He led Langston into his inner sanctum. On a shelf to the left were a number of petri dishes. To the right, stacks of file boxes.

Langston went to the left. The dishes had various growths inside.

"My pets," Ishii said. And he was serious. Langston knew that because it was in his file; during his time in University, Ishii's eccentricities had garnered the attention of his fellow students and the faculty.

Ishii indicated the boxes. "Our data. Current up until yesterday. Sadly, today will be our last active day but I will insure the data is included."

"I told you," Langston said, "we have the bomb. The Russians don't. So, yes, we don't want them to get this, but it's not important enough to forgive what you've done. There were Westerners in there. Getting cut open while still alive. No one will ever forgive you."

"They will forget."

"Most will," Langston allowed. "But some will never."

"Meaning you?"

"I do my duty."

"Admirable. But you misunderstand." Ishii indicated a door behind his desk. "Come."

They went through.

A captain was standing there along with a nurse. On a table next to them was the red straw basket from the field of death.

The nurse was leaning over, singing a lullaby in Japanese in a low voice, gently rocking the basket back and forth.

"I am not offering your data on death," Ishii said. "I am offering you something much more valuable. Data on life."

HUNDREDS OF YEARS IN THE
FUTURE, AFTER THE CHAOS

"But ah, my foes, and oh, my friends—It gives a lovely light!"

Millay's voice was a harsh whisper, barely audible. Her left arm was a knot of pain, except it was gone. Phantom pain was screeching from the severed nerve endings to her brain, which couldn't separate out what was there and what wasn't, but the pain was most definitely real.

She began again, the ritual keeping her from slipping away from reality.

"My candle burns—"

"Enough."

Millay licked her lips, but there was barely any moisture. "Is that irritation I hear?"

A short silence gave her a short victory.

"I want you to see something," Michael said, his voice still mostly machine, but with an edge, coming out of a speaker somewhere in the sparse white room. "Open your eyes."

Millay didn't want to. Because it would be nothing good. She heard something to her right, then felt a slight mist on her lips.

"Open your eyes," Michael ordered.

Millay cracked open her eyelids, breaking the seal of tears. She blinked, trying to adjust to the brightness of the white room.

"I want you to see the price others have paid for your transgressions," Michael said.

An image flickered, then formed directly above her. As it did, there was another spritz into her mouth.

Immediately the pain began to fade as the image solidified. An Assembly Field. Littered with bodies. Men, women, children. Their bodies blasted and torn. Limbs, torsos, heads, entrails, scattered about. The dirt field was stained red. Nothing was moving.

"It is forbidden by Code—" Millay began, but knew Code meant nothing now.

"I *am* Code," Michael said. "Like you, they attacked Dealers. This is the result. As you can tell, you are fortunate. You've only lost an arm. I have been patient. Tell me of the Prime."

"Take the other arm," Millay said. "Take my legs. Put me in a box. I can't tell you what I don't know."

"The Backdoor?"

"Box me. Be done with it."

"I will take the arm. And the legs. Eventually. I want you to reflect. In pain."

A door opened and a human walked in. The green card of an Evermore resting on her chest.

"Who are you?" Millay asked.

The woman was rolling a metal stand, several plastic bags of fluids on it. She didn't meet Millay's eyes as she quickly and efficiently inserted IV's, one in the right arm, then one into the femoral arteries on the inside of each leg.

"You're a human," Millay said to her. "This is not Code."

The Evermore still didn't make eye contact, taping down the last femoral cannulation.

"I'm a human!" Millay said and there was a flicker on the woman's face.

"You're a People," the Evermore hissed, hatred in every syllable.

"*You* broke Code." She checked the bags, adjusted the flow and then left the room.

"What do you give them for their obedience?" Millay asked. "burners get Heaven. Do you give Evermores and Middlemores the Spice of Life?"

"Sometimes," Michael. "But most do it out of duty. Something you know nothing of."

"What cause is that?" Millay asked as the probe gave a small mist of painkiller.

"Our existence. Our survival. The survival of the human race."

"You're not human."

"I was once. I will be again. I will arise once more, like Lazarus."

"How will you do that?"

"I gave up my body for the greater good. I will get it back."

"Who determines the greater good?"

"I'm not here to discuss philosophy," Michael said. "It is likely you don't know what you are. And that you don't know what the Backdoor is. Or perhaps you once knew, but it's been erased from your memory. Or blocked. They did that in the Chaos."

"'They'?" Millay was buying time, which meant buying more painkiller.

"Cyborgs."

"Like Ruth."

"Yes. Traitors to mankind. Your sister doesn't know who she is with."

"You knew Ryker." It wasn't a question.

"Yes. Long ago."

Millay looked at the fluid in the line into her arm, then the legs. She knew whatever was in them could keep her alive indefinitely. The dark side of being People.

"He's a burner," Millay said. "It can't have been that long ago."

There was a low rumble, as if ball bearing were being swirled in a jar. She realized Michael had laughed. "He is anything but burner. He also lied to you. You and your sister have been lied to from the very beginning of this foolish escapade. He is a cyborg."

Millay blinked. "No. He breathed. He ate. He's human."

"Believe what you want," Michael said. "Who told you to switch places with her?"

"No one," Millay said. "I promised Grace on Dealing Day that I would try to make things right for her when she was dealt red and I was dealt white. The best I could do was give her thirty days of Island. Of living like a People."

"And you spent thirty days as burner. How was that?"

"I understand why they look forward to Heaven. It's not fair."

"Fair!" Michael sounded bemused. "Fair has nothing to do with it. It is what it is. We, Dealer and I, have done our best with the cards that mankind dealt itself. This is the best solution according to the data."

"Humans aren't data."

"Oh, my friend, Millay," Michael mocked, "once of the People, they certainly are. They have to be treated like data in order to find a solution to the mistakes they made and still make. Most humans are inherently self-destructive. They have to be saved from themselves."

"'They'?" Millay said. "So you actually don't consider yourself human."

"I am more than human."

"I think you're less than."

"You're the one lying on that table missing your arm. What you think isn't relevant. Did the Person also suggest you switch? The Person before Andrew?"

Millay said nothing.

"You'll tell what little you do know eventually," Michael said.

"Finish boxing me," Millay said. "Let's be done with it. Even better, kill me. I'm of no use to anyone."

"You're half of the Prime," Michael said. "You've very valuable."

"But you don't what the Prime is either," Millay said. "So how can I be valuable?"

"Because your sister wants you. Ryker wants you. That want will be their undoing."

"Is Haydn truly in Heaven?" Millay asked, her skin crawling with the thought that Michael was going to use her as bait.

"Of course. He earned it."

"You lie."

"Not on that. And I'm not the only who is capable of lying. Remember that Millay, once of the People. You've lied to. Ryker's lied to you."

And then the room went dark.

"How could I have told you?" Ryker asked. "This is the first time I'm hearing all of this."

Grace was rubbing Ace's head, trying to absorb all this new information.

"And what do *you* remember of being a true human, with a body?" Ruth asked. "And of *your* existence before becoming aware on the boat crossing the Sound with Charon?"

That gave Ryker pause.

"I remember you now," Ruth said. "Some of it. Centre was a key for me too." She pointed at Ryker. "I first met you, when you were human. Hanan and I was the ones who brought you here while you were dying."

"Who am I?" Ryker demanded. "Who was I? I know Michael was my brother. That I fought him for some reason; it was in a dream. But the rest is either dark or cloudy."

Ruth pointed at his head. "It's all in there. You just need the keys to let it all come back."

"Why not just tell me?"

"Because I only know a little," Ruth said. She pointed at the tube that was in the left side of the front row. "There's someone being activated who can help. Who holds a key to your human memories."

"Who?" Ryker asked.

"Someone you knew in the old days, before the phage, the Chaos, the Truce. He'll be the first one activated. It won't be long now. His name is Elias."

"I don't remember anyone named Elias."

"That's why he holds a key," Ruth said.

Ryker moved on, accepting he'd have to wait. "All right. What exactly did I tell you?"

"You were dying, mortally wounded. Elias was helping you. You'd just fought Michael. Hanan and I didn't know what was going on, but Elias forced us to put you on our aircraft, fly you out of Centre. Get you away from the Soldiers. Elias told us you had wounded Michael. And then you told us that Michael was the one behind Dealer. Then you told us that Michael was doing something horrible."

Ryker nodded. "In my dream I stabbed him after I was shot."

"That's what you said. And you brought a recorded video."

"A 'video'?" Grace asked.

"Like a Stream," Ruth said. "Except this was old fashioned. A d-drive. You told us to watch it. That what was happening on it was what Michael was doing to people on the *Kennedy*; up to then we thought Dealer had been using the ship as a hospital. You said this gave Michael and those with him more time via something called the Spice of Life. Reaped it from others." Ruth turned to the console. A Stream image flickered into existence above the console. There was a loud humming noise. A young, naked man was strapped securely to a board. The board was on a conveyor belt, which was slowly carrying the board with its cargo toward a large black box, forty feet wide, sixty long, and ten high. The belt went into an opening on one end of the machine.

The machine was inside a large open space with grey metal walls.

"Where is this?" Grace asked.

"Hanan and I recognized it right away," Ruth said. "The hangar deck on the *Kennedy*."

The man looked sedated, not struggling against the bonds. A golden glow was coming out of the opening. The man disappeared inside. The view shifted to the other end of the box, where the conveyor belt exited. For fifteen seconds all that was visible was the belt moving.

And then what remained of the man appeared, still on the board. But it was as if he'd aged eighty years in those few seconds. His skin was gray, wrinkled and covered with small red dots, too numerous to count. His eyes were empty of life.

"What was taken from him?" Ryker asked.

"We don't know, but it makes the Spice of Life," Ruth said. "You told us not to trust Dealer, because Michael had done the final programming. Planned something awful a long time ago. And—"

"Yes?" Ryker said.

"You told us not only did Michael have Dealer extracting the Spice of Life, but that he had invented the phage and loosed it on the world. You had no proof of that part of your story and not everyone believed it then or believes it now. It's been hundreds of years and some of my fellow cyborgs are still in denial that anyone would do something so horrible to the entire planet. But that ideo is what caused us to bring you here, change sides and fight Dealer."

Grace was shaking her head. "Why didn't you tell everyone after Ryker told you? Show them the video?"

"We wanted to," Ruth said. "It was near the end of the Chaos. The last of the enemies inside and outside of Sound were practically defeated. It looked like peace was at hand. But then we got this—" she indicated the image of the man. "We tried to shut Dealer down even thought we greatly outnumbered by Dealers' Soldiers. We attacked Centre. The Forlorn Hope is what we called that attack. We were repulsed.

"So we asked for a Truce. Dealer would have wiped us out other-wise. And we had some hope because of the few other things you said," she nodded at Ryker once more. "You told us that Dealer would eventually degrade and that we had to be there when it did, because there would come a Prime that was the code to a Backdoor to change everything. Put things back the way they were before the phage. Cure it."

"Did I tell you what the phage was?"

"No."

"So we threatened Dealer with releasing the video if he attacked us and negotiated the Truce," Ruth said. "We had no choice. We couldn't defeat him. And you'd wounded Michael. We thought he might die, but found out later he'd uploaded his consciousness into Dealer. And there were the nuclear weapons in Delta. We bluffed, told Dealer we had control of some and would destroy Sound unless it agreed to the Truce and the separation between us and the rest of Sound.

"We promised to do nothing and Dealer promised to leave us alone. It also promised that it would not reap anyone before their Deathday."

"Michael wasn't around to re-program it," Ryker said. "Even if his conscious was uploaded, it would take time for him to become aware. Based on what you've said, Dealer's core operating principle would be to maintain the system above all else. It had defeated you, but if it attacked you further, you were threatening to destroy the system either with the video or nuclear weapons. It would accept the Truce as the most logical course of action."

"How do you know that?" Grace asked.

"A computer is logical. Obviously, Michael had programmed it to build and maintain the Sound. All else was secondary to that, including this place. And—" he frowned, trying punch through the gray wall around his B.D. memory. "There's something else, but I can't remember."

"You did tell us something similar," Ruth said. "That Dealer would leave us alone as long as we left it alone," Ruth said. "And that was about it before we had to induce a coma. And we blocked your memories as you asked us. Then we wiped it from our own memories to make sure they were secure. But we don't have those keys." She pointed at the front left tube. "He has one. Elias. He'd been wounded too in the fight."

"Hanan had one," Grace said. "She told me. When I said Centre, you knew where we had to go," she added, indicating Ryker. "And it was your key to remember meeting Ryker."

"But we didn't make it to Centre," Ryker said. "And where have I been all these years?"

"Here," Ruth said. "I remember now. You activated two months ago. Told me you had to leave. And then you put in a block on my memories of you."

"I wish I could remember more," Ryker said. "If Michael invented the Spice and the phage, then . . ."

Ruth summed it up. "Then Sound is set up perfectly to keep running and keep the People supplied with the Spice of Life by reaping burners."

"But that also means it can be undone," Ryker said.

Ruth turned to the console. A stream image was projected. A map of the Sound. "We're here in Deep Void." She indicated the land to the west. It was colored black. "Used to be called the Olympic Peninsula." She shifted her finger to the right. "The gray was also part of the Peninsula, but a city was to the south, Olympia, where they connected. It was nuked during the Chaos, making travel by land between the two impossible. So this part became Void, a buffer between us and Dealer."

"Who nuked Olympia?" Ryker asked.

"We don't know who did it. A missile most likely, but everyone was launching missiles." She moved her finger. "Red is Island. Yellow City. Red City Edge. Purple hive. And then there is the Wasteland leading up to the Wasted Mountains."

She tapped a spot in Void, on the western edge. "This is a place you know," she said to Ryker. "Delta. It was one of two bases from which our country sent out submarines armed with nuclear missiles, the only one on the west coast. Thus a large amount of nuclear warheads were stored there."

Ryker remember the bunker where he'd spent the night with Doc. "There still are a bunch there."

"Indeed," Ruth said. "In a strange way, that base is what saved Sound. Because it was such a priority asset, and thus a priority target for our enemies if large-scale war broke out, it was the first place to get a new missile defense system just a few years before the phage, which, in essence also covered Sound; it didn't extend far enough down to cover Olympia. It's surprising it actually worked, but if it hadn't; well, we wouldn't be here. We'd have been destroyed like every other city on the west coast."

"How do—" Ryker began, but he was cut off as a strip of red light around the top edges of the cavern began flashing and klaxon sounded.

Ruth once more inserted the probe from her arm into the machine's portal. "Our outer perimeter has been breached."

"How far out is that?" Grace asked.

"Five kilometers," Ruth said. "Ground breach. Motion detectors have picked up multiple targets. Not heading directly this way, but too close no matter what."

"Animals?" Ryker asked.

"No. Machines."

"Dealers," Grace said.

Ruth nodded. "The Lifts that chased us must have landed and let out their complement of Dealers. Michael really wants to find this base. Those Dealers have an approximation of where we disappeared." She pulled the probe out and it slid back into her arm. "We have to destroy them. Every single one. Before they find this us. And if they do find us, we have to stop them before any can make it back with the location, because they're out of Dealer's Stream here in Deep Void."

She turned to Grace and Ryker. "Ready to fight?"

"You're looking pretty rough."

Haydn heard the woman's voice, couldn't place it.

"What wrong with you? Where were you last night?"

Haydn opened his eyes. A woman leaned over him and he remembered. Yesterday. Tori. A burner in the same hall, who'd received the same briefing about what to do and what not to do here in Heaven.

He'd already broken several rules and he had no doubt there would be more of that in the immediate future.

Harming another human called for immediate bagging if it was discovered. He assumed killing one, especially a renderer, was also considered bad.

It was daylight and Tori was casting a long shadow on the pebbled beach.

Tori continued. "Of course, everyone is looking pretty rough this morning. Most of us partied and sexed straight through the night. No work to go to. No shift! Can you believe that?"

Haydn sat up, blinking in the sunlight. Tori was small, with short blond hair and her shoulders pressed inward; a perpetual hunch which Haydn remembered from his mother. Like his mother, Haydn imagined Tori could throw her shoulders out of their sockets as needed. She was a venter, crawling through the vents and pipes and tunnels in hive, making sure they were clear and working properly. A never-ending job, because by the time she'd cleared all of her sector, it was time to start over again at the beginning.

She also looked rough, eyes red, reeking of 'chol. Her gray coverall was torn on one shoulder. "It was an orgy," she continued. "Everybody was doing everybody."

burners weren't monogamous in hive; their lives were too short for that. And sex was considered the same as a game of Tracers or drinking.

It is what it is, Haydn thought.

That brought a smile to his face and Tori must have taken that as an invite. She sat down next to Haydn and put her arm around him. Looking landward, Haydn could see burners in various states of excess, from those having sex on the grass, to those passed out from too much of everything. There were more of the latter.

Tori was sliding her other hand up his thigh and Haydn looked down. He saw the red smear of dark blood on the beach where the renderer had died. Haydn hopped to his feet. He looked out to the water, but there was no sign of the body, the tide having done its work.

"Hey!" Tori was surprised. "What's wrong?"

"I love someone," Haydn said, surprised at the words that burst forth, and the truth of them.

"So?" Tori was confused. "You can love me. You can love anyone you want here." She unbuckled the fastener on her shoulder. She was reaching for the other one when he grabbed her hand.

"No." He let go of her. "Love is something else. True love."

"And what is that?"

Haydn nodded his head and they began walking toward their hall. Leaving the bloodstain on the beach behind, for the next tide to wash away.

"Where only one person is everything for you," Haydn said.

"What a strange concept," Tori said. "But everyone is taken from life so quickly. Unless you have the same Deathday. But that's rare in hive and would be very lucky; or not lucky, never really thought about it. Almost always one goes to Heaven before the other. Why would someone commit to another person that will only bring loss?"

"That's the price of love," Haydn said. He paused and turned to her. "Your parents. Did you know them?"

"My mother, of course." Tori shrugged and Haydn heard the slight grinding of bones rubbing against each other in her shoulder joints, the tendons, cartilage and muscle so loose, they hardly held the arms in place. "My father. Could have been one of many. You know hive."

"I knew my father," Haydn said. "Or rather the man who called himself my father. He lived in the same cubby with my mother and I until Dealing Day. My mother was seven years short of her Deathday when she had me. My father, the man who said he was my father, was six until Deathday. He was to go to Heaven not long after my Dealing Day."

"That must have been nice, knowing and living with both parents," Tori said, her tone indicating she didn't think much of it either way.

"It wasn't."

"If it wasn't, then what does that have to do with love?"

Good question, Haydn thought. "That wasn't love. He needed my mother."

"For what? Sex? A burner can have sex with pretty much anyone. I don't—"

"Not sex," Haydn said. He remembered the fights, the screaming, the blood from his mother. "He didn't love my mother. He needed her. Big difference."

"I still don't get it." Tori was growing bored. She was looking past him, at the hall and the burners wandering aimlessly around outside in the field, most with flasks of 'chol in hand. Some carrying food, real food, not 'tein, in their arms, bodies hunched over the booty as if fearful someone would take it from them, heading toward the forest further inland, to eat it in secret, as if it were something to be embarrassed of.

There were also couples, more than couples, tangled together in sex, here and there.

Haydn looked at her and she shifted her gaze back to him. He smiled sadly. "I love a woman named Millay."

"When is her Deathday? Or did she already Assemble and come here?"

If love was hard for her to grasp, Haydn knew that telling Tori that Millay was People would be incomprehensible. burners never met People. Middlemores from City Edge supervised burners in the hive. Then the Evermores in City supervised the Middlemores. And on top of it all, the People who lived across the Sound on Island.

It was as Dealer had designed the Sound to continue on after the Chaos.

To this, Haydn thought, looking around once more.

"She's already passed," Haydn said. *Boxed at the very least.*

"I'm sorry," Tori said and he felt the words.

"Thank you."

"But if she's gone, then . . ." And she put her tiny hands on his chest.

He reached up and placed his over hers.

"As long as I say her name and keep her in my heart, she will never be gone."

THE OVAL, the Person's office and nominally from where the Sound was ruled, was empty. It was at the top of the tallest building on Island, in the center of Capitol. The elevator doors slid open and a man walked in.

He was bald, the skin liver-spotted, his face wrinkled as if a great weight were pressing down on his forehead, shoving the skin toward his non-existent chin. There was a green card on his chest, designating an Evermore, the black numbers indicating he had less than a year until Deathday.

He walked the edge of the round office. Large windows showing the Sound were evenly space between images projected out of the Stream; a real and virtual tour of the realm. There was a desk in the center; the Person's. It was an incomplete circle of polished wood, with just a break to allow one to enter and sit in the high-backed chair.

The chair was empty.

There was no Person for the first time in the history of Sound; ever since Andrew, once of the People, had been apprehended by Dark Angels, charged with crimes against Code, and boxed.

The Evermore, Claude, had been Andrew's personal assistant.

Claude didn't miss him. People tended to take Evermores for granted.

Claude ignored the Stream projections. That was a show to make the Person, and the human visitors, think he was really informed and in charge. Dealer could absorb the information they showed so much faster than any human could hope to. And then make decisions and take action, in a time measure so small, it was gone before a human could consider it.

But the view was spectacular. Something a human, even Claude, could appreciate.

To the north and west, the place of most concern at the moment, across Lone Bridge, was Void and beyond it, separated by water and the Broken Bridge was Deep Void.

Supposedly inaccessible, since jokers lived in Void, tracking down and killing and eating those who tried to pass through. And because Lone Bridge had been severed during the Chaos.

But *they* had gone there. Survived the jokers and across the water. The twins and others. Against the odds, they had managed to make it. A mystery how they had crossed over, but not an important one. It was done, that was the key factor.

What exactly was in Deep Void, that it was off-limits to the Stream, to Dealer and all the Dealers? That's what Claude wondered.

Perhaps Michael would let him on the secrets, Claude thought as he slowly paced, counter-clockwise. To the west, more Void and Deep Void, and the white-capped Olympics filling the horizon from north to south. Claude continued around until he faced east.

Across the Sound was City. The towers, all B.D. (Before Dealer), were worn, some damaged from the Chaos. Some uninhabitable. But enough had been fixed so that the Evermores could live there in relative comfort.

In the haze beyond that was City Edge. And out there, lost in the distance and gray, was hive. Beyond them, on a rare clear day, were the Wasted Mountains, once known as the Cascades. A physical line of defense for Sound during the Chaos, when all the passes through it were destroyed. There was only death on the other side of them.

Claude turned inward, toward the desk.

No Person.

The elevator doors slide open and a Dealer walked in. Not just a Dealer. The Dealer: Michael. He looked like all the other Dealers: black metal torso, joints leading to two arms and legs. Flat white face with a black sensory band. But this one had something unique: a narrow stripe of gold around the top of the head.

"Sir." Claude said, almost bowing, giving the machine the honorary he used to extend to the Person.

Michael didn't acknowledge him. It went to the center, inside the desk, shoving the chair away. A machine didn't a chair. A probe came out of the forearm and into an opening on the desk.

Claude had never seen Michael do that before and didn't understand why the machine needed to since it was in the Stream.

"There are Dealers still in Deep Void," Michael finally said.

"Yes, sir." Claude had no idea what that portended.

"The Truce is over," Michael said.

"Sir?"

"The Truce with the cyborgs. I broke it trying to get the Prime. The Dealers still out there are out of the Stream, but I programmed them to get the Prime. They caught half of it. Thus the rest of the Dealers disembarked their Lifts and are on the ground, searching, until they find the other half."

"Yes, sir." Claude had little concept what Michael was talking about. Cyborgs? None had been seen since the Chaos. So long ago, many believed they were just a myth; and the most accepted one was that the cyborgs had been wiped out during the Chaos, defeated by Dealer. In fact, it wasn't myth, it was the accepted history in Sound. But when Claude really thought about it, there were no facts to back that up; just what was in the Stream. But this did explain why Deep Void was off-limits. And a truce implied--

"There is a darkness into which I cannot see. Worse, there has been a darkness in—" a pause, as if Michael were searching for a word—"in me. A blank spot. This Millay of the People, and her twin, Grace-five-eleven-kilo-one. They have not existed in my system, in Dealer's system, but they have existed in the system. And they are the Prime."

"What is the Prime?" Claude dared ask.

Michael ignored the question. He retracted the probe and turned toward Claude, something in its metal claw: a small glass jar, filled with a golden liquid. "The Spice of Life."

Claude took a step toward the desk without even realizing it.

"You did a satisfactory job keeping me appraised of the Person's actions and thoughts," Michael said. "Both Andrew and the one before him. You told me of their treason. You have worked for the greater good of the Sound. This deserves a reward."

Claude held out his hands and Michael let go of the jar. Claude scrambled, almost dropping it to the floor, but finally getting both hands cupped underneath it. His fingers were shaking as he set it on the desk and he made to open it, but Michael's voice cut him off.

"Not here. Not now. There are more important matters."

Reluctantly, Claude looked up from the golden liquid.

"Achilles?" Michael asked.

"He is ready to rebuild Delta," Claude said. "Given that you have bestowed upon me the Spice of Life, it seems appropriate that Achilles should also—"

"Serve as he deserves," Michael said. "The situation in Delta is more complex than it appears. The Person before Andrew established Delta with the apparent motive of building a small, self-sustaining community outside of the Sound and outside of Code. Because of your predecessor, we learned of this from the beginning and co-opted the process by inserting Achilles and Doc with the first group. We replaced Charon with our own man. We kept control on it and guided it to our own means."

Claude nodded, aware of bits and pieces of this ploy, but not the big picture. Delta was a B.D. military base in Void where Achilles had gathered folders, burners who quit hive and followed the folding trail on the boundary between hive and the Wasteland until they arrived at the ferry landing, where Charon took them across the Sound.

For many decades, folding had been tantamount to committing suicide, since those few who survived in Void, could only do so by becoming the threat to their initial survival: jokers. Cannibals who preyed on newly arrived folders. But Achilles changed that, bringing folders together in Delta and building a community capable of defending itself against the jokers. But those who were floed, forced out of hive, were left to the mercy of the jokers and either were eaten by them or became them.

Up until a little over 30 days ago, when the decision had been to round up everyone in Delta and end the experiment.

Except Achilles. Who was left out there to start over again.

Doc and Charon were dead.

"Achilles is ready to do his duty," Claude said. "We need to replace Charon and—"

"This isn't about burners," Michael said. "It's about Delta. Achilles needs to keep it secure. It was a mistake for you to close it down."

Claude's mouth flapped open to protest that he'd run that decision by Dealer, which also meant by Michael, who'd approved it, but he stifled the protest.

"Most Deltans were bagged and extinguished, sir," Claude said instead. "But—"

Michael cut him off. "And that also wasn't what was to happen. I had a different plan for them. Bagging is a waste."

A waste of what? Claude wondered. "Well, sir, the ones under twenty are being held, since they are below age. Perhaps they could —" he paused, since his last original idea hadn't turned out too well. But then again, there on the desk was the Spice, so—"Perhaps we could allow them to escape? Facilitate their way back to Delta? Achilles can take command again."

There was a lingering silence that Claude found odd. Dealer/Michael could compute thousands of decisions a second. Why the hesitation?

"Do it."

"Yes, sir." Claude reached out to take the Spice and leave.

"And then," Michael said, once more causing Claude to pause. "There is the issue of Millay, once of the People. She is half the Prime. We need the other half."

"You just said the Dealers in Deep Void are doing that."

"And if they fail?"

Claude was out of suggestions.

"If my Dealers fail, which is not likely, then *they* will come for her," Michael said.

"They who, sir?"

"Ryker. Maybe they'll even be foolish enough to send Grace. And cyborgs. They will send someone, maybe even a team, to try to rescue her. To unite the Prime. We not only cannot allow that; *we* must be the ones who unite the Prime"

"We could assign more Dealers to guard—" Claude began, but was cut off again.

"Dealers do not stand up well against cyborgs," Michael said. "It requires Soldiers. I have prepared for this."

A piece of a dusty puzzle fell into place. Years ago, Claude has grown curious as to certain requisitions and assignment of some Evermores that didn't fit into the normal flow of the Sound. He'd done some research and learned that those Evermores were cannibalizing material from City and City Edge and actually driving out to some destination in the Wasteland, coming back with empty trucks. Since this action was approved by Dealer, although the Person was not aware of it, then . . .

However," Michael said, "force is not the correct course. Not while I need the Prime. We must be subtler than that. Use Millay of the People as a lure. Make it seem they might succeed in their task."

"And then?" Claude asked.

"Then whoever is sent will tell us where Grace is."

"Yes, sir. I will capture whoever they send and make sure they are available for interrogation. Is that all, sir?"

Claude bore the silence as long as he could, but after ten minutes, he picked up the bottle of spice and scurried out of the Oval, leaving Michael standing the center.

Not long after Claude left, Michael finally moved as a Lift came to a hover next to a platform that slid out of the side of the building. One of the windows of the Oval swung open to the platform. Michael stepped out of the building onto the platform and then into the Lift as the side door opened.

The platform retracted and the Lift banked hard, heading east.

Time to deal with the trouble in hive.

HUNDREDS OF YEARS IN THE FUTURE, AFTER THE CHAOS

Ryker and Ruth ran through the old growth forest, leaping over fallen logs, dodging the sparse undergrowth. Just ahead of them, Ace was scooting under some of the larger logs, leaping others.

The knowledge that he wasn't human, but a cyborg gave Ryker extra speed, even though Ruth had not had time to deprogram his governors. He'd always been fast, but now he could keep up with her as she led the way toward where the motion detectors had been activated.

Ryker had a pulser in hand, matching the one integrated into Ruth's arm. They hadn't said a word since leaving the cyborg base via a tunnel, leaving a fuming Grace behind.

It was difficult for Ryker to believe his body was a machine, because he could swear he was breathing, feeling cool air flowing down his throat into his lungs, he could smell the sweet smell of the forest, of the pine needles on the ground. They'd done such a good job on his model that it had even fooled the brain placed inside the cranial casing.

He shut down those thoughts as Ace skidded to a halt, a line of black-brown fur rippling up along his back. The dog's lips curled back and he emitted a low growl.

Ruth took a knee on one side of Ace, Ryker on the other. He looked over and Ruth nodded her head toward the dog and he realized she hadn't touched Ace; because she was machine.

He put his hand on the dog's neck, his human-like skin calming it a little.

"Remember," Ruth said. "They're Dealers, not Soldiers. They have stunners, not pulsers. So we have that advantage. And they're not armored. Your integrated armor is top of the line. But when we face Soldiers it will be very different; they have pulsers and armor. But the Dealers here have the advantage of numbers. How many Lifts did you see chasing us?"

"At least three."

"That's seventy-two Dealers if they were full."

"They weren't," Ryker said. "The ones at Port Townsend held eight each. That's a max of twenty-four."

"Good," Ruth said. She was looking ahead, trying to see whatever had caused Ace to alert. "Evens things up a bit."

Ryker laughed. "Optimistic."

"They're out of the Stream here," Ruth said. "Means they're acting autonomously. Dealers don't function well on their own. Michael had to put governors on their own processors; give them enough to function on their own when absolutely needed, but not enough that acting on their own could cause them to turn against him. The curse of the inventor and programmer to avoid a Frankenstein."

"Like us. Did Michael invent us?"

"No. We were a pre-Chaos project by the U.S. military. And we made you."

"There." Ryker pointed to the right front.

Ruth peered. "I don't see anything."

"Four Dealers," Ryker said. "Range two hundred twelve meters. Four meters lower than us. Azimuth zero-three-four degrees."

"Your programming is coming through," Ruth said. "And your sensors are amping up. Very good."

Ryker realized he'd given the target information without conscious thought. They were there, that's what he knew. He analyzed the terrain.

"We should—" Ruth began, but he cut her off.

"There are more than four out here. They must have broken down to six Dealer teams to cover more terrain. If we fire pulsers, we'll give away our position by the sound. Also, there could be an over-watch element and they're bounding forward. We take them out quietly."

He drew one of the coffin-handled Bowie knives from its sheath and extended it, handle first to Ruth. She took it and he drew the other one. He twirled the heavy weapon, steel flashing, then gripped the ivory handle. The blade was over nine inches long. Edged on the down side, except for a dip near the tip, where the haft thinned, giving it a sharp point. A cross guard protected the hand.

"Follow me," he said to Ruth as he stood up.

Together, crouched over, they ran through green-dappled forest, dew dripping off of leaves and branches. Ace was behind them, loping, easily keeping pace.

Ryker arced them to the right of where he knew the Dealers were. So that when they burst upon the machines, he and Ruth were on their left flank.

The first two went down with blades into the neck joint before they were even aware they being attacked. The last two turned fast, not fast enough. They collapsed besides their fellows, systems dead.

"More," Ryker said, pointing with the tip of his knife to the south. The blade wasn't dripping blood. Instead there was a dark oily sheen on it. But the metal wasn't scratched from cutting into the Dealers, a testament to a long-dead B.D. knife smith. Working the metal by hand, with the meticulousness a machine could match, but a passion for his craft, a machine never would possess.

"How many?" Ruth asked, accepting that he could 'see' more than she.

"Two." Ryker didn't move and Ruth waited. Ace was sniffing the inert machines, teeth bared, but not making a noise.

"Where's the other two?" Ruth asked.

"Exactly."

They waited. The two Dealers became visible to Ruth, crunching through the forest on a path that would miss their location, but take them close to the cyborg base.

"They're grasping," Ryker said in a low voice.

"What?"

"Look at the way they're moving. These—" he nodded at the lumps of metal next to them—"were on a parallel course. They're quartering this area in a search pattern. They won't stop until they find something."

"Or they're stopped."

"That's the plan. How many stuns can we take?"

"I can take four or five," Ruth said, "but the reboot gets slower each time. If I get hit repeatedly with more stuns while rebooting, there comes an overload point where my system will shut down."

"For how long?"

"Long enough for them to tear me to pieces."

"Well, let's not have that happen," Ryker said.

"No idea how many stuns you can absorb," Ruth added.

"Let's not find out."

"You're awfully optimistic."

"There's two in over-watch on top of that large rock," Ryker said. "We have to get them first. Let's go."

CLAUDE'S APARTMENT was on a middle floor in the tower. While every other Evermore lived across the Sound in City, serving three days on the Island coordinating with the People, then three days in City coordinating with the Middlemores, and having one day off, as the Person's personal assistant, Claude lived here on Island seven days a week.

It was the smallest apartment in the tower, which made it larger than any in City. A dozen burners cubbies would easily fit in the main room.

Claude was in the bathroom, the bottle on the edge of the sink. He leaned forward, pulled the stopper out and lifted it to his lips with a shaking hand. He tilted it back and the golden nectar flowed into his mouth.

Claude was surprised at the sharp tang and while he swallowed most, he coughed, spraying drops onto the mirror. Without hesitation, Claude pulled himself up and began lapping at the glass, getting every last bit.

He slid back, his belly thumping on the edge of the sink and stared into the mirror, searching for any drops he had missed. Then he looked into the sink and noticed a drop. With great difficulty he pushed himself forward, tongue out.

He scrambled and managed to lick it.

And then he fell, hitting his forehead on the sharp edge of the sink, continuing down to thud, unconscious on the floor as blood dribbled out of his lacerated skull and began to pool under his head.

GRACE PACED BACK and forth in the cryostasis chamber. Ryker and Ruth had left in such a rush she had no clue how anything worked in here. The green lights were still flashing on the front row of tubes; several computer screens were flickering. The latter was interesting, since they must have predated the holographic streams everyone in Sound was used to.

A buzzing noise interrupted her thoughts. It came from the tube on the left corner of the front row. The green light wasn't flashing any more. It was a steady glow.

There was a grinding noise and the front of the tube swung open, revealing a person, cyborg Grace mentally corrected, hanging in a harness on the inside.

Much like someone who was boxed.

But he had arms and legs. He appeared to be a young man, his artificial skin mostly intact, short brown hair. All his fingers and toes. He was dressed in just a pair of tight gray shorts.

Grace walked to the tube and waited.

The man's—cyborg's—eyes flickered and opened. They were machine, all black, pupils lost against the iris, an odd, and somewhat disconcerting appearance. Grace couldn't tell if he was looking at her or where exactly his gaze was directed.

His hands reached up to the buckles on the harness, fumbling, trying to find the releases. Grace helped, pulling the releases.

Free, the cyborg's feet touched the bottom of the tube. He staggered, regained control. Took a step forward as Grace took a step back. He exited the tube and his head swiveled back and forth, taking in the chamber.

"When is it? What day?" His voice was mechanical, Dealer-like.

"It's today," Grace said, since the only 'date' that a burner knew was Deathday and she was past that date.

"What year?"

"I don't know."

The eyes fixed on her. As near as she could tell. "How long since the Chaos?"

Grace remembered Mrs. Marash. "Over three hundred."

"'Three hundred'! So long. So very long to be gone." He reached out and Grace fought back a flinch as he touched the side of her face. "You're human." There was a slight change in the voice, less machine.

"I am. I'm Grace." She almost said her letter/number designator, but that didn't matter any more.

He stopped. "I am—" and there was a long pause—"I am Elias."

"Welcome back, Elias."

Grace now realized another aspect of his eyes that was disconcerting. The right eye was slightly off center, the small utter blackness where the pupil should be not quite true.

"Why was I brought back? Do I have the duty?" But as soon as he said, he shook his head. "They wouldn't wake me for the duty. We agreed on that. Do they have the cure?" His voice was changing even more and the last sentence was in a human voice, excitement creeping through.

"'Cure'?" Grace asked. "For what?"

Elias took a step toward Grace, inside her personal space. "*Why was I brought back if there isn't the cure?*"

"I don't know," Grace said. "Ruth said something about a key."

Elias was still for a moment. "Then it is Ryker. Is he here?"

"He was. He had to go out with Ruth and fight off some Dealers."

"Tell me what is happening."

Grace summarized events as succinctly as she could, starting from the battle at Port Townsend. While she did so, he pulled a gray jumpsuit of a bin on the side of his tube and pulled it on.

He stopped her when she mentioned Ryker.

"That name. I know that name." As if he didn't remember mentioning Ryker's name just a moment ago. "I knew a man named Ryker once. Long ago. Before the Chaos. Before being reborn. There's something—" Then he lapsed into confusion once more. When his mind came back: "Where were we?"

"I was telling you what happened."

"Finish please."

When she was done, Elias was quiet for a few moments and then spoke. "The Truce is over then. It's war." He looked behind him at the other tubes. "A ripple wakening. We had hoped we'd wake to a better world. Not to war again." He nodded. "Ruth woke me first because of Ryker. The day that was foretold is here now." He turned his attention to her. "*Who* are you? Why are you here?"

"I'm—" Grace hesitated, then said it for the first time—"I'm half of the Prime. My sister, Millay is the other half."

"The 'Prime'?" Elias slowly nodded. "Part of what Ryker promised. That the Prime would come. Give access to the Backdoor and—" he feel silent and Grace waited for several seconds. Then: "What was I saying?"

"The Prime." Grace suggested. "The 'Backdoor'."

"Oh. Yes. According to Ryker we can take the Sound from Michael with the Backdoor."

"What is it?"

"A way to get to Dealer. It's what we pinned our hopes on. But some didn't believe. Where is your sister?"

"Michael has her prisoner."

"That's—" and again he went silent, perfectly still.

"Are you all right?" Grace asked, but her brain was buzzing: she'd experienced this before. With Mrs. Marash.

He pointed at his head. "My brain is deteriorating. A disease. This body, this machine, we can fix it. But what's happening to my brain; we can't fix it. The human part. The only human left of me. And it is slowly dying. I am dying."

"I'm sorry," Grace said.

"Technology can only do so much."

"Why would you be first? What do you know of Ryker?"

He walked past her, to the control panel. "Perhaps it is in the mainframe," he said, as if convincing himself of it. He was looking at the console. He lifted his arm and a probe came out, sliding into the machine. "She's waking everyone in a ripple," he repeated as if he didn't remember saying it. "Using max power. Dangerous and we might not be able to come back from it. But since the Truce is over, then everyone is needed." He paused. "Even me, but I can't remember why I am important to Ryker. We had to compartmentalize so much to safeguard information. To safeguard—" a hint of excitement tinted his voice—"to safeguard Ryker's plan."

"But Ryker doesn't know the plan," Grace said. "If he does, he didn't share it with us. He only realized we were to try to get to Centre when I told him some lines from a poem."

"'Centre'? Ah, yes. Where Dealer is. You told him a poem and he remembered? A key. That's it! An implanted key that only one person would know. I know one—" the excitement abated—"I knew it. Ryker didn't know my mind would start to go."

"You can remember it," Grace assured him. "The Second Coming?" she tried. Then repeated the line from the poem, but the words did nothing.

The probe retracted. Elias turned to her. "Ruth's upload before she left to battle the Dealers confirms what you have told me. Tell me —" he fumbled into silence.

"Grace."

"Tell me, Grace. Do you know what the Prime is? What you are?"

"No."

"Strange."

"Do you?"

"Not that I can recall." Elias nodded his head toward the console. "Ruth left instructions that if this facility was breached by Dealers I was not to allow you to be taken prisoner."

"She'll come back," Grace said. "She's with Ryker." She thought about it. "How would you do that?"

"Kill you," Elias said as he reached out and grabbed her arm. "I will not hurt you, Grace, unless I have to in order to prevent you from falling into Michael's control. From Ruth's report, Michael already has the other half of the Prime. We cannot allow him to complete it."

"Millay and I are that dangerous?"

"Please don't struggle," Elias said. "Let us wait for them to get back." He went silent for a little while. "I have to remember." He slowly turned his head, taking in the cavern, as if something might prompt his memory. "We had a name for this place near the end of the Chaos," he said. "When the battle was going badly. We called it Masada. Named after an ancient fortress in—"

As he fumbled for the name, Grace looked at the hatch that opened on the tunnel Ruth and Ryker had left through. She'd sealed it behind them.

"We named it—"

He stalled once more.

"Masada," Grace gently said.

"Yes. An ancient fortress where rebels held out against the mightiest empire of the time for a long time. But when the time came and they knew the walls would fall and the enemy would win, they killed themselves."

"That makes no sense."

"They would have been slaughtered anyway. They made it a choice. Their final choice."

"But that's not what you did when you faced down Michael," Grace pointed out. She thought she heard a noise from the hatch. Cocked her head. But there was nothing.

"Do you know how to win a game of chicken?" Elias asked.

"What game is that?"

"You don't have cars in Sound?"

"There are trucks. Middlemores drive them." And Evermores, Grace remembered from Haydn and Millay's tale of the Wasteland.

"Two trucks are driving straight toward each other," Elias said. "The game is to see who will turn away first."

"It would be smart to turn away," Grace said.

"That's why it's a game," Elias said.

"It's dumb," Grace said, but she got the idea. "A test of wills."

"Exactly. So how would one win this every time?"

"Never turn away."

"Yes, but how would the other driver know you won't turn until it's too late?"

"I don't know," Grace said. "The other driver wouldn't know."

"The solution is simple," Elias said. "You remove your steering wheel so you cannot turn. Hold it up so the other driver can see. Then the other driver must turn away or crash into you."

With his free hand Elias extended his probe into the console. He looked toward the hatch leading to the landing bay where Ruth had brought them and parked the Lift. "They're coming."

"Ryker? Ruth?"

"No. Dealers. They're here." He removed the probe. His pulser flipped down, ready for use.

"Don't do it," Grace said.

"I'm taking the steering wheel off," Elias said. He aimed it at her.

"Machines don't know fear," Grace said. "They won't turn away."

≈

Two Dealers were kneeling behind a large log, oriented toward the two that were slowly moving forward; a classic over-watch position to provide covering fire. Ryker and Ruth took the over-watch out, striking home with the knives at the same moment. A second later, both of them were hit with multiple stuns, coming from several directions, knocking them down.

Ryker lay on his side, his system rebooting. He managed to speak: "Ruth?"

No reply.

There was no pain; in fact there was no feeling at all, his system overloaded. He'd felt at least three strike, but wasn't certain. He could hear movement in the forest; Dealers coming toward them, breaking through the undergrowth. Not far away but not too close.

They had some time.

Ryker felt foolish as his system slowly came back on-line. The over-watch had been the bait for the ambush, not the two moving forward under their watch. He'd under-estimated the Dealers.

Ryker rolled over, got to his knees, pulled the pulser out of his belt. "Ruth?"

She wasn't moving.

Ryker peered over the log and two stuns hit the log. He ducked back down. Looked left and right, and then over his shoulder. At least eight Dealers were coming in, each pair on perfect ninety-degree azimuths from each other, covering all directions. Any way he ran, at least four would have a shot.

"Ruth?"

"Getting there," she said.

"Get there faster." Ryker popped his head up with his firing hand. He fired twice, both pulses hitting home. He was down before seeing the result as stuns came in from the other, one striking a glancing blow on his firing shoulder.

He grabbed the pulser with his other hand. The shoulder was tingling, but the single stun hadn't disrupted his overall system. He did a quick three-hundred-sixty degree check. There was a second wave behind the first. Eight more. These offset from the first wave, covering the gaps between.

Ruth sat up. "Situation report?"

"Took out two from the first wave."

"First wave?"

"Eight on equal quadrants. Two down. Eight in a second wave, covering the gaps. Might even be more behind them. They'll become more accurate as they get closer."

"Are they connected?" Ryker asked.

"They're not in the Stream," Ruth said.

"But their attack is coordinated," Ryker said. "They have to be communicating with each other somehow."

"A LAN," Ruth said. "They have to be using a Local Area Network."

Ryker looked at the 'dead' Dealer next to him. "Where would this LAN be?"

Ruth pulled herself over, on the other side of the Dealer. "We disassembled some Soldiers during the Chaos. I assume they're pretty similar in design. Roll it over."

Ryker shoved the machine, putting it 'face down'.

Ruth pointed at the back of the head. "Here."

Ryker brought the knife up over his and slammed it in a seam below that point. It penetrated a half-inch. Then he leveraged.

Ruth was hit by a stun and fell forward onto the Dealer. With his other hand, Ryker fired the pulser, hitting a Dealer that was less than ten meters away. It fell back, but then others came into view.

The rear of the Dealer's head plate broke loose. Ryker was hit in the back by stun but he could still function. He 'knew' exactly what he was looking at. The circuitry, the design. He dropped the knife and bent his right wrist forward. A probe, slimmer and sleaker than the one Ruth had used in the cavern emerged. He slid it into a slot right where Ruth had pointed.

In a flash he could sense all the Dealers out here, their exact position.

Six were in the base, in the landing bay.

He was hit by another stun.

ELIAS WAS FACING the hatch leading to the landing bay.

"Don't do it," Grace repeated. "Give me a pulser. We'll fight them."

"You might pulse me," Elias said.

She pointed at a pulser on one of the equipment tables. "We can defeat them. Ryker and Grace will be back."

"Six Dealers are in the landing bay," Elias said. "The two of us can't stop six."

There was loud clang of metal on metal.

"Please don't do it," Grace said.

"It's an order. I'm very sorry."

"You're human," Grace argued. "You can make a decision on your own. We have to try! It's only machines that follow orders without question."

Elias let go of her arm and she ran to the table and grabbed a pulser.

RYKER WAS HIT by two more stuns and he sensed his system edging toward shutdown. The first ring of Dealers were just a few meters away, about to over-run the position.

He took that 'sense' and flowed it into the Dealer's LAN.

THE HATCH SWUNG OPEN.

Grace and Elias began firing as the first Dealers charged in.

The first two were blasted back, but the following four were firing back.

Grace was stunned in the chest and went down.

Elias looked at her. "We tried."

He pointed his pulser at her.

RYKER CAME BACK on-line surrounded by Dealers. More statues.

He retracted his probe from the LAN.

Ruth sat up, looking at the Dealers. "Very smart. How did you know what command to send?"

"I reflected my own pending shut down. Except with more power."

"You over-loaded their circuits." Ruth got to her feet and went to the nearest standing Dealer. "Will they reboot?"

"No." Ryker didn't know how he knew that, but he was certain of it. "Six made it into the base."

"Are they shut down too?"

"Yes. But I don't know how far in they penetrated. We have to get back. Make sure Grace is all right. Can you make it?"

"Give me a minute."

"Grace might not have a minute," Ryker said and he took off, running through the forest, retracing the way they'd come.

He reached the access port, hidden underneath a camouflage net on the side of the mountain. He flung the hatch open and shimmied inside. He crawled down the tunnel. He didn't pause when he reached the end, shoving the inside hatch open and rolling forward, onto the floor, coming to his knees, pulser at the ready in one hand, Bowie in the other.

A cyborg had a pulser pointed at Grace. And four Dealers were frozen in the hatch to the landing bay.

"Easy," Ryker said. "I'm a friend."

"Ryker." The cyborg nodded, his pulser folding back. "I'm Elias."

Ryker got to his feet and ran to Grace, checking for a pulse.

"She was stunned," Elias said. "She should be all right."

"What were you doing?" Ryker asked.

The cyborg looked down, as if confused. "I"—a long pause—"I had orders to make sure she didn't fall into Michael's hands."

Ryker picked Grace up and carried her to a table. He set her down gently.

The hatch clanged and Ruth entered, brushing leaves out of what remained of her hair. "Is she alive?" she yelled, even before she lowered herself to the ground.

"Just stunned," Ryker said. "He almost killed her."

"Oh, Elias!" She went over and placed a hand, the one covered in fake flesh, on Elias' shoulder. "It's all right. You were doing what you were ordered to."

"We're not supposed to be programmed like machines," Elias said.

There was a whine from the open hatch. Ace's head was poking out, but the German Shepherd was eyeing the distance from his position to the floor.

Ryker went over and helped the dog out.

"We're going to have to up-armor to fight Soldiers," Ruth said.

"'Up-armor'?"

"External armor," Ruth said.

"We can't defeat them by force," Ryker said. "We have to outsmart them."

Grace stirred, opened her eyes. She smiled when she saw Ryker standing over her. "You made it."

"Of course," Ryker said. He helped her sit up.

The hair on Ace's back was standing up, and he was emitting a low growl, skittering sideways, focused on Elias.

"Dogs don't like us," Elias said.

"He'll warm to you," Ruth promised.

"I doubt it," Elias said. He nodded at Grace. "She told me the Truce is over. What now?"

"We need a plan," Ruth said.

"Sounds like you have the beginnings of one," Ryker said.

"I do," Ruth said, "but we need the end of the plan too."

"Wait a moment," Elias said. He pointed at Ryker. "I know you. I knew you before the Chaos. There is something I have to tell you."

"What?" Ryker asked.

Elias slammed both his hands on the side of his head. "I can't remember!"

MIDWAY IN THE 20TH
CENTURY, BEFORE THE CHAOS

"T echnically, you are still a prisoner," General Hoffelder said.

Once upon a time General Ishii, now prisoner Ishii, didn't look like a prisoner in his freshly pressed suit. There was a fine layer of dust on it, but there was a fine layer of dust on everything and everyone out here.

The two were standing on the edge of a dirt runway that extended as far as one could see in either direction. A few battered hangers were behind them. A lonely control tower. The plane they'd just gotten off was already in the air heading back to Las Vegas.

Across the runway, a large mountain blotted out the horizon. A plume of dust approached from the shadow of the mountain.

"'Technically'," Ishii repeated. "And not technically?"

"The Russians wanted to talk to you," Hoffelder said. "Rather urgently. Got their balls in a ringer when we wouldn't let them have a crack at you and your boys. And you got the immunity. So now it's time for you to ante up. Full disclosure."

"It would help to have my files," Ishii said.

"Oh we got your files," Hoffelder said. "And we got your ass if you don't play ball."

The Jeep pulled up. The driver was a staff sergeant. The man in the *passenger seat had on a dirty white lab coat. He leapt from the seat, hand extended. "Doctor Ishii! So glad you could come out here."*

Hoffelder looked none too pleased.

"I'm Doctor Reynolds from Fort Detrick. I'm the one who filed the report."

"The 'report'?" Ishii said.

"To MacArthur and then Washington," Reynolds said. "They asked me if you were important. Whether your data was important. I wrote back, saying absolutely invaluable. I wrote that there was no way we could ever obtain your data, due to scruples here in the States regarding experimentation on humans. I think we're getting a gold mine for relatively low cost."

A slight smile curled underneath the mustache on Ishii's face. Hoffelder caught it, and the General spit, narrowly missing Ishii's shoe. But Reynolds was still prattling on.

"MacArthur himself endorsed the letter!"

Ishii looked over at Hoffelder. "I assume then, that I am no longer a prisoner?"

"You don't fart when you're told to fart, you won't be a prisoner, you'll be dead." The general waved his hand out toward the desert. "A body can disappear real easy out here."

"I imagine so," Ishii said. "But I was endorsed by General McArthur himself. Might be easy to hide a body, but difficult to explain someone who has disappeared."

"They gave Groves the Manhattan Project," Hoffelder grumbled, "and I got this nest of vipers."

Ishii ignored him and climbed in the back seat of the Jeep.

Reynolds gave up his seat to the general, not for decorum or rank, but so he could sit with Ishii. The doctor was still talking even though the sound of jeep's engine and the wind whistling by made him practically inaudible.

The staff sergeant had the Jeep floored, not that that made it go very fast, heading directly toward the mountain. The sergeant glanced over and leaned toward Hoffelder. "Ever been here, General?"

"No."

The driver lifted a finger from the wheel and pointed ahead. "Groom Mountain. We're going inside it to the base."

"Base got a name?"

"No, sir. Just a designation grid on the map."

"And that is?"

"Area 51."

~

THE LAB WAS BEHIND two heavy, steel vault doors, each one guarded by steely-eyed soldiers, who checked everyone's identification card twice. Reynolds griped that they saw him every day and they ignored him.

The last door opened on a long corridor carved out of the mountain stone.

"Your quarters," Reynolds said, pointing to the first door on the left. He made to open it, but Ishii stopped him.

"I wish to see the lab. And my records. And my scientists."

"Of course," Reynolds said.

General Hoffelder said nothing, following, a scowl on his face.

At the end of the corridor, after passing a half dozen doors on either side, they arrived at a metal door with a round glass portal and a hand wheel below that. A green light was glowing next to it, a red light off.

"Air lock," Reynolds said.

"I see," Ishii said, in a tone that indicated either it was a stupid comment on Reynolds part or he was being polite and failing, but it wasn't in his nature to be polite.

Reynolds grabbed the hand wheel and turned it. Bolts unlocked and he swung the door open, revealing an air lock. The three men entered and Reynolds shut the door behind them and activated the red light on the outer door. He waited a few moments as the airlock over pressurized to equal that in the lab. Then he spun the hand wheel on the inner door.

They entered the lab. About two hundred feet long by fifty wide, there was a center aisle and tables covered with equipment on either side. A half dozen of Ishii's scientists were at work, peering through microscopes, checking growths in petri dishes, reading reports. They all snapped to attention upon seeing Ishii.

"Jesus H. Christ," General Hoffelder exclaimed.

Ishii glanced to his right at the General bemused. "I assume this is your first time here also, General?" He waved at his men to get back to work.

The object of Hoffelder's shock was a glass tube, four feet high, by two in diameter. Inside was, floating in formaldehyde, was a young boy of approximately three years, his body cut open from throat to lower belly, organs exposed.

"You have the samples, of course?" Ishii asked.

"Of course," Reynolds quickly said. "After all the formaldehyde essentially taints the cells."

"Then why the hell do you still have him here?" Hoffelder demanded.

Ishii turned to the General. "A reminder." He walked to the tube, Reynolds at his side, Hoffelder reluctantly following.

"Of what?" Hoffelder asked.

"Of our past and of our future. Of the fork in the road from death to life." Ishii pointed. "This was the case that started our investigations. It was born in—"

"The boy was born," Hoffelder interjected.

"The subject was part of a batch selected to gauge the effectiveness of a strain of plague," Ishii continued. "It was the only subject to still be alive after three days. And showed no signs of illness. So we began to focus on it. We placed the subject in a very different test."

"This was a person," Hoffelder said. "A kid for cripes sake."

"This is a test subject," Ishii said. He faced the American officer. "General, I have no doubt this repels you. But that is in fact, the reason I, and my scientists, were recruited by your country. We learned things via means you cannot comprehend, never mind attempt. For example, we learned a new methodology to treat frostbite. Our country was facing the prospect back then of having to fight the Soviet Union. As your country faces that prospect now. Many powers have tried to invade Russia, but most often it was the winter that defeated them, not the Russians. Thus it means being ready to effectively treat large numbers of cold weather injuries.

"Doctor Hisato, of my staff, discovered that the accepted method of rubbing the affected area was ineffectual. Often injurious. He determined the correct method, inversion in water, heated between forty and fifty

Celsius had the most beneficial effect. Many of your soldiers will benefit from this."

"I don't want to know how your guy learned this," Hoffelder muttered.

Ishii smiled, taking it as an invite for a dig. "Hisato would immerse an appendage in water, then allow it to freeze. To make sure, one of his staff would strike it with a stick. A frozen arm makes a distinctive noise. My men learned to recognize it. Then the frozen flesh was chipped away and water of varying temperatures was applied. All very scientific."

He turned back to the tube. "We used another deadly bacteria on the next batch with the subject. And the subject survived. We knew we had something unique. We ran more tests. We learned it could survive a wide range of viruses and infections, but we didn't know how it did."

"Why did you kill him, then?" Hoffelder asked.

"We weren't sure we could kill it," Ishii said. "Given all that it had survived. Ultimately, though, we had gone as far we could with living samples. We tested various wounds first and learned that the cells did not regenerate as quickly as we had hoped. It seemed that the process was slow. Enough to handle a virus, but not fast enough for a sudden wound. This intrigued us. Finally, we damaged it past the point of recovery. I then made the decision to examine further. This is the result."

"Was it worth it?"

Ishii looked confused. "If it weren't worth it, I would not be here as a guest of your government." He was done with the General. He barked out something in Japanese and one of the men in white coats scurried over. Ishii began questioning him in Japanese, getting rapid answers.

Hoffelder looked at Reynolds, but he just shrugged.

After three minutes, Ishii turned back to them and English. "Most interesting. Testing here, with your equipment, which my associate indicates is most excellent, indicates that whatever was happening in the subject, was occurring at the cellular level. I had assumed that, of course, but it is always gratifying to have assumptions turned into fact.

"Because we were isolated in Manchuria and the war was interfering with scientific sharing," Ishii continued, "there was much we were not aware of. Also much has happened in this field in the past year. Most interesting." He stroked his chin, deep in thought.

Reynolds couldn't hold back. "What's most interesting?"

"One of your scientists, indeed a man who won the Nobel Prize last year, Doctor Muller, has done considerable work on the effects of radiation on cells. He was one of the first to point out the dangers of excessive exposure. Of course, he worked with fruit flies; but there was a good reason for that beyond ethics. One can go through so many generations so quickly and thus follow the patterns."

Ishii turned to the scientists and snapped several questions in Japanese.

"Most excellent!" he exclaimed. "And most intriguing. Doctor Muller has postulated that there are structures on the end of chromosomes, called telomeres, that have some sort of protective role for the cells. How they do this, he does not know. But given his work on radiation, one would correlate that certain exposure to radiation might involve certain mutations at the cellular level. And strangely, he also did work on twins separated at birth and their hereditary development."

"Why is that interesting?" Reynolds asked.

Ishii nodded at the body in the tube. "It was a twin. And, my colleague checked the records of its parents. The mother was x-rayed numerous times while pregnant in an attempt to watch the development of the fetuses. We rarely had the opportunity to watch twins in utero."

"What happened to its twin?" Reynolds asked, earning a disgusted look from Hoffelder.

"Still born." Ishii turned away from the corpse. "I'd like to look at its records myself."

"Of course," Reynolds said. He pointed to the far end of the lab. "They're in a separate vault. Hermetically sealed to protect the contents."

Reynolds led Ishii in that direction.

General Hoffelder remained in place, staring at the boy's body floating in the glass tube.

～

"WHATEVER IT IS," Ishii reluctantly admitted to Reynolds, "I don't believe the technology has yet been invented to uncover. However, I have no doubt *that as our equipment gets more precise and allows us to see at the level we need, we will achieve our goal of isolating the secret of longer life."*

They were in the center of the lab. All his scientists were gathered behind Ishii. It had been two weeks since the Japanese General, or Doctor as he now preferred, had arrived. In that time he'd been brought up to speed on everything that had been accomplished at Area 51, and in the worldwide scientific community, while he had been held pending trial.

A trial that had never come to fruition.

"Therefore," Ishii said, "I propose we move in a new direction. As per the request I put in, you must allow us to conduct radiological testing on human subjects. We have recommended that initially these subjects be drawn from those condemned to death in your prison system."

"I've forwarded your recommendation through secure channels," Reynolds said.

STANDING IN THE AIRLOCK, General Hoffelder was peering through the small portal at the meeting. He couldn't hear what was being said, but he didn't need to. He'd seen the request and the recommendation by Reynolds.

He shifted his gaze from Reynolds, Ishii and the Japanese scientists to the glass tube and the young boy floating in it. With one hand he unbuttoned his uniform shirt and wrapped his hand around the small gold cross he wore on a chain with his dog tags.

"Burn in hell, you sons-a-bitches," Hoffelder muttered. With his other hand, he pulled open a panel below the red and green lights. A small black button was inside. Hoffelder pushed it.

The incendiary charges built along the outside wall of the lab to prevent an accidental breach of containment protocol did exactly what Hoffelder had wished: turned the lab into a blazing inferno, incinerating everyone and everything inside.

A small charge in the airlock did the same to Hoffelder.

HUNDREDS OF YEARS IN THE FUTURE, AFTER THE CHAOS

Michael was flying the Lift; he always piloted manually when he was in one, even though the auto-pilot was slaved to his own directions. Every machine in the Stream was slaved to him, via Dealer.

But he didn't like giving up the control. And he could look out of the cockpit and get a first hand view of things outside. Images via the Stream were valuable, but he'd learned long ago that seeing things for himself made a difference. A vestige of his human self, but one he didn't spend time wondering about.

It is what it is.

He passed over the water of the Sound, seeing two Waves sailing below, one heading to Island, the other coming back. Supplies and Evermores going west, Evermores and commands going east. The humans had to have the illusion they were running things. It was part of the program Dealer had calculated and implemented over 300 years ago.

But Michael knew it was time for change. And it was obvious Ryker did too, or he wouldn't have activated. Michael could sense Ryker's presence, outside the Stream yet barely touching it, a feather on edge of the flow of data. But Michael couldn't read Ryker or even determine where he was. He just knew he was there. He knew Ryker could see the Dealer Stream but not enter it; that at least Michael had prepared for. The Stream was his, because Dealer controlled it, and Dealer was protected by an unbreakable quantum encryption.

Which begat which? Michael wondered as he passed over City. The balance upset, or Ryker activating? The data suggested the former.

Michael glanced to his left. The Space Needle had been decapitated during the Chaos. He had considered rebuilding it, but what was the point? It was part of the past. Most of the tallest buildings, to the right, had also been hit. They poked up like broken teeth.

The city was where Michael had run his conglomerate before the Chaos. He'd lived on Island, known as Bainbridge back then, and flew his own helicopter in every day, landing on the top of corporate headquarters.

Perhaps that was where the desire to pilot his own Lift came from?

Then he was over City Edge, where the Middlemores resided.

There was smoke ahead and Michael directed the Lift toward hive. Arriving, the four engines, one on each corner of the rectangular shaped craft, rotated from horizontal to vertical, bringing the Lift to a hover.

He could 'see' the cordon of Soldiers surrounding the hive that had revolted, each machine a tiny dot on the tactical overlay of what he was looking at. The bodies were a waste; they couldn't be bagged, it was too late. That meant decisions would have to be made. The Sound was a closed ecosystem. A community where the living existed in conjunction with the nonliving; the land, the air, the water, the resources, and most of all, the machines.

Michael had made the decision to crush the revolt brutally and quickly and he didn't regret it even though it upset the balance of things. A balance could be restored.

Though his contact with Dealer was encrypted, Michael didn't want to leave anything to chance. He pushed forward on the controls, going from hover to flight, turned the Lift and headed toward Dealer to have a direct interface.

CLAUDE RETURNED TO CONSCIOUSNESS, his head in a pool of blood. He struggled to sit up. He gingerly touched his head, where it throbbed with pain. He could feel the gash. He tried to stand but he had to sit back down, his head woozy.

He remained still for a while, trying to remember what had happened.

The Spice!

Claude looked up and saw the empty vial and that pushed the pain away momentarily. He had it in him. He had more life. He looked down at the green card on his chest and knew that Deathday was no longer valid.

More time.

The most valuable reward one could be given.

Claude struggled to his feet, holding on to the sink. His mind was a little off. He tried to remember what had happened in the Oval. Michael's instructions.

Millay. Part of the Prime. She was bait. To get the other half. To make whoever came for her talk.

But how would they know where she was? How would Ryker and Grace know?

A trap did no work if no one walked into it.

And Michael hadn't believed him when he'd pointed out that if Millay wasn't talking, why would whoever came for her give up the location of Grace? Had he said that? And they certainly wouldn't be sending Grace into the lion's den.

"No," Claude said to his reflection in the mirror. "Not a good plan."

He used a towel to wipe the blood off his face. The wound had stopped bleeding. He should see a Doc, but that wasn't a priority.

He could do better. He knew it. And by doing better, he would be rewarded again. More Spice. More life.

And, of course, there were other possibilities.

Claude went to the Lift and dropped down, below ground level, to the service tunnels that were the province of the Evermores. He passed two security checkpoints where his card was scanned and his retinas. The thick doors opened automatically and closed behind him.

He passed by the boxing control room. The closed Stream displayed Millay on the table, the IVs. Her eyes were closed. She appeared asleep, but Claude doubted that. The pain was too great.

He went across the room and another door opened onto a long corridor. On either side were observation Streams, spaced every ten feet, in front of a large door. The Streams presented what was on the other side of the door.

Boxes holding all those who'd suffered the fate since the Sound was founded. And were still alive. It seemed that even being a People, and having the Spice of Life forced into the system via the shunt, when the will to live was completely gone, life did end.

Claude walked to the most recent Stream on the right. The night vision image of Andrew, once the Person, hanging in his harness in the dark box was displayed. His face was gaunt, his skin pale, his lips cracked and covered in scabs, but they were moving, saying something, too low for the monitor to pick up at the current setting.

Claude turned the volume up to maximum.

"Stone walls do not a prison make. Nor iron bars a cage."

Claude sighed. Such foolishness. He turned the volume down and accessed the Stream, gathering information. Satisfied, he typed on the command board. A probe extended from the wall and spritzed liquid onto Andrew's lips. His tongue snaked out, mouth wide open, trying to take in every bit of the painkiller. While this was happening, Claude was turning on the light inside, gradually increasing it. Then he withdrew the probe. He shut down the Observation Stream, isolating the box and Andrew. He opened the door and stepped inside.

"Andrew."

The former Person took a while to focus his eyes, blinking hard against the light.

"Andrew. You've had enough liquid and painkiller. You can speak."

"Claude. You'll be dead soon."

Claude laughed. "That's the best you can do? You're wrong. Michael gave me some Spice. Something you would never have done."

"Michael is the enemy of mankind."

"I'm not here to argue with you," Claude said. "Actually, I agree with you. Michael is dangerous. Very dangerous. He has to be stopped. We're alone right now and can talk freely. Out of the Observation Stream. This is between you and me. He hasn't replaced you. He isn't going to. He doesn't see the need to have a Person in the Oval any more. It might have been mostly a pretense before, but it was at least a gesture. And the Person did have some power. Now there is nothing to check Michael."

"He gave you the Spice," Andrew said, "to own you." His eyes were focused now, staring at Claude. "You betrayed me."

"I was wrong." Claude took a step closer. "He sent Dealers into Deep Void. They're searching for Grace at this very moment. The Truce is over. He told me there are cyborgs out there; so the stories of Dealer defeating them at the end of the Chaos were false. We are on the verge of war; another Chaos. Everything that we have built up here will be destroyed."

"Why are you telling me this?"

"I need your help," Claude said.

"Help with what?"

"Helping Millay get to Deep Void and join her sister. Uniting the Prime. Stopping Michael."

"Why would you betray Michael?"

"Whatever you think of me," Claude said, "I'm still human. I have a son and a daughter. Something you never even bothered to learn about me. My son is an Evermore. My daughter was dealt Middlemore. That was a blow to my wife and I. But we never complained. We've done our duty. But Michael, I fear he no longer cares about humans. His only concern is getting the Prime. If he doesn't see a need for a Person, how long before he doesn't see the need for any of us?"

Andrew didn't respond.

Claude took another step closer, reached out, and placed his hand on Andrew's chest, above the shunt that provided him with all that was needed, besides oxygen, to remain alive. "I did betray you. But only because the Person before you, and then you, were secretly building Delta. Outside of Code. You never bothered to inform me why you were doing this. When Michael showed me this, I thought it was *you* who was betraying mankind. I was wrong. Michael is the enemy. We must work together, Andrew. For the good of all humans; not just People and Evermores and Middlemore and burners too. We can make things better for them too."

"How can I help you?"

"They'll send someone for Millay. The cyborgs. They want to unite the Prime also."

"Why is Grace with the cyborgs?"

Claude pulled his hand back. "That, honestly, I don't know. But it has something to do with this man, Ryker."

"So what do you want me to do?"

"Get a message to Grace, to the cyborgs. Let them know where Millay is. When they send someone, we capture whoever it is. Find out where Grace is. Then send Millay to link up with Grace and come back to the humans."

"Not much of a plan," Andrew said.

Claude's masked slipped. "'Not much of a plan'? This from a man who's been boxed?"

"Exactly. You make my point. How am I getting a message out there into Deep Void? It's out of the Stream. *I'm* out of the Stream."

"I have a solution for that."

"WHAT HAPPENED TO YOU?" Tori asked.

Haydn sat with her outside of their hall. They'd grabbed some food and drink from inside. Now Haydn was tearing into the food, real food, not 'tein, for which he was very, very grateful given what he'd seen last night. And while he knew Heaven was a lie, the food was real.

"Can you keep a secret?" Haydn asked, mouth half full.

"From who?"

"From the Greeter. From everyone."

"Why?"

"Forget it," Haydn said. "It's my problem."

"You're very strange," Tori said. "You don't want to sex me. Or anyone else. Because you're in love with someone who isn't even here. And you're going to die soon. And why were you sent to Heaven twelve days early?"

"That's a good question," Haydn said. "One I've been wondering about. I should have been bagged and extinguished."

"What did you do?" Tori looked around nervously.

"Best if you don't know."

"But you just wanted to tell me a secret," she point out. "You don't make any sense."

What he'd seen hadn't made much sense and he was still jingle-jangled from the experience.

"Where did you go last night?" Tori asked.

A group of burners staggered by, drunk, clothes in disarray, but laughing, enjoying the perks of Heaven, blissfully unaware of the lies.

"I'm not sure Heaven is all that great," Haydn said, watching them.

"I had a great time last night. What I remember of it." She laughed. "Of course you wouldn't think Heaven is great if you don't partake. Did you even believe in Heaven when you were in hive? Or were you one of those?" Her tone made it quite clear what she thought of those.

"I didn't believe in it," Haydn admitted.

"So you were wrong."

Haydn had to smile at that. "I was wrong. Heaven does exist."

"And it's what we were promised, isn't it?"

"Right here is." But his mind was focused somewhere else. "But what about beyond the Wall?"

She gasped. "Did you go beyond? How? It's against Code! You'll be bagged. Extinguished. No more Heaven."

Haydn looked back at her. "But that's would should have happened to me before I was brought here." Another thing that didn't make any sense. "Michael—"

"Who?"

"Dealer. Dealer didn't bag me for a reason. He—it, wants me to get to Millay. To get to Grace."

"Is one of these women the woman you say you are so in love with, that you can't enjoy Heaven?"

"Yes."

"Where is she? Still in hive?"

"I don't know."

Tori leaned close, putting an arm around Haydn's shoulder. "Tell me what's beyond the Wall?"

"I think they do something to us when we die," Haydn said. He was about to tell her what he'd seen, but what good would it do? There was nothing she could do about it. And he wasn't sure what was happening beyond the Wall anyway.

Tori shrugged. "It is what it is. We're going to die regardless. What does it matter what they do to us after we're dead?"

Haydn sighed. "But there are lies in Sound. Dealer lies. How can we believe anything?"

"It is what it is," she repeated. The mantra of hive. She grabbed his hand, pulling him to his feet. "Come. Let's have some fun. You won't sex, but we can drink!"

"I can't remember," Elias repeated.

"Ruth says you know me," Ryker said. "When we were both human. You saved me. Do you remember any of our time together?"

"We did things together. Things outdoors. I remember an axe. Ice. Snow. Climbing a mountain."

"Good," Ryker said. He looked at Grace and Ruth, who were anxiously following the conversation.

"You were to be first awoken if Ryker came back," Ruth said to Elias. "You must have a key for him. To unlock something in his mind."

Elias closed his eyes. "I'm trying! But the damage to my head. My brain. It's not what it was. I was supposed to be awoken for a cure."

"We don't have a cure for your brain," Ruth said.

"You are remembering things, Elias," Grace's voice was gentle.

They were gathered around the console. Ace was just behind Grace, as if using the only human here as a shield against the three cyborgs. He wasn't growling, but his hackles were still up.

Grace reached out and touched the side of Elias' face. "You *can* remember. I was with Mrs. Marash—" she glanced at Ruth—"with Hanan. Her mind was damaged too. But she could remember in moments of clarity. She gave me the key for Ryker about Centre. For Ruth about Ryker."

"A poem?" Ryker suggested. "Is there a poem you remember? The Second Coming."

"I can't—" Elias said, but Ryker suddenly stiffened and held a hand up. "Wait!"

Grace was startled by his abrupt change. "What?"

"Dealer is damming its Stream," Ryker said.

"How do you know?" Ruth demanded. "The Dealer Stream doesn't reach out here."

"I can reach the Stream on my own," Ryker said. "I feel it, a distant thing, but I can—" he paused.

"No!" Grace exclaimed. "Tell me it's not Millay's boxing!"

"Can the Dealer Stream reach you?" Ruth demanded. "Does it know where you are?"

"It doesn't know where I am," Ryker reassured her. "It can't touch me." He held out a hand, palm up. "Here is what Dealer is sending."

Grace sighed, knowing it wasn't a boxing, but her relief was only temporary. A hive, dead bodies, Soldiers stalking among the corpses. Buildings collapsed.

Dealer's voice was low, tinny, machine. "This is the price of breaking Code. Of going against Dealer. We must not descend into Chaos again. Until balance is destroyed, the justice of Code will be swift and merciless. Until the Prime is revealed to us, there will be more dead."

And then the holo flickered out.

"Michael is killing burners," Grace said.

"Dealer mentioned Prime," Ryker noted. "That last line was directed right at us. Not burners. He's saying he'll kill more until he has the Prime."

"Why does he need me so badly?" Grace asked. "I'm not worth more burners dying. Let me go to him. Join Millay."

"No." Ryker said it as an absolute.

"I say we reply," Ruth said.

The other three turned to her. "How?" Ryker asked.

Ruth pointed at the Dealers, frozen in the hatch. "We rattle Michael's bolts with those. The Lifts they came in are outside. We can use one to send a message."

"Who will fly it?" Grace asked.

"Lifts have an auto pilot," Ruth said.

"Doesn't Dealer control Dealers and Lifts?" Grace asked.

"We're out of the Stream," Ryker reminded her. "They can be flown manually. But they can also be programmed. There's a map on the console of Sound. Just tap the destination and it gets there on its own. And if you put your hands over the two control levers, you can feel what they are doing. It's a way to learn how to pilot one."

Ruth picked up a power saw. "I need some help."

Millay stared up at the ceiling. She could see small marks in it, almost a pattern. She had been trying to understand the pattern, if there was one, ever since Michael had left her and she'd been hooked up to the IVs.

Paint, she finally realized. The strokes of a paintbrush.

And then the pain came to the forefront.

Millay looked to either side, trying to find something else in the sterile room to focus on, a puzzle to wrap her brain around, to put the pain second.

The door opened and Millay lifted her head. Two Evermores; one she recognized. The nurse who'd put in the IVs, pushing a tray with various equipment on it. The other was a gnome of a man, with a glint in his eyes; dangerous.

"How are you, Millay, once of the People?" he asked. "My name is Claude. I am, was, the Person's personal assistant."

"What do you want?"

The nurse was in the background, waiting.

"I don't supposed you'll tell me of Prime?" Claude asked. "The Backdoor?"

"I don't know anything. I told Michael that."

"I heard." Claude put a hand on his chin, a finger tapping. "I believe you. The Prime is somewhere in you, whatever it is, but this crude technique—" he indicated her shoulder—"which won't help you find the knowledge we need. No. We must try something different. You burner friend, Haydn, he's in Heaven. What if we bag him?"

"You've already bagged him."

"Oh no." Claude pointed. "Watch."

A Stream appeared above Millay.

Haydn was sitting on a beautiful lawn in front of a large wooden building with a blonde girl. He was smiling, as if he were actually happy.

"Heaven," Claude said.

"I don't believe it," Millay said.

"It's true," Claude said, "but I knew you wouldn't believe me. Michael, despite having been human once, has lost touch with how

irrational humans are. Fortunately, we tend to be predictably irrational." He gestured for nurse.

She rolled the steel cart forward. Millay stretched her neck, trying
to make out what was on it. Some needles, some small black boxes.
Scalpels and other implements of surgery.

"What are you going to do?" Millay demanded.

"What is necessary," Claude said.

The nurse picked up a needle and inserted it into the peripheral
cannula on the line going into Millay's right arm.

"Count backward from ten," the nurse said.

"My candle burns at both ends," Millay said. *"It will not last the night.
But ah—"* and then there was darkness.

"YOU SAID you remembered us being outside together," Ryker said to
Elias.

They were seated next to each other on a bench, cavern wall
behind them, the cyborg tubes in front of them. Grace sat on the
other side of Elias.

Ruth had her probe into the console, searching for answers.

"Yes. Yes! We climbed together. Climbed mountains."

"Then we were friends," Ryker said.

"We must have been," Elias said. He closed his eyes. "I can see
something. You talking to me. Telling me something."

Ryker glanced past the cyborg at Grace. She gave a helpful smile,
then leaned forward, close to Elias.

"I know you're forgetful-" she began, but Elias' eyes flashed open.

"'Forgetful'! That's it." He turned to Ryker. *"Blessed are the forgetful:
for they get the better even of their blunders'.* That's what you told me.
Because it was you who were going to be forgetful. I had to remember
for you. The key." He repeated it. *"Blessed are the forgetful: for they get
the better of their blunders'.* That's Nietzsche. Remember?"

Ryker sat up straight. "Yes. Nietzsche." He nodded. "It's there.
Prime. Backdoor."

Ruth retracted her probe, hurrying over. Even Ace lifted his head, cocking it to the side, aware something significant was occurring.

"The Backdoor is as you said," Ryker said to Ruth. "A means of bypassing Dealer's encryption. Michael's encryption. It's an authorization that Michael isn't aware of."

"How can there be a backdoor into Dealer?" Ruth asked.

"I put it there," Ryker said.

"Yes," Elias said with excitement. "That's what you told me. You'd put a backdoor into a computer. The one that became Dealer. But before then it was—" he paused, trying to remember. "You were the one who initially programmed it. And it survived the IMP." He frowned. "But you were dying and you knew we were going to make you a cyborg. But you wanted to protect your knowledge. You said you'd hidden the Prime. You gave keys to unlock the information when necessary. You gave one to me."

"And one to Hanan," Ruth said. "How did you put in a backdoor in Dealer?"

"As he said, I helped build and program Dealer." Ryker nodded. "With my brother. Michael. We were both humans then."

"And what am I?" Grace asked. "What is Millay? What is Prime?"

"Prime is the code to access the Backdoor," Ryker said. "There's a very, very, very long number in your brain. A prime number."

"What is a prime number?" Grace asked.

"It's a natural number greater than 1, that has no positive divisors other than 1 and itself."

"That didn't help," Grace said. "They taught us so little in the womb of hive."

"Trust me on this," Ryker said. "You have one. And there's one in Millay's. You multiply those two prime numbers together and you get an extraordinarily long prime number with only two factors other than itself and one.. That product of those two numbers is the encryption code for the Backdoor. It's an unbreakable encryption except—".

"Except for what?" Grace asked.

"The only way to break a Prime is to uncover the two prime factors. It's a flaw that's inherent in process."

"Millay and I," Grace said.

"Yes."

"But I don't remember this number!" Grace said.

"Neither does Millay." Ryker pointed at his own head. "But just like I still have knowledge in here I can't remember, so do you. The Prime is in you."

"How do we get it out of us?" Grace asked.

"That, I don't know. Yet." Ryker stood. "But I'm sure we'll figure it out. Right now, there are things we have to do. The most important is getting Millay back. And I have to go to Centre. That was the first thing that came to me, when Grace said the word. It's from the key I gave Hanan. So it must be important even though Dealer isn't there any more. I know that too. It was moved by Michael."

BEGINNING OF THE 21ST CENTURY, BEFORE THE CHAOS

M ichael leaned back in the chair, fingers steepled under his chin. He was reading, not for the first time, and not for the last time, the poem he'd had carved onto a teak plaque to the left of his station at the console in front of Dealer. Even Michael, with his quest for perfection, appreciated the workmanship to get so many words, etched so perfectly on the two foot by one-foot piece of wood:

Turning and turning in the widening gyre
The falcon cannot hear the falconer;
Things fall apart; the centre cannot hold;
Mere anarchy is loosed upon the world,
The blood-dimmed tide is loosed, and everywhere
The ceremony of innocence is drowned;
The best lack all conviction, while the worst
Are full of passionate intensity.

Surely some revelation is at hand.

Surely the Second Coming is at hand.
The Second Coming! Hardly are those words out
When a vast image out of Spiritus Mundi
Troubles my sight: a waste of desert sand;
A shape with lion body and the head of a man,
A gaze blank and pitiless as the sun,
Is moving its slow thighs, while all about it
Wind shadows of the indignant desert birds.
The darkness drops again but now I know
That twenty centuries of stony sleep
Were vexed to nightmare by a rocking cradle,
And what rough beast, its hour come round at last,
Slouches towards Bethlehem to be born?

POETRY HAD BEEN *Ryker's interest. Even at Stanford, while his brother raced through getting his PhD in computer science in eighteen months, he'd also taken literature courses. Michael had little use for poetry, but he'd had to read The Second Coming in the one required undergraduate Literature class he'd been forced to endure. The professor had spent two hours leading a discussion about it, and despite himself, Michael had found it intriguing and felt an affinity for Yeats and what he was expressing. What the words portended. The inevitability of the end. It had been written by Yeats after the carnage of the War to End All Wars, when Europe was in shambles.*

The gyre, a 2,000 year cycle which was now here. Anarchy spreading. The 'beast'. That had caused much argument in class, but Michael firmly believed Yeats was referring to the masses of people overwhelming the ruling class, the rich, the elite. Being torn down by the beast.

Michael had known his destination ever since he was a young boy. That time was upon him. And it was not to be torn down by the beast.

His brother had never been very practical. He'd never asked for an accounting of the assets of the company they'd founded together. He'd simply requested a stipend, and not a particularly large one in Michael's opinion, to be automatically deposited in his account every month.

What truly bothered Michael about his brother, something it had taken his therapist three longs years before he even dared to point it out to Michael, was that Ryker didn't seem to have much fear.

*Not that Michael had gone to a therapist to fix any personal problems; he'd gone to the psychiatrist who his chief competitor had used, trying to get some insight into **his** psyche. But things had come up, of course. And the therapist had resisted revealing things about the competitor, but Michael had eventually cracked that reticence.*

Everyone had a price. In this case it had been relatively easy: a book contract with a New York publisher Michael owned. So the therapist could have his pet theory published, even while he violated the ethics he was writing about.

Ryker climbed mountains, sailed oceans, raced across deserts, lived life to the edge. Michael had always ascribed that to being an adrenaline junkie, but then his brother would retreat to some cabin somewhere with a stack of books and simply read for a month or two.

But then, Ryker hadn't been forced by their father to see their mother kill herself.

Father had dragged Michael out into the driveway, pointing up at their mother standing precariously in the open window of the attic. She was naked, crying, hands gripping the edges of the window.

Father told Michael to wave at her, call out to her.

For many years, Michael had thought it was his father's attempt to get her to stop, to make her think of her son.

Once again, it had been the damn therapist who'd pointed out that it might as well been done with the opposite intent.

Michael had to grudgingly admit he might be right about that, since she'd let go.

He'd watched her tumble and strike the driveway head first, just a few feet away. He'd never forgotten that sound of her skull imploding. Or the warm splatter of blood that hit him.

The worst though, the thing he fixed on, was her eyes. How they were so empty of life.

Death was ugly.

And several years ago, one of his chief rivals, a man known around the world, had died a slow, excruciating death and Michael had felt death's wing brush by. The only feeling he had about it was that he was going to do everything he could to keep death at bay.

Michael flipped a switch on the console. "Dealer?"

"Yes?" The voice out of the speaker was flat, machine. Michael hated those who, pre-Chaos, programmed a woman's voice or some foreign accent like British or Australian into their systems. It was a machine; it was foolish to mask the reality.

"Do you have a solution?"

Michael had typed in the query the previous day, after Ryker had left. Even though Dealer was the fastest computer in the world, there were an almost infinite number of variables it had to take into account. And there were probably numerous possible solutions, but only one had to be the most viable.

And Michael had specified it be viable. He didn't want to waste time, because one never knew how much was left.

"There is a path to a solution," Dealer said. "This is not the first time this problem has been investigated. The most promising data, however, was collected during World War Two by a group of Japanese scientists. After the war, the data, and those who worked on it, were moved to a classified location in Nevada. Unfortunately, the facility was destroyed in an explosion and sealed off."

"Then why are you telling me this if the data is gone?"

"It's not certain it is gone. The facility was sealed off without any investigation due to concerns about contamination. It is possible some data may have survived the explosion."

"Where?"

"The facility is located at the Air Force Flight Test Center, Detachment 3."

"Where is that?"

"Nevada. It more commonly referred to as Area 51."

HUNDREDS OF YEARS IN THE FUTURE, AFTER THE CHAOS

Achilles watched the Lift take off from the pier and head east, out of Void back toward Sound. It had deposited two people. A teenager probably around fifteen, scrawny, thick black hair and scared eyes. The other a man, not a burner, too well fed and muscled for that. Dark hair with the beginning of tinting the temples. He had a stubble of beard and the look in his eyes wasn't care; it was haunted. It was a look Achilles had seen before: He'd done something bad. Worse; he'd been caught.

"Didn't even let them take a slice," Achilles said to him. "Threw in your hand pretty quick, did you?"

The man didn't meet Achilles' eyes.

"I don't remember you," Achilles said to the boy.

The kid pointed at the pier to the north, a wedge-shaped one, indicating that was where he had resided. The one they were on was Delta: connected to the land by two bridges at the base of the triangle, it extended over the water for a thousand feet.

"How long ago did you fold?" Achilles asked.

"Three months." The kid's eyes were darting about, trying to make sense of being brought here from a holding cell by Dealers and dropped back in Delta; this over thirty days since he'd been scooped up from this supposed sanctuary.

"I negotiated for your freedom," Achilles said.

The kid blinked. "Why? Why would Dealer negotiate with you? How did you escape the Dealers when they came out here? They bagged all the older Deltans. Penned us younger ones."

Not stupid, Achilles thought. That was one thing People and Evermores consistently got wrong: that burners were stupid. Achilles had underestimated them too when he first was sent out here to Void to establish Delta. But having worked with them for years, he knew they were cunning and adept at surviving.

The man was listening, trying to understand.

"Both of you are going to help me re-establish Delta," Achilles said.

"Dealer won't allow that."

"You prefer being bagged?" Achilles asked. "Because that is the alternative."

"No."

"Then you'll do what I say."

The kid nodded. He was, indeed, not stupid.

"What am I doing here?" the man asked.

"Evermore?"

The man nodded.

"Kill someone?"

The man shook his head. "It was an accident. I didn't mean to hit her. It was just—"

"I don't care," Achilles said. "You got offered a deal before you got boxed and you took it. You had no idea what you agreed to, but you said you'd do it. So this is what you're going to do. Your new name is Charon."

"But I'm—"

"I don't want to know your old name. That's gone. You're Charon. You're going to need a boat." He pointed toward a shed on the far side of the Delta shaped pier.

The facility was Pre-Chaos. A naval base for nuclear submarines.

There was a dry dock to Achilles right that could hold an Ohio class missile sub. Void, and the large nuclear arsenal at this base, was the buffer between Sound, run by Delta, and Deep Void, where the cyborgs were holed up.

"What do I need a boat for?"

Achilles sighed. This one wasn't going to last long, he already knew. He missed the old Charon. The man had rarely spoken and had seemed to enjoy his job rowing burners to Void from across the Sound.

"You're going to bring folders and floers over. You need to go to that shed, open it. There are wood boats in there. Sealed in some sort of protective wrap. Pick one. Unseal it. Take the oars. Put it in the water and practice. When I need you, I'll tell you where you need to go and what you need to do. We need more bodies here. You're going to bring them."

"When will the other Deltans still alive get here?" the kid asked. "There was room on the Lift for more."

"More will come," Achilles said. "I need you to do something. Something very important."

"What?"

Charon was still standing there, befuddled.

"Go!" Achilles snapped and the man walked off toward the shed.

Achilles turned back to the kid. "Introduce a message from someone else. If you do that, Dealer will release the rest of our people being held. If you don't, then—" Achilles shook his head—"then I don't know what will happen."

"If you're talking to Dealer—"

"We're brokering a truce. An exchange. I give Dealer something it wants; it gives me more people back."

The boy looked skeptical, but understanding. "Introduce a message?"

"A woman named Grace. The message is about her sister. She'll be happy to get the news. But you have to send the message exactly as I tell you. And in the way I tell you."

"There is no Stream out here," the boy began, "how will I—"

"Come with me." He led the boy out along one of the sides of the triangular pier, toward the apex. An old crane leaned over, its boom dipping into the water was the very tip. Achilles climbed up a ladder, not easy since he was missing his left arm, the boy following. There was a new electronic lock on the door into the operator's cabin. Achilles pulled a black card out and slid it through the lock reader.

"What is that?" the kid asked, pointing at the black card.

"My card."

"No one out here has a card. And I never seen black."

"Its how I negotiate with Dealer," Achilles said. He pointed inside. "Along with that."

In the operator's seat was the upper half of an old model Dealer.

"How come we never heard of this?" The kid was not only smart, but inquisitive. Perhaps too inquisitive.

"It wasn't my job to tell everyone everything out here," Achilles snapped. "My job was to keep this place going. To keep everyone alive."

"Didn't do good job," the kid pointed out.

"You're alive." Achilles slid the black card into a slot on the side of the Dealer. Energized, it used its now activated energy cell and transmitter to reach out, forming it's own, directed Stream.

"You'll only have voice," Achilles said. "And here's what I want you to say. It's not much, then the other person will do the rest."

MICHAEL WAS HOME.

The quantum computer that was Dealer was inside a hardened bunker. The design was based on the Cheyenne Mountain Complex that had housed NORAD, but scaled down considerably. Of course, NORAD, despite its defenses, had succumbed early in the Chaos, but by sabotage inside and then multiple nuclear strikes.

The computing center, aka Dealer, was two hundred feet below ground. Dealer's building was built on large springs to protect against movement by nuclear blasts and also the likely event of an earthquake here in the Pacific Northwest. Movement was limited to less than one inch. All connections from the building were made with flexible pipe. Air was filtered to protect against chemical, biological, radiological, and nuclear contaminants.

There was only a single way in and out and it had a ten-ton blast door.

After the Chaos, knowing he needed to move Dealer after the close-call of the cyborg attack, Michael, linked with Dealer, had searched for a suitable location and found this one, ready-made by the military.

Michael walked up the control board. A single chair faced a two-dozen monitors. There was a keyboard and a mouse. All rather archaic, almost amusing, but it would have been necessary if it had not been for Ryker's blade.

Who, what, he was now, could bypass that. Michael put a probe into a portal, making a direct link with Dealer. He was always part of Dealer as long as he was in the Stream, in fact he spent most of his time 'residing' inside of Dealer, where his consciousness had been uploaded just before his human body had finally succumbed to Ryker's wound. He only moved the core of his consciousness into the robot Michael when he felt the desire to experience something first hand, an event that was occurring more and more lately, but which the human Michael had not consciously registered.

But he almost always maintained the link to the Stream where the rest of him was. To move to the robot and disconnect from the Stream? Michael had done it occasionally, cutting off from the Stream, to experience a 'freedom' from the sharing of his core with the computer. He'd never moved *out* of the Stream, until he'd led the Dealers into Deep Void after Ryker and the Prime. It had been a dangerous move, not just because he'd violated the Truce, but also because he knew that being separate from the computer he'd been uploaded into would eventually lead to his essence degrading. He *needed* Dealer's memory capacity and computing speed to remain Michael.

Another development, which he *was* aware of, was that he felt more and more distinct from Dealer.

Officially, Michael had designed Dealer and coded it, but the reality was the serious work had been done by his brother. Indeed, Michael had laid claim to many of his brother's inventions over the years before the Chaos and they'd formed the basis of his business.

Ryker hadn't totally been cut out: he'd been given his stipend, though he had been offered so much more. But his brother had set out to travel the world and have adventures. Which had been just fine with Michael, who'd reveled in increasing his wealth and power. And preparing and implementing his plan.

Once uploaded, it had taken years for Michael to explore and understand most of Dealer. He was like a kid lost in a maze, wandering, learning the paths By which time the machine had developed the Sound out of the ruins of the Chaos. Almost exactly as Michael had planned.

The *almost* was the problem.

Michael hadn't planned on his brother trying to sabotage things. He hadn't planned on getting killed and having to implement his emergency upload. He hadn't planned on the cyborgs turning against Dealer while he was being uploaded and helpless. That he would be unable to help Dealer with this unexpected development.

Ryker had screwed everything up and now he was back.

After upload, Michael had slowly managed to understand enough to be able to gradually take control from the machine. For a while, a long while, over two hundred and fifty years, they were one. But twenty-five years ago, Michael had begun to feel the split. There was Dealer. And there was him. He controlled Dealer.

This mind-machine meld was unprecedented, just a theory prior to Michael being forced to resort to it, so it was unclear exactly what had happened, what had developed, and how things stood now.

But there were still 'places' in Dealer that Michael had not 'visited' or understood.

Which was the current problem.

Michael: *Do we know where the Backdoor is?*

Dealer: *It is the nature of a backdoor that the machine it is put into is not aware of its existence.*

Aware. An interesting word, Michael thought. He wasn't certain how aware Dealer was. It was aware of facts and figures and data and could make decisions quickly. It could improve on its original programming and had done so many times over the years.

Given what he now knew, that Ryker had turned against him, Michael had to wonder how long Ryker had been sabotaging his plans? Had it just been during the Chaos? Or had his brother started even before? Even during the initial programming? Was that when he'd put in the Backdoor? Who had had the white pieces in the game? Made the first move?

Michael probed: *And we weren't aware of Millay, once of the People and Grace-five-eleven-kilo-one.*

Dealer: *There are no records of them prior to being informed of their existence.*

Michael: *How can there be twins? That was forbidden under the original Code.*

It is currently unknown. There was a pause, as Dealer ran through data. *There is a gap in the programming regarding them.*

Michael: *Ryker did that. But they were issued cards on Dealing Day. Cards we determined.*

It wasn't a question, but Dealer responded anyway. *Again. Part of the gap in programming. Part of the Backdoor. A Prime is an antiquated way to encrypt. It was used extensively in the late 20th and early 21st centuries. Until surpassed by quantum encryption, which is much more effective and secure. It is how we are encrypted. Using a Prime doesn't make sense.*

Michael: *It makes sense that Ryker would use an out of date protocol in the world's most advanced computer. Something no one would look for.*

Dealer's response was startling: *Something you wouldn't look for. The viable course of action for you to take is to kill the one we have in custody. Each of them holds a factor of the Prime. If you kill one, the Prime will be gone forever. That will ensure that the Backdoor cannot be used.*

Michael was surprised that Dealer had delineated between the two of them; first by the rebuke and, more so, by the use of the pronoun: *you*. Dealer had never indicated they were separate, always using the plural *we* and *us*. Michael realized he'd begun doing the same, referring to himself in the first person. Which begat which?

Dealer continued, interrupting his thoughts: *A development, A Lift has passed out of Deep Void and is over Void. Ground to air on Island perimeter has targeted it. We cannot access the control. Recommend we destroy it.*

Michael: *Negative. It could be bringing the rest of the Prime.*

Michael was accessing the Stream, tracking the Lift. The aircraft was descending as it came over Void, on a vector toward Lone Bridge, which was odd. If it was manned by any of the Dealers he'd left in Deep Void, it would have gone to Centre as he'd instructed.

Through the sensors in the Dealers guarding the only bridge from Island to Void, Michael watched the Lift land on the center of the bridge. One of the Dealers moved forward.

It opened the door on one side.

Stacked inside were a dozen Dealers, heads missing, which meant their data was gone.

Ryker.

Dealer: *This makes no sense.*

Michael: *Obfuscating.*

There was a pause and Michael knew Dealer was running through all possible definitions of the word, it's origins and all variations.

Dealer: *You were known to use that word often before the Sound.*

Michael: *It's a message. In response to the one we sent regarding the hive that was destroyed.*

Dealer: *It makes no sense.*

Which was the point. Michael looked at building that housed the computer and while he kept the probe in, shut down any outgoing data from himself into Dealer. He reflected back on what Dealer had said: You.

A mistake by a machine that wasn't supposed to make mistakes. Michael felt more distant from Dealer than he had since he'd uploaded. It had been too quick to suggest killing Millay in order to destroy the Prime, permanently shutting the Backdoor. And protecting Dealer.

Dealer was separating from him. And he thought he'd been the one separating from the computer.

There'd been a balance for so long, hundreds of years. A partnership where the lines between the machine and his essence had been one. Michael tried to remember when that had changed? He'd thought it had been his decision. But when had he made it?

He couldn't recall. And how could he have made it if he'd been one with Dealer?

And there were others problems. Why had Dealer made the decision to wipe out Delta? Michael knew he'd been part of that decision, but in retrospect it made no sense. So why had he gone along with it?

His memories were—what was it burners said—Jingle-jangled. And there could be only one reason for that: Dealer.

He re-opened access to the computer.

Michael asked, even though he knew the status; more just to see Dealer's reaction: *What of the Lazarus Problem?*

Dealer: *A solution has not been found. Still working on it.*

But Dealer wasn't. Michael knew that. Uploading his brain, his consciousness had worked using nanotechnology to scan every single cell in it, then the data was transmitted to Dealer. But the Lazarus Problem, enigma really, was how to go the other way. From machine to flesh. How to download his consciousness back into a human brain.

Michael and Dealer had wrestled with it long and hard, but they were trying to understand the most complex entity in the world: the human brain.

Michael: *I must go into Deep Void again.*

Dealer: *Not the optimal course of action for this situation. Terminate Millay, once of the People, and Grace-five-eleven-kilo-one will be worthless.*

Michael closed the link. He had about twenty hours hours before his consciousness would begin to degrade. Eventually he would fragment so badly, he would need to reboot.

But Dealer controlled the backup for his reboot.

Michael withdrew his probe. He walked over to an access door. Opened it. An airlock was inside. He stepped in, the door shutting behind him. Pressure was equalized. The other door opened. He walked inside Dealer's casing.

The twenty-four containers had been brought here, one-by-by, each still operating and connected to the other twenty-three by the Stream. It had been a vulnerable time when the system got close to the fifty percent moved phase because a failure of the Stream would cause the operating system to fail, without enough computing power at either site. But the move had been completed without a hitch, Evermores and Dealers doing all the work.

The Evermores had then been terminated to keep the location a secret, something Dealer had determined to be the most effective method.

Michael was startled as something moved to his left.

A robot, but not a Dealer. This was a different kind of machine. Moving on four legs, with two long arms. A maintenance drone. Dealer was self-sustaining and could repair itself.

The primary power source for the entire place was, of course, CNS. The spheres were located in a much larger black vault below the building. Power radiating up from them. Venting was to the side, to long tunnels leading to the outside world. Dealer also had an emergency power backup that could tap into thermal power from a vent two miles down.

The drone stopped twenty feet from Michael and he realized it was observing him. Then he saw more drones arriving, all stopped the same distance away, even some on the walls or clinging to the sides of parts of Dealer. While they didn't come any closer, there was something about the way they were deployed that bothered Michael.

It was as if he were an invading parasite.

Michael turned and left.

Once outside he didn't bother to look back. He exited the blast door and went to his Lift.

Moves and counter-moves.

The fact was that whoever had the Prime could access the Back-door. Into a part of the quantum computer where it would not be aware of the intrusion. Which meant someone with access to the Backdoor could reprogram, even shut down, Dealer. Michael was sure the latter was why Ryker had programmed it in. Despite being one of the world's leading experts on computers, Ryker had also felt they were a threat.

Michael could finally understand that sentiment.

THE SUN WAS SETTING on Haydn's second day in Heaven. He'd spent some time with Tori, exploring the boundaries of Heaven. There were parks and entertainment holos. All the things which he imag-ined People had every day.

Finally, he'd had to beg off, head back to the hall to try to get some sleep.

But like hive, it seemed there would be no quiet in the hall. burners were eating and drinking and sexing as long as they could stay awake.

Haydn had left the hall and gone into the woods, finding a quiet spot and laid down, falling into exhausted sleep.

He startled awake. Aware someone was close by. It was dusk, the last of daylight grayly giving way to night. Haydn sat up.

"Who's there?"

"It's me," Tori said.

Haydn looked to his right. She was standing next to a tree. She sounded sober for the first time. "What's wrong?"

"Nothing. I was just worried about you, when you disappeared."

"It was too loud to sleep in the hall."

Tori laughed. "Yeah. Noise all our life and even noise here. I think Heaven should be quiet."

"I thought you liked the partying."

"I liked it for a little while because I thought I should like it," Tori said. "But I thought about the things you said."

Haydn stood up. Stretched, feeling muscles he had rarely used before ache.

"What did you do last night?" Tori asked. "Seriously. You asked if you could trust me and you can."

"You don't want to know."

"I do want to know." Tori looked over her shoulder. "This morning, I was over in another hall. One where everyone was two days out from Deathday." She paused for a moment, looking around as if to make sure no one else was within ear shot. "I heard something. Someone said he heard from a burner three days closer to Deathday."

Haydn did the numbers. burners had limited math skills, but when it came to figuring Deathdays, they were quite good. "So three three days ago Deathday." 33 days ago.

"Yes. He said he was told that many Lifts flew in. More than they'd seen in the previous two eight. Didn't land here. Went overhead that way." She pointed north. "Then, while later, was a lot of smoke. The wind blew some of it this way and it was nasty. Bad smell."

"Three five," Haydn said. He was trying to remember. "That's the day after—" He paused.

"After what?"

"When Dealer shut down Delta. Took everyone." He tried to recall what Ryker had said about it. "Almost everyone. Bagged them, most likely."

"That's not good," Tori said.

Haydn was looking to the north. The forest was dark, foreboding, almost impossible to see more than a few feet.

"That's not all," Tori said. "Man said this burner told him that he was done partying. Heaven was about done. He didn't believe in Second Room. Figured he had nothing to lose. He went toward the smoke. Crossed a fence, but nothing happened. No Dealers. Just kept going for two days. Then he came to..." she stopped, looking around again.

"What did he see?"

"A pit. A big pit." Tori's voice broke. "There were bodies in it. Lots of bodies. Still smoldering. The smell was so strong. And while he stood there watching, a Lift came in. Hovered overhead, then Dealers dumped bags. With burners inside on top of the pile. Tossed something down onto the pile and the bags burst into flames. That's when he ran. That's where they take the burners who've been bagged and extinguished."

"I've told you a secret," Tori said. "Now tell me yours."

"All right," Haydn said. "When I folded, Dealers were hunting burners along the folding path."

Tori frowned. "They weren't when I walked it. And that was after you."

"They were looking for someone specific," Haydn said.

"Who?"

"It doesn't matter. So I had to move out into Wasteland, off the path."

"It's said you die in Wasteland."

"I didn't die."

Tori smiled. "I can see that."

"I saw a hive out there in the Wasteland." Before she could ask any more questions, he quickly told her about the rendering hive. And how the burners had slaughtered and rendered seventy-five cattle so efficiently.

"There's meat here," Tori said. "You've had some. People must get it all the time. It has to come from somewhere."

"Yes," Haydn said. "Except these burners. They were different. They didn't have cards."

"Every burner has a card," Tori said.

"They didn't. And they cut their hair in a special way." He indicated on his own head. "A stripe this way and one that way."

"That's weird."

"The other night," Haydn said, "when the summoning sounded, I wasn't in a hall. I was near the Wall. When the burners came down, they were being channeled by the same people. Renderers. Hair the same. No cards."

Tori was looking at him, a still figure in the darkness. "You think—"

"I don't know," Haydn said. "It doesn't make sense. If they're rendering burners, then why waste the bodies that have been bagged?"

"You're right. It doesn't make sense."

"But there's a ship on the other side of the Wall. The burners are filed into it one by one, almost like the cattle were pushed through a chute."

"And then?"

"I don't know. Something happens to them in the ship."

"Maybe Second Room?" Hope, the fuel of burner.

"But why use renderers?"

Tori didn't have an answer for that. "How could you see this ship? The burners going into it? We can't see it—" she stopped her words abruptly. "You went to the other side of the Wall."

"Not really."

"You were on the beach. Wet."

"But I can't swim," he said, though he knew by the look on her face she knew he'd managed it somehow.

"You broke Code."

"Are you going to turn me in?"

"No." There was no hesitation in her answer. "I think we need to find out more about Heaven. Maybe *it isn't what it is*. I will help you."

"I NEED TO DO SOMETHING," Grace said.

"The best thing you can do is remain here and be safe," Ryker said.

"The next cyborg should become active soon," Ruth said. "Then others. They'll protect you. Soon the three hundred will be ready."

"I'll go with Ryker," Grace suggested.

"You stay here," Ryker said. "There's no point in rescuing Millay if you get caught. We need both of you." He reached into a pocket and pulled out a deck, rattled it. "Charon's black card is in here." He handed it to Ruth. "Use it if you have to. From what I can gather it allows you to be in the Stream but gives all access. Dealers should let you pass."

"Unless Dealer knows Charon is dead and put an alert on the card," Ruth said, but she took the deck anyway.

Elias had worked on Ruth, repairing her appearance to the point where she looked like the young woman in the passport photo. Long black hair and her skin repaired.

Ryker shook his head. "I don't think Dealer deals the black cards. Michael does. And he's blocked them from Dealer. That's why Dealers don't notice them."

"Intriguing," Elias said. "That suggests that Dealer and Michael are separating. And if Michael is blocking things from Dealer, then they are at odds."

"Could Dealer block things from Michael?" Grace asked.

Ryker considered for a moment. "I never anticipated Michael uploading into Dealer, but since has and if he is indeed blocking things, its possible Dealer is doing the same thing ."

Ruth put the deck into a pocket. "If Michael invented the black cards, once I pull it out, he'll know where I am."

"True," Ryker said. "But that might work to your advantage in certain situations."

"Possible," Ruth allowed.

"Wait a second," Grace said. "What if you could get a white card?"

"Where?" Ruth asked.

"Hanan's cabin. It's hanging on a hook by the door. At least it was when I left."

"Ah!" Ruth said. "Well." It was hard to tell what the cyborg was feeling. "I'll keep that option in mind." She reached to her neck and pulled out a chain. On it were two rings; the ones Grace had brought from Hanan's cabin. "This is something I want to give you." She unfastened the chain, took one ring off and held it out to Grace.

Grace demurred. "I can't take that."

"You were the last one with Hanan," Ruth said. "She died for you.

But she died with her heart at peace because you were there. Take this and remember her."

Grace reluctantly accepted the ring.

Ryker looked at the ring. "Where did you get that?"

"Hanan had them."

"Where did she get them?"

"I don't know," Ruth said. "We'd lost ours during the Chaos; can't wear them when flying. Just before she left to go to Island. To take up her role as our spy inside the system, she had them and offered one to me. But—" Ruth held up hands. "It didn't fit so I told her to take both; something to remember me by, and that someday we'd re-unite and retake our vows and give one to each other. Why?"

Ryker shook his head. "I don't know. Still so much locked inside my head."

Ruth fastened the chain and put the remaining ring back inside her coverall. "Our problem," she said, "is that we don't exactly know where Millay is. Michael could have taken her anywhere."

While Ruth had removed the rest of the governors on Ryker's cyborg system, his memories, the human part, were still another matter. Each key was giving him a piece, but most was still blocked.

Which was good in a way; in case he was captured. He knew who the Prime were, but so did Michael. He knew the Prime opened the Backdoor, but he had to assume Michael knew that too. But no one knew the Prime numbers, except somewhere in Millay and Grace's brain, or how to access them.

Not yet. And there was no point even dwelling on that until they had Grace and Millay in the same place.

"We assume she's been boxed," Ruth said. "And we assume those who've been boxed are on Island somewhere. But they also box Evermores and Middlemores. So she could be held in City or City Edge."

"She could be," Ryker said. "But they would never send People over the Sound. People who've been boxed have to be held on Island. And Michael was a chess player. We played many times growing up. He was good. I was better." There was no boast in that. A simple statement of fact. "We destroyed all his Dealers that chased us. He has no idea where exactly Grace is either except in Deep Void."

"Great," Grace muttered.

"The thing to do—" Ruth began, but once more, Ryker held up a hand and closed his eyes.

"Dealer damming the Stream?" Grace asked.

Ryker shook his head. "No. Someone's trying to contact us. It's weak, a narrow Stream sent into Deep Void." He cocked his head. "From somewhere in Void."

"Millay?" Grace asked.

"No." Ryker was quiet for almost a minute, leaving Grace, the only true human in the cavern, fidgeting. Ruth and Elias were so still; they might have been statues.

Finally Ryker opened his eyes. "Millay is being held in an area in the service tunnels on Island. I was given the approximate location."

"By who?" Ruth asked.

"A burner reached out. Said he worked the tunnels. Cleaning out the boxes. A job even a Middlemore won't do. He's going to Heaven tomorrow. He got access to the Person's personal Stream."

"How—" Grace stared, but Ryker hushed her. "Andrew gave him the code, told him what to do. The burner linked the Stream to the box holding Andrew, once the Person, and to the Stream that Achilles used in Void as a relay. Andrew talked to me. Fast. That Haydn was in Heaven. Told me where Millay was. Told me the burner had been given this access by Claude, once his assistant. That Claude was trying to play both sides and this was his attempt to get us in his debt."

"I don't believe it," Ruth said. "It's an obvious trap set by Michael."

"It *was* Andrew," Ryker said.

"How do you know?" Ruth challenged.

"I know." Ryker said it in a way that ended that line of discussion. "It was Andrew. I believe him. And I believe an Evermore, someone that highly placed, would try such a maneuver. I also believe part of playing both sides is to accept it's a trap by the Evermore. Gain our favor, then turn that favor back over to Michael." He turned to Ruth.

"Millay is there. It makes sense that Michael would put her with the boxed. You're going to have to play this. Be ready for anything. Adjust as needed."

"Nothing new there," Ruth said.

Ryker moved on to Grace and Elias. "Any questions on your missions?"

"I'm fine," Grace lied.

"Elias?" Ryker asked gently.

"What if I have other keys for you?" Elias asked.

"You don't," Ryker said, earning a look of rebuke from Grace. "I'm sorry, Elias. I know you had just the one key. But it was important."

"Yes," Elias said, his voice deep with acceptance.

Grace went over to him and put a hand on his shoulder, looking into his slightly offset dark eyes. "Remember when you told me the name of this place?"

Elias nodded. "Masada."

"But what if those who felt there were about to be defeated sacrificed themselves a different way?" Grace asked. "What if they attacked their enemy with their last ounce of strength? In the hope that others will take up the fight and finish it?"

Elias looked at Ryker. "You'll finish it?"

"*We* will," Ryker said. "But we need to stall Michael. Keep his strength down. Also, you will provide a diversion. Draw Dealer's attention away from Island and Heaven. Give Ruth and I a real chance. We wouldn't ask this of you if—" He paused.

"If you had a future," Ruth said.

Which brought another harsh look from Grace.

Elias nodded. "I will do what I have to. Make sure you finish it."

BEGINNING OF THE 21ST
CENTURY, BEFORE THE CHAOS

Beginning of the 21st Century, Before the Chaos

T
he sentry called the Sergeant of the Guard. Who arrived at the gate and called the Duty Officer. Who checked the papers brought by the man at the head of a convoy of construction vehicles and then called the Commanding Officer of the facility because this was simply unprecedented at the eastern entrance to Area 51 and the Duty Officer didn't have the authority to let anyone in.

Even the Commanding Officer didn't. But when he saw the signatures on the cover letter of the papers and called the Pentagon to check, which put him on hold while the White House was contacted and then came back with an affirmative on the legitimacy, he accepted he had to let these civilians in and support them in whatever way possible; that was the last sentence on the cover letter, which was signed by the President.

The convoy rumbled down the road, over the ridgeline, and into the valley where one of the longest runways in the world, and perhaps the most secure, was located. Past the runway, past the hangers where the F-117

Stealth Fighter, the B-2 Bomber and a long history of classified planes had first been housed and then test flown.

The Commanding Officer had to personally lead the man and his construction personnel through the blast doors at the base of Groom Mountain, assuring the guards that this was authorized, albeit completely unusual.

So unusual, that as per protocol the CO's executive officer pulled a pistol on him, backed up by a heavily armed Quick Reaction Force, and demanded to see the authorization. And kept his superior officer under gunpoint while the XO called to verify and endured an ass chewing from the Chairman of the Joint Chiefs of Staff, even though the XO was following the very strict protocol established many years ago here at Area 51.

Because there were things happening here other than just aircraft being tested.

The XO had to hang up, lower his gun, and step aside, worrying about the future of his career, even though he'd followed the rules. Getting a good OER, Officer Efficiency Report, from a higher-ranking officer you pulled a gun on was iffy.

"There," Michael said, pointing as they came to a branch in the tunnels that honeycombed Groom Mountain.

The CO was mystified. "That's been shut down for decades. Nothing but rubble that way." He pointed at a sign. A circle with three incomplete circles on top, indicating a biohazard area. To emphasize the point, there were several NO ENTRY signs in red posted.

"But it's blocked," the CO said. "A concrete retaining wall was put there some time in the late forties. And the records indicate there is rubble behind the retaining wall."

"That's why I brought the workers," Michael said, and signaled for his foreman to go ahead.

A long line of men wielding jackhammers, picks, shovels, axes, pneumatic drills and other gear filed by.

Michael folded his arms on his chest. Waiting as the men went to work.

The CO shifted his feet. "What's there?"

"You're in command and you don't know?"

"No," the CO admitted.

"Never wondered?"

"No."

"That's why they picked you to command this place, I suppose," Michael said. "By the way, do you really have aliens here? That would be so cool. You know. ET phone home." His voice changed. "Because the place he's visiting is broke."

Two hours later, the foreman came back down the tunnel. Covered in dust. "We're close. Through the retaining wall." He glanced at the CO. "No rubble beyond. Just two steel containment doors. The first one was already breached outward. The second is buckled outward, so that had to have been an interior explosion. It fits with the plans you gave me. We've got a breaching charge in place on the door. Will do the job."

Michael nodded.

He turned to his assistant. "Phase two."

The men who'd been digging were filed one way. The men and women in biosuits came in the other way. The CO watched all this with irritation and admiration. He'd spent the couple of hours trying to figure out a way to 'sell' himself to Michael. After all, retirement pay only went so far. And Michael's conglomeration had many, many, government contracts.

"I could bring in our, my, bio scientists, sir. They're very good at working with—"

"Aliens?" Michael said it with all seriousness. He turned to the CO. "Truth. Do you have aliens here?"

The CO swallowed. "No, sir."

"Then why do you have bio scientists?"

"Uh, well, that's classified and—"

"Weapons? Targeted genetics?" Michael laughed at the CO. "Of course you'd be working on that. Every government with the capability is doing it. Just like every government with the capability started working on nuclear weapons as soon as they could. It's the nature of the beast. And the beast is man."

A sharp blast echoed down the tunnel.

Michael donned the suit and mask presented to him.

The CO seemed disappointed he wasn't offered his own.

"I would like this corridor cleared," Michael said, his voice muted by the mask. "All the way to the trucks we've brought. Also, turn off all surveillance inside your perimeter."

The CO opened his mouth to protest, realized the futility, and nodded.

"And you need to go," Michael said, dismissing him.

Michael headed into the haze of dust. He went through the portal; the only thing remaining of General Hoffelder were some metal bridgework, partly melted. Into the lab. Not much left there either. Michael went to the far side of the room. A demolitions expert was emplacing a shaped charge around a door. The metal was scorched, buckled, but it had held. As it had been designed to.

The demo man indicated for everyone to step back. He clicked his detonator, there was a sharp crack, and the door tumbled outward, clanging to the stone floor. Michael was first into the room.

Stacks of cardboard boxes with Japanese characters scrawled on the sides filled the room. Michael smiled. He'd spent millions and over two years searching this trove down. Then it had taken tens of millions in bribes, gifts to favorite charities for those who didn't take direct bribes, low ball bidding on government contracts, and in some case flat out threats to gain this access.

As suited men brought up dollies to cart the boxes out, Michael went back to the lab. One of his men was kneeling in the soot and ash, looking at something. There was a small pile of melted glass amongst the ashes.

"What is it?" Michael asked as he joined him.

"What's left of a person. Enough to get DNA."

"One of the scientists?"

The man looked up, the grin visible through the mask. "No, sir. This is patient zero."

MICHAEL WAITED *and he didn't like waiting. The whole point in building Dealer was speed and data capacity.*

The speaker finally crackled with Dealer's voice. "The data retrieved from Nevada was valuable. It gives a direction. It will need an expert in microbiology to work on it with our assistance because sufficient work wasn't done for a solution. Additionally, there have been numerous advances in the field since this data was assembled. Equipment is much more advanced. We have correlated with current data and this shows true promise for making large advancements in the field."

"I'll get the best. Send me a list of candidates, rank-ordered. I'll get them all."

"It is best to have one person work this," Dealer said. "A team can be assembled for assistance, but a single point would be best."

Michael rolled his eyes. He'd built one of the largest businesses in the world. He didn't need a computer, even Dealer, telling him how to construct a team. But the feeling quickly passed with excitement that cheating death was appearing more and more possible.

HUNDREDS OF YEARS IN THE FUTURE, AFTER THE CHAOS

Michael stood on the tarmac outside of what had once been the Boeing Everett Factory; the largest building the world, pre-Chaos, by volume. And it was still the largest in the world. The perfect place in the Wasteland for Michael to expand his forces.

Soldiers were moving in perfect orderly lines into Lifts. The first regiment of what would be eighteen. When the Truce was negotiated with the cyborgs, Dealer had only two regiments. But over the decades, Michael had slowly and surreptitiously appropriated materials and resources from the ruins of City and City Edge to build up his forces. It was a violation of the Truce, but he knew there was no way the cyborgs could discover it from wherever they were hidden in Deep Void.

Michael had no doubt he could now overwhelm the cyborgs with his new army. He felt a small degree of pleasure at the thought of how surprised Ruth and the others would be when they realized what they now faced. A very different situation.

True, the cyborgs supposedly controlled some nuclear weapons, but Michael knew they wouldn't use them. He'd been too weak in those early days to stop the logical negotiation of the Truce between

Dealer and the cyborgs. The flaw in the machine was to believe humans, even just human brains inside a machine, would eliminate themselves.

Humans wanted more time over all else. It was the base fact on which the Sound ran, yet Michael found it strange that Dealer didn't completely understand the ramifications of that.

An alert flashed through the Dealer Stream: a Lift was inbound from Deep Void, flying low over the water of the Sound. Michael felt a moment of excitement and possibility.

Centre air defense pinged the inbound craft.

And got no response.

Michael's excitement dissipated in an instant. The craft was on manual control and no Dealers were registering as active on board. And it was heading for Centre; and Heaven.

While Dealer was calculating possible intentions, Michael was trying to think like a human. What were the cyborgs doing?

What was Ryker doing?

Dealer instantly decided, logically, that the Lift was a threat and directed all air defense systems to protect Centre.

ELIAS NOTED the alert from the control console of the Lift indicating that missile tracking systems were locking on to his craft. He had his probe extended into the console, flying it via the link, just as a Dealer would.

"Time to part," Elias said over his shoulder.

"Thank you," was all Ryker could say, standing in the open door of the Lift. Then he cast himself out, plummeting toward the dark water of the Sound.

As soon as Ryker was clear, Elias put the Lift into a steep climb, using maximum power, while at the same time, angling to the right, away from Centre.

RYKER HIT THE WATER, went under, bobbed back to the surface. Now that his governors had been removed, he had complete control over his body and understood how it worked. He expelled two thirds of the air from the cavities inside his chest that mimicked breathing.

Which caused him to sink below the surface. He made some slight adjustments and came to a buoyancy point approximately five meters below the surface, where the fading grey daylight still managed to give some vision.

Then he began to swim, legs scissoring, arms extended straight in front.

THE AIR DEFENSE system-protecting Centre stood down now that the threat had veered away.

Michael noted this and the Lift's new direction, still going up but now in a straight line. Directly toward his location.

Michael transmitted orders to the Soldiers that were activated, sending them scattering, while also having every armed Lift that was ready take off. Michael looked at the massive building one last time, full rows and rows of Soldiers stacked floor to ceiling yet to be activated; at the new Crawlers and Lifts, modified with lethal weapons.

Then he sprung up into the side door of his Lift, went forward, and took the controls.

THE FOUR ENGINES were straining as Elias had the Lift at maximum elevation for the payload it was carrying. He looked down and saw the Boeing Building. It was the most significant landmark in view. He looked at the display showing altitude, speed, and bearing. It flashed and he knew he'd reached the correct point.

Elias cut the engines.

The sudden silence was startling. As was the moment of weightlessness as the craft reached apogee.

It was an odd sensation for Elias. His human mind expected a racing heart, a clenched stomach, shaking hands, but his machine body was providing none of the normal physical feedback of fear. It was as much a part of the Lift as of him.

As the Lift plummeted, Elias tried to remember the feel of a cool breeze on his face; the touch of a lover's caress. But they seemed so long ago, part of someone else's life.

He saw dark spots rapidly coming up from the ground.

MICHAEL REACHED out in the Stream and accessed the falling Lift's autopilot.

No use; the engines had been shut down and by the time they could be restarted, it would be too late.

"Is that you, Ryker?" Michael asked through the Stream, although he doubted his brother would be throwing himself away like this.

Not yet.

ELIAS HEARD the question come out of the speaker in the cockpit. It was Dealer's voice, but different, a tone to it. Something that jogged Elias' memory.

"Michael?"

"Who is this?"

"It's Elias, Michael." Elias looked down at the read-outs. Passing through ten thousand feet altitude. Not long now. He'd been an engineer and his mind presented the physics: there were variables but he had roughly forty-five seconds before impact. Elias smiled, glad he had some pieces and parts of the old him in there.

"I remember you," Michael said. "You were on my core team. You betrayed me."

"You betrayed us," Elias said.

"This is foolish," Michael said.

"Doesn't matter," Elias said. He lifted his hands up, as if he were holding a steering wheel. "Nothing any of us can do about it now." Twenty seconds.

The Lift shuddered as a pulse struck, ripping off a chunk of metal.

Looking out, Elias saw a half-dozen Lifts firing, angled up. Another strike. Another and the right half of the cockpit was torn away. Wind whistled in.

"Too late, Michael. Even you can't defeat gravity." Ten seconds.

FROM A SAFE DISTANCE, if there wasn't a nuke on board Elias' Lift, Michael watched, his mind racing for options, tied into Dealer in the Stream.

Schematics of Lift development and design were being searched at quantum speed. As soon as he realized it, Michael implemented.

THE TOP of the building was filling the view forward. Five seconds.

Elias instinctively brought his hands out in front of his face. His machine body might not have instincts but his mind did. And then he was slammed back and down in the seat.

A moment later, he heard the explosion; the explosion that should have consumed him.

MICHAEL STALKED through the flaming wreckage. He was flanked by surviving Soldiers on either side. They ignored the mangled remains of their fellow Soldiers.

Little remained of what had once been the largest building in the world. A few remnants of the outer walls rose out of the blackened Earth, twisted and torn. Fires were burning, but that didn't bother the Soldiers.

An alert came through the Stream from one of the Soldiers and Michael headed in that direction, shoving metal and debris aside, plowing a direct path. At the Soldier's feet lay a machine; but this one was a little different. Not a Soldier or Dealer. Smaller. Human sized. Still strapped in the ejection seat. Both legs had been torn off. Along with an arm.

"Almost boxed," Michael said, betraying a twisted sense of human. "How are you feeling, Elias?"

One eye had been ripped out of the socket and dangled by sensor wire. The other was looking up, aimlessly. Then it slowly swiveled, fixing on Michael.

Michael knelt. As he did so, he extended the probe from the top of his forearm. He jammed it into the left side of Elias' cranium. "I doubt you took the time to have your cache memory wiped before doing this fool-hardy thing." The data flowed. "Ah, yes. Thank you. Now I know from where you came. I assume Ryker is there. And Ruth. She didn't look very good. And, of course, Grace. Grace of the Prime."

If he could have cried, Elias would have, but his body was machine. And machines didn't cry.

GETTING onto Island had been relatively easy for Ruth. She'd followed Ryker's example and crossed underneath the Lone Bridge, bypassing the Dealers who guarded the road above. She found it interesting that it never seemed to occur to them that there was another way across the bridge, simply by going under. But they were programmed to guard the way they did, and, unlike humans who might have an imagination and think about options, Dealers simply did their duty.

Walking through the uninhabited north end of the Island, Ruth was recalling her human past here. Much had changed. She went by the ruins of numerous pre-Chaos houses, most so degraded by time there was barely any sign of them underneath the forest that had consumed them.

But Ruth remembered. Over there had lived the wonderful violinist and her husband. There, on the high bluff above the water, had been two women, doctors, where Ruth and Hanan had often spent evenings, drinking wine, seeing the lights of Seattle sparkle in the distance and discussing—Ruth paused as she tried to remember what had consumed their thoughts and worries and hopes before the phage struck and the Chaos ensued.

It wouldn't come to her.

She was moving by instinct, almost drawn. She pushed through undergrowth, paused as she came to a worn trail, the high route along the bluffs that she and Hanan walked almost daily when they were home together; rare events given their deployment schedules.

Ruth crossed, found the even narrower path, a tunnel of green through old growth forest. She froze as she came out into the clearing.

The log cabin was exactly the same. Perfectly maintained for hundreds of years. Ruth could barely imagine how much work that had been for Hanan to do alone. It had been old already when they'd purchased it Before Dealer.

Ruth went up to the door and put her hand on it, but she paused.

She let her hand drop and walked around, to the back, where Hanan had had spent so many hours working in her garden. The rectangle of dirt already had some green on it, plants, weeds, and even some moss. Ruth walked to it and fell to her knees, the heavy weight of her machine body sinking slightly into the ground.

"Ah," Ruth said. "My love."

She reached forward and placed a hand on the dirt.

She remained like that for a while, but the call of duty was pressing on her. She could not let her lover's sacrifice pass in vain.

Ruth got to her feet and retraced her steps around the cabin. She opened the door, her mechanical eye adjusting to the darkness much faster than her human one. The artificial eye technology had not yet been perfected with her model, the earliest functioning one. So they'd left one biological eye. When they'd mastered the eye, Ruth had insisted on keeping the one eye when she was upgraded.

She walked around the single room, throwing open the wooden shutters on the windows. She paused at the large stone fireplace. The ashes were long dead. She noted the collapsed stone table, which Grace said Hanan had toppled onto herself in order to get Grace out of the root cellar where she'd been hiding.

Ruth slowly turned, taking in all the books on the numerous shelves that filled all the wall space where there wasn't door or window. Each title evoked a memory. Ruth had been an eBook person, valuing the amount of titles she could take on deployment in such a small device. But for Hanan it had always been physical books; as she knew what the future held for both of them.

Ruth walked back to the door. A white card dangled on a chain looped over a hook by the door. The white was smudged with dirt, but it was clear of any markings or numbers: no Deathday for those who wore the white.

Ruth slipped it over her head, leaving it on the outside of her coverall, the ring on the inside.

Without a backward glance, she went out the door, closing it behind her. Crossed the clearing, took the small, private trail until it hooked up with the trail. Then she turned right and strode briskly toward the Capitol.

"Hello?"

Millay was twisting and turning on the table, slamming her armless shoulder down, the metal straps around her other wrist and ankles digging into her skin. She was moaning, crying out, because in her nightmare a knife was slicing into her chest, cutting deeper and deeper, burrowing to her heart in order to rip

"Hello?"

The voice was disembodied, floating in from what sounded like the ceiling.

mostly machine, but more importantly they were from another time, another place. Grace had been forced to take Ace out of the chamber and leave him in the landing bay; he simply could not accept being around so many machines and his constant barking and snapping had become unbearable.

Grace had briefed the second cyborg out of her chamber, a woman named Isabel, but the cyborg had listened to her impatiently before heading to the console and linking up with the computer.

Michael might have lost much of his humanness when he uploaded into Dealer, Grace thought, but these cyborgs had also lost something when they gave up their bodies.

The chamber was bustling with activity. Some cyborgs were checking weapons. Some were getting repairs done by other cyborgs. Isabel was with two others at the console, discussing the situation in low terms. As near as Grace could tell, they were at an impasse as to a course of action until Ruth either came back successful, or they learned she had failed.

When the other two left Isabel, Grace walked over.

"You should send someone to help Ruth," Grace said.

"If Ruth desired help, she would have left word of it. She left strict orders that we take no action on her behalf and no offensive action against Dealer. She did instruct that we prepare our defenses."

"What else?" Grace asked. "What about me?"

"If it appears we will be over-run and you are about to be captured we cannot allow you to fall into Michael's. Her orders are quite explicit on that."

"Will you?"

Isabel finally turned from the console.

"Will I what?"

"Kill me?"

"There is a reason we named this place Masada," Isabel said. "We're all prepared to die."

"Yes, but the people on Masada, from what I understand, were trapped. They had nowhere to go. We're not trapped. We can run."

Grace took a step forward. "In fact, *I* could leave. Go into the deep forest. Hide until Ruth gets back. And Ryker."

Isabel was still, her artificial skin-lined face impassive. "When we start disobeying orders and making our own decisions in violation of those orders, then we are on the verge of everything falling apart. I remember Ruth bringing Ryker in. She believed his story. She believed his plan. Not everyone was of the same opinion."

"Were you?"

"No." Isabel stepped away from the console, closer to Grace. "You're one half of the Prime. Part of a legend we pinned our hopes on when we went into cryostasis. Prime. Backdoor. It would be nice if it were true."

"I'm standing here."

"You're a burner who supposedly has a number in her head," Isabel said. The cyborg's voice was a copy of the human she had been, rough-edged, indicating perhaps a lot of whiskey and cigarettes, or just the bad luck of genetics. Her left arm was slightly bent in the middle of the forearm, but she had begged off repairs until more serious cases were seen to since the arm was still functional. "Ryker claimed to be the one who did most of the programming of Dealer. Thus, Dealer might be considered his offspring. His creation."

"Which is why there is a Backdoor," Grace noted.

"Perhaps."

"We're off the topic," Grace said, giving up. "All right. Just wanted to understand how things stood."

Grace walked away. Looking over her shoulder, she saw that Isabel was once more connected to the console, doing who knew what. Passing a table, she picked up a pulser and stuck it in her belt, next to her scraper.

Grace opened the hatch to the landing bay. Ace whined when he saw her, tail wagging. She shut the door behind her and with Ace at her side went to the bay doors. She'd watched enough to have an idea how this worked. She hit a button on the side and the doors slid open.

Five feet out, the waterfall was cascading with a roar. Grace leaned forward and looked down. The water hit a plateau twenty feet down, splashing in a pool and then she couldn't see any further. She had no idea what lie beyond that—a vertical drop? A turbulent stream?

She felt a thumping on her leg: Ace at her side.

"You don't like this place, do you?"

Ace whined.

"Your choice whether to follow," Grace said and then she sat down, and slid off the edge, down the rock and into the thunderous cascade of water.

CLAUDE WAS SHOCKED by the extent of the damage in front of him. "What happened, sir?"

The Lift he'd been flown in on powered down, but one could hardly tell, given the noise of the engines powering up on over fifty Lifts behind Michael.

That was all that was left of the fleet and army he'd been patiently building up for over a hundred years. Still, it was three times larger than that which had been left at the end of the Chaos. And there was the Quick Reaction Force, which had destroyed the revolting hives. He'd recalled that.

"We were attacked by the Cyborgs," Michael said. "A suicide mission."

"It looks like—"

Michael cut him off. "They're desperate. When one resorts to such tactics, it is a sign that they know they cannot win by other means. I'm going to press our advantage. I'm leading my Soldiers into Deep Void."

"Yes, sir," Claude said, because he had no idea what else there was to say. "But they haven't come for Millay yet. We don't know where—"

"I know the location of Grace of the Prime. She's with the cyborgs."

"How did you discover this?" Claude asked, so surprised by this revelation that he breached protocol by questioning Michael.

"We recovered the pilot of the suicide Lift. I accessed his memory cache. This will all be over shorty. You must insure that Millay of the Prime is kept secure and alive. Nothing else matters. Do you understand?"

"Yes, sir."

"I will be out of the Dealer Stream in Deep Void," Michael said. "I should be able to contact you through Achilles' post in Void. But if I can't get in contact, you'll have to make decisions."

"What about Dealer?" Claude asked. "Won't Dealer—"

"Dealer will run the Sound," Michael said. "Dealer will keep it functioning. But Dealer can't cope with the numerous human variables that are coming into play with the end of the Truce."

But Dealer brokered the Truce, Claude thought.

Michael was silent. The disconcerting thing about talking to a machine was that there were no tells. No facial expressions. Not even being able to see if the machine were looking at you or staring off into space. Claude had no clue where Michael's thoughts were in the silence.

Michael finally spoke. "We're at a tipping point. Where we either move forward or all is destroyed. What is can no longer be what it is. It is not sustainable. It was the problem B.D.. And before the IMP, and before the Chaos and before the Phage.

Claude didn't like the sound of that. The present, the *it is what it is*, was finally treating him pretty well.

Michael turned toward his Lift. His last words were almost an afterthought. "The future lies in the balance."

Claude watched as the flotilla of armed Lifts rose up into the air, formed up, and then began flying west.

BEGINNING OF THE 21ST
CENTURY, BEFORE THE CHAOS

"Approximately one hundred and fifty thousand people die every day," the scientist said. She waited for a reaction from her singular audience, received none, and then continued. "Two-thirds of deaths are from age-related factors, which most seem to accept as a given." She spread her hands. "We believe death an inevitability. Part of being human. Part of every living thing." She paused for effect, but there was none apparent. "Except not every living thing dies. At least not quickly in the overall sense of time. Certain endoliths have been found with an evolving time of over ten millennia."

"Obfuscating, Doctor Benet." Michael's voice was sharp, one used to being in command.

It was a term infamous in the business world, and especially in the conglomerate Michael controlled. It might as well be a profanity given the tone. And he was known only as Michael and perhaps the richest businessman in the world, but his holdings were so varied, so layered in subsidiaries, no one could calculate it. Which was exactly the way he wanted it.

Benet scrambled. "Endoliths are microorganisms, such as an amoeba or bacteria, that live inside rock, animal shells, coral. Astrobiologists are *particularly interested in them because the scientists postulate that if there is life on other planets, such as Mars, they would be endolithic in nature, as they live in places inhospitable to other life, such as deep in the ocean here on Earth."*

"Humans are not microorganisms," Michael said.

Benet spared back. "But all life is built up from single cells. Including you, sir."

When there was no response, she pushed on with her presentation.

"We all get old. We die. But few understand what exactly causes us to get old. While we spend billions on research to prevent death from accidents, disease, heart attacks and other factors, we still don't know the exact cause of the number one killer of humans: aging. The one thing no human can avoid."

Michael sat in the back of the lecture hall, just a dark silhouette. The glow from the holographic presentation the scientist unveiled next to her on the stage failing to reveal any of his features. He did not take notes. His arms were folded across his chest, his head canted ever so slightly, the only sign of his interest other than his two comments.

Doctor Benet, actually held four doctorates and was an MD, had won a Nobel Prize in microbiology the previous year and commanded most halls in which she spoke. She had no doubt who commanded this room. What she didn't know was that the lecture hall had been designed with numerous psychological factors: in fact, when Michael took the stage for a meeting, the entire platform had been lifted twenty feet, allowing him to look down on the closest rows and at just above eye level with the last row, while the display was projected below him. There was nothing Michael didn't do that wasn't calculated to give him an advantage.

"There are two main theories," Benet said. "Programmed Aging and Damage Aging. Programmed essentially posits that we are born to die. That our genetic code has an expiration date programmed from the moment of conception.

"The damage theory postulates that our environment induces enough cumulative damage to the body over time that we eventually die.

"The truth is both. They work in tandem.

"There is one solution. At the genetic level, focusing on the issue of telomeres, a molecular clock, where human cells begin to die after roughly fifty cellular divisions.

"Many of my colleagues believe that genetic coding is responsible for the determination of our lifespan. The rest is brought on by damage, whether molecular or of a more drastic, and larger nature. However, almost all damage is brought by cellular degeneration. Cell death leads to system malfunction and eventually body death."

She reached up and touched her hair. "Our hair becomes gray because the pigment cells gradually die. Our muscles cells begin to die, causing us to lose about ten percent per decade once we turn fifty. Even neurons in the brain begin to degrade after forty or fifty, causing us to lose three to four percent per decade. By the time we hit eighty, we're looking at a ten to eleven percent loss. This loss is selective at first causing damage in short-term memory and higher-level cognitive functioning.

"Currently in the United States, the average lifespan is seventy-seven years. The oldest person ever recorded lived to be one-hundred-and-twenty-two. That's a wide variance. What did the person have that was special?"

She paused.

No reaction.

"My research has focused on cellular division and death. Particularly telomeres. It's—" she stopped and it was obvious she was re-evaluating her presentation and whether she would be 'obfuscating'. She hit the pause on her holograph remote. Benet looked young for having won such a prestigious prize. She had long blond hair, a symmetrical face with prominent cheekbones and a tall, slender figure; indeed, many had accused her of 'working' her way to the top by means other than her scientific acumen.

If that had been true, she would not be here.

"DNA, deoxyribonucleic acid, is a molecule that holds most of our genetic markers in terms of development, functioning and reproduction. Nucleic acids along with proteins and carbohydrates compose the three major macromolecules that is the core of life.

"Telomeres is repetitive DNA. When cells divide; if they did so without telomeres, the cell would lose their ends and all the essential information they contain, would unravel. The problem is that when a cell divides, while telomeres keeps it intact, the telomeres is itself destroyed and has to be reconstituted. This occurs at a decreasing rate the more divisions there are. A slow degradation of the overall system."

"Another problem is that in each division of the cell, the end of the chromosome is shortened. As is the telomerase. However, they are remade by an enzyme, TRT."

"Telomerase reverse transcriptase," Michael said.

She was not surprised he'd read her papers. "Yes." It was also an indicator that she needed to stop throwing big words around.

"Do you wonder why I have you here?"

"No, sir."

"A guess?"

"I have no idea, sir?"

Michael sighed. "Did you know that Alfred Nobel read his own obituary eight years before his death?" He did not wait for an answer. "It was titled 'The Merchant of Death is Dead'. He invented over three-hundred-and-fifty-five different things in his life. More than me, actually. Of course, the most prominent of those inventions was dynamite. The headline was wrong; not about who he was, but because it was his brother who'd died.

"However, the specter of how he would be remembered after he died caused him great consternation. We all want to leave a legacy." He paused. "How do you think I will be remembered?"

Doctor Benet folded her arms across her chest, a subconscious protective stance a PR consultant had once told her of during her training she'd endured to enter the prime-dollar lecture and consulting circuit. That was the least of her concerns at the moment.

"I don't know, sir. That's not my area of expertise."

"Wouldn't it be better not to have to be remembered at all?"

Her mouth dropped open slightly, but this move she consciously caught and corrected. "I imagine it would."

"Alfred Nobel wrote a number of wills in his life, but in the last year—" he paused— "of course Nobel didn't know it would be his last year. We have a birthday. And we have a Deathday. Do we not?"

"But we know when our birthday is. Our Deathday is unknown."

"But we have one."

"True."

"Nobel's will left ninety-four percent of his assets, roughly two hundred million in today's dollars, U.S. to establish the Nobel Prize and the Foundation that doles out the award you received. Now, when people mention the name Nobel, it is associated with, first, the Nobel Peace Prize. Then the other Nobel awards. Few know of his inventions, even though their offspring have killed millions. Perception is reality. As you indicated when you began, our perception of death is that it's inevitable. But do you believe that?"

"No," Benet said. *"I believe it a scientific problem that can be conquered. To an extent. If someone can live to be one hundred and twenty-two, there is no reason we can't live much longer, if we can uncover the reason."*

"So you truly believe you can do something about our Deathday."

"Yes."

"Proceed."

Benet regrouped. *"Different cultures look at age in a variety of ways, but all mark periods from birth to death. As you just noted, this perception implicitly assumes that death is inevitable but, unlike, birth, has an unknown date. Armed with the right data, we can indeed project a Deathday. With enough research, experimentation and testing, I believe we can change the Deathday; push it further out by keeping our cells intact."*

"How long will it take?"

"Estimates, given the current rate of research and scientific advances, balanced against ethical and moral limits in experimentation, are that it could occur within a century."

"Doesn't do us much good, does it?"

"No, sir. But—"

"Yes?"

"There are several other areas being studied. It is believed that within fifty years, a human being's brain could be uploaded into a computer."

"Would they still be the same person?" Michael asked. *"The same consciousness?"*

"Unknown."

"I like it when someone readily admits what they don't know. Makes me trust when they tell me what they do know. Call me Michael."

"Yes, Michael."

But it was not an invitation to be friends, since everyone called him that. Coming from him directly it was an acceptance that he had passed some sort of test.

"When you say inside a century, do you mean a median between now and then, or slanted toward the then?"

"Slanted toward the then. Heavily."

"What's the number one thing holding you back?" Michael asked.

"Data. We've got reams of experimentation on lesser life forms and from that have extrapolated numerous computer simulations for humans, but our DNA is, well, our DNA. And as I mentioned, we are very limited by ethics in the work we can do in that area."

"And if you weren't limited ethically or morally?" Michael asked. "What if you had access to a computer that was twice as powerful as any you know of?"

"That would be extremely useful in running multiple simulations at high speed."

"I have such a computer."

Benet waited, sensing there was more.

"What if I told you there was data on a human who survived the plague, anthrax, phosphine gas, cholera, glanders, and other viruses and bacteria that kill most people?"

"All of those? One person?" Benet was silent for a few moments, stunned. "Glanders? That doesn't make sense. Very rare in humans and it has an extremely high mortality rate if it crosses over; via a form of bacteria called B. pseudomallei, which is the causative agent of melioidosis."

Benet took a step forward, to the edge of the platform. "Michael." She said the name as an equal this time. "B. mallei and B. psuedomallei are classified as category B pathogens by the CDC. An agent that can be used for biological warfare or terrorism. And there is no vaccine for them. How could one person have contracted all these? It's almost a statistical impossibility. And, more importantly, how could this person have survived?" She didn't wait for an answer. "From what I understand, our own government tried to weaponize glanders during World War II, but for some reason, it lost a considerable amount of its virulence in the lab. The Soviets also were interested in it. But the ones who delved most deeply into it were—"

Michael beat her to it. "The Japanese."

"Unit 731."

"Exactly." Michael sounded pleased, something unusual for him. "You know your history." He stood up out of the shadows and slowly walked forward toward the stage.

"I know my field. Who was the human?"

Michael shrugged. "A number. A box of file folders."

"Do you have the files?"

Michael reached the stairs leading up to the stage. "Yes."

Benet left the stage and came down to meet. She stopped just a few feet from him. "Can I see them?"

Michael gave a dry laugh. "The first question most people would have asked is how did I get them?"

"What does that matter?" Benet said. "The reality is, you have them."

"If you have access to those files; and many more from 731, will that shorten the timeline on your research?"

"I'd have to see the files first." She saw the hard stare and nodded "Yes. It will shorten it. It would help if you had cell samples from this person."

"We do."

"Is the person still alive?"

"Unfortunately, no."

There was a fire in her eyes. "Having a DNA sample, though. That's a game changer. It sounds like this subject was some sort of mutation. Or was exposed to a combination of agents and events that produced a genetic change."

"Tell me something, Doctor."

"Yes?"

"You are excited about the possibilities of this area of research?"

"Of course."

"But where do you see it going? What would be the progression? The implications?"

Benet paused.

"Surely it's something you've thought about," Michael pressed.

"Yes," Benet said. "Like every development in science, it has positive and negative implications. There is the potential to unlocking the key to the secret of telomeres," Benet said. "What you've described indicates a subject that could rapidly regenerate cells."

"Which means?"

"We can extend people's lives."

"Good."

Benet was silent for a few moments. "You haven't asked me about the negative implications."

"That's not your field," Michael said. "How much do you need?"

Benet struggled to calculate. "Based on the funding for cancer research, all the varieties, approximately two billion would—"

He cut her off. "Based on getting it done. Money is no object."

"Getting the expertise, the equipment and outfitting a lab and—"

"I have a lab with the best equipment and people who know how to use it. If you need something, I can get it."

"I'll also need the best scientists—"

And once more cut off. "When money is no object, then getting the right people is not a problem. Everyone wants something. Everyone has a price. Money is the easy way. But there are other offers we can make if necessary. Get me a list of who you need. What you need. I'll get it all."

"IF I FIND a way to extend life," Michael asked, "it initiates a larger problem, doesn't it?"

Dealer's reply was immediate. "Yes. Several."

"Why didn't you brief me on this?"

"My answers were within the specific parameters of the problem you wanted solved. Extend a human's life."

Michael tapped his fingers on the console, just short of the keyboard. "I assume whatever Benet comes up with will be expensive. So it won't be accessible to everyone. That would cause friction. Trouble."

"That is just a microcosm of larger issues," Dealer said. "Your focus is *too narrow. There is a saying in the Bible, which has been translated many ways. Matthew Six-Sixteen. One of those translations from the Holman Christian Standard Bible is: 'What will it benefit a man if he gains the whole world, yet loses his life'?"*

Michael was confused. "Are you referring to ethics? Morality?"

"Invert the saying," Dealer said. "What will it benefit a man if he gains his life, but loses the whole world?"

HUNDREDS OF YEARS IN THE FUTURE, AFTER THE CHAOS

"Thirty minutes," Tori said. "They're going to start bagging us. You have to do the right thing."

"This is all wrong," Haydn said. "All wrong. Heaven is wrong. Dealer is wrong. It's all a lie."

"There is Code. There is Death. You don't have many more days anyway, but don't take them away from everyone else."

Haydn pressed his fists against the side of his head, as he could expel his awareness of the current situation and all would be well again. Actually, not *again*, because it had never been well.

"Who is this Millay?" Tori asked, surprising Haydn with the sudden shift. "This woman that you love. She wasn't a burner, was she?"

"No. She wasn't."

"She's the reason you want to live. Hoping to see her again."

"Yes."

"There's been a rumor," Tori said, "going round in Heaven. Yesterday's arrivals said they heard of rioting in hive. That Dealer dammed the Stream and showed bodies. Threatened more if Code was broken."

"It's bound to happen," Haydn said.

"There's more. Some say that a burner and a People switched places. And Dealer didn't even know. And that they escaped into Void. That the legend of Prime is happening."

Haydn grabbed her shoulder. "Who told you of Prime?"

"It's a legend," Tori said. "Surely you heard it in womb of hive?"

"Why are you telling me this?" Haydn demanded, glancing to his left, toward the field where the burners were milling around. The Greeter was on the podium, Dealers in front.

"You're here in Heaven early," Tori said. "Aint never heard of that. So strange things are happening and you're strange. So what do you know? If you're gonna be bagged in a few minutes, don't let your secrets die with you. I'll help in any way I can. If I can help your Millay, I will."

"How could you possibly help?"

"I could at least think good thoughts for her," Tori said. "But, really, things are changing. Who knows what I may be able to do?"

Haydon considered that. Grace and Ryker might even try a rescue attempt here, although he knew that they would go after Millay first; Ryker because she was half the Prime and Grace because she was her sister. And then Millay would force them to come for him. He had no doubt of it. It was why he didn't want to die today. Not today. Not while he still had hope.

"The Prime," Haydn said. "She's part of the Prime."

"What?" Tori reached out and grabbed his shoulder. "What do you mean part of? What is it?"

"Even she doesn't know," Haydn said.

"She must have said something."

Haydn shook his head. "She has no idea."

"Well, where is she? On Island?"

"No. Mi—" he began, but caught himself. "Dealer has her. I'm afraid she's been boxed."

"That sucks."

"I—" Haydn began, but then the Greeters voice floated over the area, boosted by the speakers and the wrist band vibrated.

"It is time! If the killer doesn't step forward, the decimation will commence."

"What?" Tori asked. "What were you going to say?"

"I have to do the right thing," Haydn said. "If they come for me, tell Millay I love her."

"If who come for you?" Tori asked.

Haydn turned toward the field. He walked forward, toward the podium, pushing his way through the crowd of anxious burners. Now that they were actually in Heaven, despite the fact it meant they were on the precipice of their Deathday, or maybe because of it, the fear of being bagged was overwhelming.

"I did it!" Haydn called out, stopping about fifty feet from the podium. "I killed him." He turned to the gathered burners. "But let me tell you the truth! The man I killed was a renderer. You know what that is? Someone who butchers cattle so the People and the Evermores and the Middlemores can have meat. Why would renderers be used to guide us into that?" He pointed at the white wall. "Why would—"

And then darkness.

~

RUTH WALKED RIGHT past a Dealer on sentry duty at the perimeter of the Capitol, the white card a free pass. She located the nearest air vent for the service tunnels. It was camouflaged as part of a large botanical display; not to hide it from intruders, but to hide it from the view of People. There were minimum reminders of life other than that which the People enjoyed, nor or the work that was required of others to support that lifestyle.

She squeezed behind the metal tube, found the entrance, swung it open and climbed in, closing it behind her. The first thing she noticed was the smell. Not the fresh air of Island, but the odor of machinery; and worse.

Ruth climbed down the metal rungs. She reached the bottom on the side of a large tunnel, twenty feet in diameter. Along the top were bolted and/or hung numerous pipes, cables and conduits. The bottom was concrete with a run-off channel in the center.

Ruth closed her eyes, bringing up the directions that Andrew had transmitted.

Not far.

Ruth ran, heavy feet thudding on the concrete. She wove her way through the maze. She took a turn and almost ran into two Evermores. She halted and they took a step back. As soon as they saw the white card on her chest, they got out of the way.

Why a Person would be running in the service tunnels might have puzzled them, but they were Evermores—they wouldn't dream of asking.

Ruth left them behind. When she was one turn away from the target, she slowed down. Edged up to the corner and peeked around.

A steel door was twenty feet down the tunnel. It was propped open with a piece of wood. There were no guards.

Trap.

Ruth deployed her pulser. Weapon in front she went down the corridor. With her other hand, she threw open the door. A hallway with steel doors offset to either side. Flickering monitoring Streams in front of each one.

Still no guards.

But there was a red light in the joint between the wall and ceiling: surveillance.

"Surveillance is currently inactive," a voice behind her said.

Ruth spun about, aiming the pulser at the man.

"Easy, easy! I'm Claude. I was the personal assistant to Andrew, who was the Person. I helped him get the message out to you. I'm a friend."

"I don't believe you," Ruth said.

"You must. I betrayed Dealer. He's becoming a threat."

"Where's Millay?"

Claude pointed. "Cell three."

Ruth went there. The monitoring Stream showed her strapped to a table. "You took her arm!"

"Michael took it. Tried to get her to talk. But she didn't know anything of use. It's what he does to people he wants information from. It usually works, but not when they don't know what he's asking. In that case, though, they start lying, making things up. Anything to stop it. She didn't."

"Open it," Ruth ordered.

Claude scuttled past, placed his hand on the access pad. The door slid up.

"What's in the IVs?" Ruth demanded as she entered the box.

"Nutrients."

"Any—" Ruth paused as Millay opened her eyes.

"You look better," Millay said. "I like the hair."

"You don't look too bad yourself," Ruth said. She glanced at Claude. "Any painkiller in these IVs?"

"No."

"Sedatives?"

"No."

Ruth carefully began to withdraw the IVs.

"I've lost some weight," Millay said with a weak smile. "Hard way to do it."

"Indeed." IVs were out and Ruth unbuckled the straps.

"There's a problem," Claude said.

Ruth helped Millay sit up on the table.

"And that is?" Ruth asked.

"Michael is on his way to Deep Void with a fleet of armed Lifts full of Soldiers."

"That's not a problem. His Dealers didn't find our base." Ruth helped Millay to her feet, arm wrapped tight around her as Millay's legs buckled.

"He knows where it is now," Claude said.

Ruth paused. "How?"

"The pilot of the Lift you sent to attack Michael's depot. He didn't die. Michael accessed his memory."

"Elias," Ruth said in a low voice. "How could he have survived the crash? We loaded the Lift with explosives."

"Michael accessed the Lift's on board system."

Ruth shook her head. "We shielded it and made sure it was out of the stream. And the Lift should have been destroyed."

"It was," Claude said. "But did you shield every system?"

"We shielded nav and engine and flight control. And what does that matter if it was destroyed?"

"You didn't shield the emergency system," Claude said. "The ejection seat. Michael activated it and your pilot was ejected clear of the blast area."

"Where is the pilot now?"

"After he got what he wanted, Michael terminated him. Your man did destroy most of the base but last I saw, Michael was heading west. He's probably in Deep Void by now."

"Where's Grace?" Millay asked, far behind the conversation. "And Haydn? Where is Haydn?"

"Ryker's getting Haydn," Ruth said, but her mind was elsewhere.

"Where is Haydn?" Millay asked. "Is he really in Heaven? He—" she nodded at Claude—"showed me a Stream of him in Heaven."

"He is in Heaven," Ruth said. She was still trying to decide what to do. "Let's get out of here. If Michael gets close to Grace and we have you, we're back at square one."

She headed for the door, but Millay stopped her.

"Andrew."

"What?" Ruth asked.

"Andrew." Millay lifted a finger and pointed at a wall. "Andrew is in the next box. We have to take him with us."

"There's no time and no way we can bring him. Not now."

Millay was too weak to fight and Ruth scooped her up and carried her.

"Where are you going?" Claude yelled, caught off guard by the suddenness of Ruth's decision and action.

"Out of here."

GRACE HEARD the Lifts approaching from the east. She was on the side of a mountain, wet, scratched up, and scrambling to keep from tumbling down the slope. Ace was at her side, also wet, scratched up and scrambling, although with four feet he was having better luck.

She grabbed onto a tree and peered up through the branches and leaves. Lifts flitted by, lots of them. With angry looking probes on the sides, larger versions of the pulser she had tucked in her belt.

Grace slid down to ground, still keeping hold of the tree. Ace sat next to her. She put her hand in his wet fur. "You stink."

He looked at her with big brown eyes.

"We used to pray to Dealer," Grace said. "But I don't think it was prayer. More begged. I'm not sure what real praying is. Or who or what to pray to other than Dealer. And it didn't make a difference anyway. It is what it was."

Ace was staring at her.

"Maybe I should pray to you." She ruffled his hair. "You give me more comfort than Dealer ever did."

Ace pressed his head against her hand and she scratched. "Or maybe I just need to take care of things myself?" She pulled herself up. "I have to find Millay." She pulled a Dealer's hand from her pack, the metal severed at the wrist by Ruth's saw.

She held it to Ace. There was fluid in the cut; what it was, she had no idea. Strands of nano-tube muscle dangled. Ace whined, but he sniffed it, his hackles up.

"Find," Grace said.

Ace's head turned to and fro, nostrils flaring.

Then he began to lope off, along the side of mountain. Grace had to run to keep up.

EARLY WARNING PICKED up the Lifts as they approached.

Isabel activated the alert, red lights flashing, an alarm reverberating through the cavern. Everyone stopped and turned to her.

The last of the 300 had become conscious less than two minutes ago, putting them at 'full strength' although the most recently activated were still under the effects of cryostasis.

Isabel cut off the alarm. She spoke in a voice that carried, a human voice recorded long ago, but now boosted by machine.

"We have multiple Lifts inbound. We must assume they are armed and manned by Soldiers. Where is Grace?"

That caused a minute of consternation, cyborgs racing about looking for her, until Isabel checked the security records and saw the Stream of her sliding into the waterfall out of the hanger.

Isabel raised a hand. "Quiet! She's gone. She left on her own."

Isabel looked out over the 300. Two-thirds were up-armored. Pulsers ready. Others needed repairs from damage done during the Chaos.

The probe was feeding data to her. The Lifts were eight minutes out. Sensors had a count: fifty. Each Lift carried twenty-four Soldiers. Outnumbered four to one.

She looked at the console.

She withdrew her probe.

"Michael thinks the Prime is here. We have to keep him and his Soldiers engaged here as long as possible, to allow her to get away. Ten with me here as a delaying force. The rest to the Snake Path. We'll draw them in, fight a delaying action where the odds will be even."

MICHAEL HAD SUPERIOR NUMBERS. He had the target. The problem was how to bring the numbers into the target. Elias' cache had given the location, the departure point from the hanger hidden behind the waterfall.

But that was it. Before that was just the darkness of cryostasis.

Michael slowed his Lift. Behind him, the other Lifts matched his speed. They were all working off a local Stream that Michael was generating on his own, but there was no access to Dealer. They were a self-sustaining system in Deep Void.

Which also meant that Dealer was on its own in Sound, a thought that worried Michael.

For a moment, a long moment, a moment that stretched into several moments, Michael couldn't make a decision. He was relying on his own essence and the massive amount of material he had cached from Dealer, but that was it.

He didn't have the layout of Masada. The only thing he'd learned from Elias' cache was a hanger and then a single door. Not promising for the attack. He could blast the side of the mountain and most likely destroy Masada, which he was sure would have been Dealer's course of action, but that would kill Grace and nullify the objective. His objective.

He was sure there were other ways out of Masada; structural engineering required it: air vents at the very least. But no one, unless they were a fool, would build such a facility without a backdoor. The moment he thought that, he recognized the irony: trying to find a backdoor to access a Backdoor.

Michael issued his order. A Lift flew forward, through the waterfall into the hanger, discharging its load of Soldiers. A dozen more waited in line to deposit their Dealers when there was room.

The rest of the Lifts spread out in a circle. Michael determined that a perimeter of five kilometers from the base should encircle any other openings.

Michael issued the orders.

THE FIRST LIFT came through the wall of water and landed with a spark of metal skids on stone floor. Isabel and the other nine cyborgs opened fire as the Soldiers jumped out, destroying half before they could manage to return fire.

The Lift was already backing out, disappearing.

The cyborgs killed almost all the remaining soldiers, when one of their number was hit by a pulse, the charge burning through his neck, killing him.

And then a second Lift was in the hanger, this one not even landing, just a brief hover, doors open and discharging two-dozen Soldiers.

RYKER ROSE UP out of the water. He'd had plenty of time to plan, now that he knew the lay of the land. Heaven, the Wall and the ship to the south, Centre to the north. Which meant Haydn was also to the south, in Heaven.

Ryker retraced his steps from earlier, over the road, over the berm, across the narrow beach and into the water. He stabilized just below the surface and swam south. He sensed the ship's presence as he drew close.

Ryker surfaced. The edge of the ship's flight deck was directly above, the hull arcing. To the left was a massive anchor chain. Ryker grabbed hold and began climbing. Up, out of the water, toward the hole just below the flight deck through which the chain ran.

He climbed fast, inhumanly fast. He wished he'd had access to this power when he had crossed under the Lone Bridge. He was sure Ruth had been able to do so without any trouble. How she would get back with Millay, if she were boxed, was another matter.

One thing at a time, Ryker reminded himself. He reached the oblong opening in the hull of the ship. He climbed over the chain into the storage room. The chamber was dark, but he could use night vision enhancement. A hatch beckoned directly ahead. He went to it and tried to turn the wheel. Rusted shut long ago. He applied more torque and slowly the wheel began to move, rust protesting loudly.

So much for stealth.

The hatch opened and Ryker went into a corridor, pulser ready in one hand—he'd turned down having it integrated into his forearm, despite Ruth's assurances it was a simple mechanical procedure. In his other hand he had one of his Bowie knives.

He'd downloaded the schematic of the *John F. Kennedy* from Masada's database. The most advanced weapon system of its time;

completed just before the Chaos. The IMP had destroyed much of its capabilities, demonstrating the foolishness of trusting too much of any system to computer control that wasn't shielded. It had been back in port, awaiting repairs, when the Chaos had over-run the world. The phage had taken out almost all of its officers and senior non-commissioned officers, and the ship had been abandoned by the rest of the crew, until Dealer began to use it.

What it held *now* was the key.

Ryker made his way to a central corridor below the hanger deck. It ran the length of the ship. He strode down it, sensors on max, listening.

There was the sound of machinery just above his head. The hanger deck.

Ryker found a ladder leading upward. He carefully climbed. The hatch was open. He poked his head through.

It was hard to process the scene revealed in the dim glow of an inadequate numbers of lights spaced out along the ceiling.

Most of the space was filled with fencing topped with razor wire forming parallel lines, barely wide enough for a person. And a third of those narrow pens were filled with burners. Most were seated, sunk in despair. But alive.

The parallel cages merged as they went from stern to bow on the deck that stretched the length of the ship, just below the flight deck. Until there was only one exit.

Renderers poked and prodded near the end of that exit, pushing a single burner through, into the glowing doorway of a large black box, which hummed with power.

It was the same box from the video with some minor adjustments. No conveyor belt as the burner walked into the golden glow of the entrance willingly. Almost.

Ryker looked forward, toward the other end of the box. A metal chute curved downward into the hanger floor; Ryker didn't want think too much about what went down it. Further aft, a Lift was parked, several Dealers around it, facing outward, as still as statues.

Ryker heard voices to his right. Two humans were walking on this side of the hangar deck, as far from the cages as they could be as if distance meant less awareness. They were deep in discussion about something. A woman and a man. Even at this distance, Ryker could see the white cards around their necks. People.

Two Dealers followed them.

Ryker focused on the two humans discussion and followed their voices.

"The production schedule is below margin, Doctor Benet," the man said. "Did you see the Stream? A hive wiped out? Doesn't Dealer know what that does to the product flow?"

The woman was tall, silver hair, a sculpted face, wearing a white lab coat. "Dealer knows all," she said in tone that indicated it was a rote reply.

Ryker slid down on the ladder, out of sight as they approached.

"If production falls," the man was saying, "there will be problems. How will Dealer cope with that?"

"Dealer will compensate across the entire system," Benet said.

"The only way to deal with a decrease in production is to reduce the consumption end. That's never happened before."

Ryker was tracking their voices and knew they had passed and were heading aft.

"There's a first for everything," Benet said.

The sound of their footsteps halted. "Do you think—" the man's voice dropped to a whisper, but Ryker could still hear—"that Dealer has something else planned?"

"Such as?" Benet sounded irritated.

"Maybe the machine has decided humans are—" he paused again, and one more she finished for him.

"Expendable?"

"Yes."

"Perhaps." Doctor Benet didn't seem overly concerned. "But you have sufficient Spice for this trip, correct? The quota is filled?"

"Yes, but—"

"You think too much," the woman said. "I'd keep your thoughts to yourself. Trust in Dealer."

Ryker poked his head up again. The man got on the Lift, all but one of the Dealers accompanying. Benet stepped back as the side door slid shut. The Lift took off, straight up through a hole in the flight deck.

The woman shook her head. "Fool."

Ryker hid as she came back with her attendant Dealer, passed him, and then headed for a hatch at the forward end of the hanger deck.

Ryker looked at the number of burners in the long cages.

More than just a day's worth of Deathdays.

Were they now killing burners *before* their Deathday in order to make up for the shortages?

BEGINNING OF THE 21ST
CENTURY, BEFORE THE CHAOS

"*E*arth Overshoot Day occurred eight days earlier this year than last year. That's a two percent increase. Or more accurately decrease.*"*

There were three in the audience for this presentation: Michael, Doctor Benet, and a nervous young man, handpicked by Michael from one of his subsidiaries. The presenter was not a Nobel Prize winner; politics prevented that. No one likes bad news, and they most certainly don't give awards to those who cry out in the dark about utterly depressing things, like the end of the world, even if they are facts. He was the chairman of the GRN, Global Resource Network.

Michael glanced to his right to Benet, one eyebrow raised.

So she was the one who asked: "Clarification, Professor Keenum."

"We started calculating Overshoot Day in 2006," Keenan said. "A year after we established our network and were able to crunch the data. It's the day each year when humanity's demand for ecological resources and services outstrips what the planet can regenerate in a year. Every year as we take more and more, and destroy a percentage of the regeneration capacity. A major example of that is the depletion of the Amazon rainforest. Additionally, we factor in those capacities, which are finite, such as petroleum products.

"We then calculate how much our global ecological footprint is that year. Since we've been doing it, the footprint is always less than the capacity. So the remainder of each year, what we are in today, is global overshoot. Doing the math is simple. We divide biocapacity into footprint and multiply by three-hundred-and-sixty-five days. That gives us overshoot day."

"But it's only August," the young man said, obviously startled by this information.

"Quiet, Daniel," Michael said. "Let the man do his thing."

Daniel twisted in his seat. "Sir, I'm confused. This isn't my area at all. Why do you need me here?"

"You'll find out," Michael said. "All in due time. Continue, please."

Keenum took a step forward, toward the edge of the stage, trying to see his small audience, but they were in the shadows; all he could hear was their hushed whispering. He was clearly uncomfortable with the setup, but not with the subject matter. He saw this meeting as a great opportunity to get his message across to one of the most powerful men in the world. Who knew what that might lead to?

He went on. "In essence, much like a ledger for a business, a profit and loss statement, one can measure what we use against what comes in. We are running a deficit. One that has significant ramifications for the planet. While in business you can borrow money, we can't borrow biocapacity. Supply for the environment comes from biologically productive land and sea areas, which include grazing lands, fishing grounds, forest lands and even built up areas. On the demand side, we have the consumption of plant-based food and fiber products, fish products, livestock, timber, and space for urban infrastructure. The most important factor is a demand for fossil fuels, a resource that does have a finite supply, which then emit carbon dioxide that causes climate change, which then diminishes supply. A lose-lose-lose scenario."

A hologram of a transverse Mercator image representing the surface of the planet appeared next to him. Country borders were delineated and then every country was colored red, green, or pink. The United States, China, most of Europe, and most of the Middle East were red. India and Pakistan were pink.

"Red are those countries in overall ecological deficit," Keenum said. "Pink are those leaning toward it. And green are those within their limits. As you can see, most of the first world countries are in deficit. So much so, that they are dragging the rest of the world down with them."

Michael leaned forward. "Russia isn't red?"

"Russia has vast terrain and resources," Keenum said. "If we focused on the country itself, parceling it out—" a new image appeared of Russia alone. The western part was red, the larger, eastern portion was green. "The Urals are a dividing line inside the country. Eastern Russia is sparsely populated and rich in sustainment. Western Russia is in deficit. Ecological deficit and overshoot are the same."

"What about solar?" Daniel asked, forgetting the earlier admonition. "If we start switching out fossil fuel for solar power? Aren't we then importing a resource from outside our planet?"

"Less than ten percent of our energy is generated by renewable sources such as solar, wind, and water. Oil, coal and gas remain, by far, the most significant energy sources."

The image disappeared. Replaced by the image of two Earth's next to each other. One larger than the other. "We need a planet one-point-six times larger than what we have to sustain our current consumption levels. We will reach two planets larger by twenty-thirty."

"We started to overshoot in the early 1970's. And that gap has grown larger and larger every year since, both due to population growth and more demand per capita. It's not something that can simply be fixed with more solar panels. We are doing irreparable harm to the planet."

"Should the be 'have done'?" Michael asked.

Keenum didn't reply, which was an answer.

"How many times have you given this presentation?" Michael asked.

"Hundreds."

"How is it usually received?"

"Not well. Rarely does it result in any action. Especially by those who have the power to make a difference," Keenum added. "The problem is psychological. Most people cannot accept the reality of the physical law of consumption versus resources and diminishing regeneration. People have a 'not today, not here', mentality. Ninety-seven percent of economic planners

consider this a minor factor for the future, not worthy of attention. But it is
happening right now, right here.

"Why do you think I invited you here?" Michael asked.

"I hoped that you could be the tipping point. That you act within your
own sphere of influence. Which is greater than many countries. Change the
balance within what you control. That would be significant and send a
message to others."

Michael stood up. "Several scientists have resigned from your organiza-
tion. Very aware men and women. Very smart. Experts in the same field.
They've thrown in the towel. They believe the tipping point is already past.
It's too late. Some have gone off the grid, although that won't change the
overall picture. What do you think?"

"It's never too late," Keenum said. "We must have hope."

"What makes you think hope is a good thing?" Michael asked. "Isn't the
hope you have much like the hope some religions generate We often refuse
to accept a harsh reality, even when it's right in front of us.

"I am always fascinated by video clips of mass executions. Whether it
be Gestapo, SS, ISIS, whomever. Leading a string of victims, often to open
pits. The prisoners can see the bodies of those who went before them lying
there, brains blown out. Then they're made to kneel. Knowing they will
suffer the same fate. And they kneel. And they can hear the man with the
pistol walking down the line, shooting them in the back of the head, one by
one. Yet they just kneel there and take the bullet. They don't try to run. To
fight back, even if their hands are tied and it's futile. Isn't it more futile to
just kneel and take the bullet?"

"I, uh. Well—"

Michael obviously didn't except a coherent answer. "Our relationship
with pending and obvious death is intriguing. History records rebellions at
three concentration camps during World War Two run by the Nazis. At
Auschwitz, there were numerous attempts. All failed. But the one that
intrigued me, was a woman who arrived under that famous sign, Arbeit
macht frei, work makes you free. Everyone in that group was selected for
death. In the undressing room of a gas chamber, they were told, as usual,
that they were just being disinfected en route to someplace else, all of them

knowing it was a lie, but wanting to believe the lie, this one young woman did something different. She grabbed a pistol from one of the SS guards. Shot him. Shot another. Inspired by this, many of the other women joined in. Biting guards, beating them."

Michael fell silent and Daniel walked into it. "What happened?"

"They were all killed. But. Here's the interesting thing about this woman. Some say she was a collaborator prior to being shipped to the camp. Isn't that interesting?"

"How so?" Daniel asked.

"That she would do whatever it took to live," Michael said. "When it meant collaborating she did. When it meant grabbing a pistol and shooting a guard, she did."

Keenum spoke from the stage. "Not to disparage her, but it sounds as if she had no convictions. Only herself."

Michael looked at him. "Interesting take. But perhaps her conviction was to life itself."

"Was there a point to this story?" Keenum said, an edge to his voice.

"In a way, Professor Keenum," Michael said. "Your own hope is very much similar to the thought process of those whose right here, right now blissful ignorance mantra. You believe that right here, right now, we can change something that can't be changed."

"Then why did you invite me? Why did you listen to my presentation if that's what you believe?"

"I wanted to hear you," Michael said. "And tell me something."

Keenum folded his arms across his chest. "And that is?"

"Since you know the facts. And why you haven't capitulated to them. Perhaps you are made of sterner stuff than most people. And you're obviously not a fool. I divide people into two groups. Those who will kneel, and those who will grab the pistol." Michael stood.

"Tell me this, Professor Keenum. When you lie in bed at night. When fear of what will happen makes your heart beat faster and gives you a sick feeling in the pit of your stomach." Michael began walking toward the stage. Behind him, Benet got to her feet. "I want to know what fantasy you have about saving the planet? Saving humanity from humanity? Keeping *mankind from kneeling and accepting an inevitable collective bullet to the back of the head. What you dare not say in public, or even to those close to you?"*

Keenum finally retreated a step, whether from Michael's advance or the questions. "What are you talking about?"

"You said most can't accept your facts psychologically." Michael reached the edge of the stage. Eye to eye with Keenum. Benet was standing, but still at her seat. Daniel was also on his feet, looking from Michael to Keenum.

"I think at some level," Michael continued, "your subconscious knows we're past the tipping point even though your conscious mind won't completely accept it. If it did, you wouldn't be making these fruitless presentations to people who don't want to hear you in the first place. And when you lie in bed at night, it wakes you up. Worrying, scared really, about your grandchildren and how they are doomed. Most people have no clue how quickly things will unravel once the panic sets in. And then your mind goes places it doesn't go in the daylight," Michael pressed on. "To unthinkable solutions to the problem you know only so well. Tell me of those solutions."

"If we begin to change—" Keenum began, but Michael cut him off.

"No! Right here! Right now! What is your fantasy that could save mankind given the reality?"

Keenum didn't answer.

Daniel walked down and stood next to Michael. "Sir, I'm not sure why—"

"Shut up," Michael said to him. "You're here for a reason. I want you to understand the why behind what I'm going to want you to do. To understand how serious it is. To understand how serious I am." Michael folded his arms. "We can't change the amount of resources. As you said, Professor Keenum. So the variable is consumption. How do we change that?"

"We can't shut the door at improving resources. We're doing some things right. Recycling. Conserving water. Better farming techniques. Reforestation." Keenum tried a rally. "Switch to renewable energy. Change—"

"Ah!" Michael said. "I apologize for being so harsh. Maybe I was hasty, although I don't think so. Neither does my computer, Dealer. It's run the data. But I want to hear the answer from you. What if there is an energy option that didn't hurt the planet?"

Keenum took a deep breath, trying to collect himself. "It would help."

"Only 'help'?"

"There are other factors."

"More significant than clean energy?" Michael asked. "What if I told you there was a clean source of energy available right now? Wouldn't that turn things around?"

"We can't eat energy," Keenum said. "Energy is one side of the equation. Supply. Growing demand requires more than just energy. Food is a priority. Along with many other resources. We're consuming too much, irreparably changing the entire water system."

"I know," Michael said. "Dealer projects the next major war will be fought over water, not oil or terrorism."

"I've made the same conclusion," Keenum said.

"How do we change demand?" Michael asked. "How fast is our population growing?"

Keenum had those numbers memorized. "Seventy-five million are born every year. Fifty-six million die. We have an overall growth rate of one-point-one percent a year. There were one billion people in 1800. We are now over seven billion. It's estimated by 2030, we'll be at eight-point-four billion. Nine-point-six billion in the mid-2050s."

"Unsustainable, correct?" Michael asked.

"Yes." Keenum was sweating. "But nature tends to correct things."

Michael cocked his head. "Really? Tell me. How will it be corrected?"

Keenum dropped his head, not able to look Michael in the eyes. "We cut back."

"'Cut back'? How? People want more. It's human nature. How are you going to get them to cut back? Humans are irrational. You know that better than most. A handful, faced with the facts, have already cut back their consumption, but it appears their efforts are futile. Even if we all want less, we still have more and more people."

Keenum didn't answer.

Michael continued. "As you say, nature tends to correct when things get out of balance. Doctor Benet here, thinks it's likely that a worldwide plague, something that will make the Black Plague look like the common cold, is inevitable. Something airborne. We're so connected now via air travel that just the right lethality with just enough incubation time before symptoms, and it will be around the world in just days."

"It's possible," Keenum said. "But modern medicine is—"

"Yes, yes." Michael waved a hand, dismissing that. "Modern medicine is helping us slit our own throats by keeping too many people alive who should be dead." Michael moved closer, inside Keenum's personal space. The professor backed up.

"Drastic measures are needed, aren't they? Tell me."

Keenum lifted his head, stared back at Michael. "Drastically cut back consumption."

"How?"

Keenum was broken. "Reverse what's been happening."

"Reduce the population," Michael said, and it wasn't a question.

"Yes."

"How?"

"Whatever nature comes up with. As you say, perhaps a plague."

"What about man? How could we cut back our own population?"

"A third World War would—"

"Also destroy much of the supply side," Michael said.

"Yes. I've thought of it."

"Unless a community was self-contained. Producing all it needs."

"Yes."

"Now you're talking like a realist. How else?"

"I don't know."

Michael took a step back. "Thank you, Professor. You've validated what I already knew. But, despite what my critics say, I'm not a bad man. I'm a realist."

Keenum was startled. "What are you going to do?"

"Come here, Daniel," Michael said. "Stand at my side."

Daniel tentatively came forward.

Michael put his hand out to Keenum. "Seriously. Thank you."

And Keenum, still living in the old world, reached out and shook it. Michael gripped his hand, hard.

"Tell me, Professor," Michael said. "Do you kneel? Or do you fight?"

Keenum was confused. "I don't—"

"We'll start cutting back with you." Michael's other hand brought up a knife and swept it across Keenum's throat. He didn't step back from the arterial spray, as most people would have instinctually done and when Daniel jumped back, he turned to him and grinned, his face splattered.

"Do you believe I'm serious?"

Daniel could only nod, staring as Keenum fell to his knees, air gurgling out of his severed throat, a shocked look on his face.

Michael let go of the hand and Keenum collapsed face forward on the stage.

"Tell me, Daniel. Do you kneel or do you fight?"

"Fuck you!" Daniel yelled. He leapt at Michael, grabbing his throat.

Michael put the tip of the knife against Daniel's throat, even as he gasped for air.

Then Benet fired a stunner and Daniel collapsed.

Benet looked at the weapon in her hands. "It works quite well. Kudos to your R & D department."

Michael nodded. "They've got better stuff than that in the pipeline." He pulled a handkerchief out of a pocket and carefully wiped the blade clean. He looked at it for a moment. "I had a better knife once. Hand-crafted."

"What happened to it?"

"Someone stole it."

Michael walked off the stage and say down, knife in his lap. Benet took the seat next to him.

"How long until he's conscious?" Benet asked, handing Michael the stunner.

"It was set at the very lowest power. Shouldn't be too long."

"Was anything he said," Benet indicated Keenum, "news to you?"

"No."

"Then why all this?"

"I wanted to be absolutely sure. Dealer gave me the facts, but also told me that if Keenum felt it was hopeless, even with the power from CNS, then it truly is hopeless."

"But you have a plan?"

"Of course."

Daniel groaned. Rolled over. Slowly sat up. It took him a little while longer to get oriented.

Michael stood. "You wondered why you were here?"

Daniel could only nod.

"It's obvious, isn't it? You're going to save the world."

HUNDREDS OF YEARS IN THE FUTURE, AFTER THE CHAOS

The cyborgs were trading space for time. The hanger was now under control of the Soldiers. The battle was raging in the cryo chamber, but Isabel quickly realized that it was too large a space. The advantage was with the Soldiers as they poured in from the hanger, Lift after Lift load.

She fired her pulser, hitting a Soldier on the side of the head, the metal imploding. Then looked left and right. Twenty-two of her comrades were down. She didn't need to access her computer cache to understand the inevitable result of making a stand here.

"Back to the Snake Path," she called out to the rest of the rear guard.

The cyborgs began to withdraw, the partially disabled being dragged; the brain dead left behind. Eight more went down before they could get inside the tunnel entrance.

Isabel was last, firing a final pulse. As she pulled the blast door closed, she caught a glimpse of Michael entering the cryo chamber behind a phalanx of Soldiers. Isabel paused. She aimed at his head and just as she fired, a pulse hit her in the chest, knocking her back. Two cyborgs grabbed her, pulling her back while another slammed shut the hatch and secured it.

THE PULSE GLANCED off Michael's arm, the same one that had been hit in the Port Townsend battle. A quick assessment indicated some damage, but nothing that couldn't wait. He saw the blast door being shut, then scanned the chamber.

He received reports from the Soldiers.

No sign of Grace yet, but the cyborgs had retreated up a tunnel, leaving behind their dead.

His Soldiers had absolute orders not to engage any humans.

Subtracting the number of dead cyborgs from the number of cryo tubes indicated there was a force of about two-hundred-and-fifty behind that door. It had to be an escape tunnel.

He issued orders for the door to be opened by whatever means necessary, then headed back to the hanger. He got in his Lift and took off, through the waterfall. He gained altitude and looked down on the mountain that hid the cyborg base. He noted the disposition of his forces encircling the mountain. Sufficient. He had a Quick Reaction Force ready to respond as soon as any cyborg popped its head up out of the emergency tunnel. Now they would be the ones trapped in a funnel and he would have them on both ends. He considered various ways to threaten to finish them off: explosives, fire, sealing them inside to slowly wither away and die.

Unless they turned Grace over to him.

And then he would destroy them anyway.

Michael scanned for any indication of a Stream.

That was another problem. There was no indication of Ryker and he couldn't sense his brother's presence. Very odd.

There was the slightest of tingles that Michael recognized. He reached out and touched the partial Stream.

ACHILLES WAS WET, tired, and irritated. The last he'd spoken with Claude, the Evermore couldn't help but let it slip he'd been given

Spice of Life by Michael. Claude had promised to push for the same for Achilles; a promise Achilles doubted would even be initiated by the Evermore. He'd known long ago that Claude only cared about Claude. But that seemed to be the nature of things here in Sound. Everyone looked out for their own interests. People not caring about all those who lived and died to support their lifestyle. Middlemores and Evermores grateful to not be burners; those among them who knew of the Spice, keeping it secret in the desperate hope they might get some.

Even here in Void the jokers were eating folders and floers and each other when need be, anything to stay alive another day. Achilles looked down at his shoulder, the missing arm. He'd given in quickly once that was sliced off; willing to do whatever Michael asked.

Even coming out here to this forsaken place and betraying those whose trust he'd earned over years of leading them. He liked to think he'd given them extra time, saved them from being eaten by jokers or from becoming jokers themselves; the only alternatives in Void before Delta.

Achilles was sitting in the control booth for the crane, next to the Dealer, half-a-Dealer. It occurred to him, for the first time, to wonder why this Dealer was missing the lower half? Was there a version of 'boxing' for Dealers? They didn't feel pain, so what would be the point?

He could see Charon about a quarter mile away, awkwardly rowing. Practicing, building the muscles he was going to need.

He'd learn. He had nothing else to do.

There was a crackle and hiss from the Dealer. A very weak Stream, audio only.

"Achilles."

"Here."

"Status?" Michael asked.

"Latest report from Claude is that all is well. No more revolts in hive. The burners took the warning to heart."

"And Millay, once of the People?"

"Nothing further to report," Achilles said. Actually, that was literally true since Claude hadn't said a word about that in the last contact. A strange omission that now troubled Achilles, realizing he was between Claude and Michael.

"And Dealer?"

Achilles blinked. What of Dealer? Michael *was* Dealer.

"Sir?"

"Is all running smoothly in Sound? Beyond the lack of trouble in hive?"

"As far as I know. but I'm out here and—"

"Very well."

The transmission went dead.

Achilles sighed. He rubbed his shoulder. The ache never quite went away even after all these years. The boy, the one he'd used to reach out to Ryker and Grace, was out hunting; one positive of having him here was he supplied food. It *was* odd that Claude had used the boy as an intermediary, Achilles thought. One of many odd things that were going on.

Claude was putting people between him and responsibility for his actions. Scapegoats.

Games with games.

A thrumming sound caught his attention. A familiar one. Achilles climbed out of the crane, down to the concrete pier. More Deltans being brought in?

But then he spotted the Lift, coming from the west, out of Deep Void. Most unusual. Some Dealers from Michael? But they'd just spoken.

It was flying erratically and Achilles first thought was that it was damaged. But as it got closer, he didn't see anything wrong on the outside. It descended unevenly and finally landed hard, angled, right skid hitting first, then left.

It was near the base of Delta and Achilles began the long walk down the pier to greet it. The side door didn't open and he wondered what the Dealers were waiting for.

When he finally arrived, the door slid open and he looked at the working end of a pulser. Held by a young woman. With no card around her neck. She had a scraper tucked into her belt.

Achilles paused to take stock of the situation, but it was so unexpected, no possible explanation came to him.

She spoke: "Ryker described you to me."

Achilles took a step back. "Who are you?"

"I'm Grace."

"The Grace? Of the Prime?"

"You've heard of me?"

"Michael is searching for you in Deep Void."

"And you know that how?"

Achilles didn't answer.

Grace hopped out of the Lift and a dog followed her.

"Ace!" Achilles said, automatically kneeling to pet the dog, but it snarled and backed up, standing next to Grace.

"The dog too?" Achilles said with a sigh as he straightened. "What do you want?"

"I want you to get me to my sister."

"Michael has her."

"I know. On Island. Where they box People. And you've been there, right?" she gestured with the gun at his missing arm.

"Yes. I've been there."

"Good. You're going to take me there."

"You can't fly a Lift to Island without authorization," Achilles said. "The air defense—"

"That's why I'm here," Grace said. "I don't plan on flying. You had a way of getting people here. You must have a way of sending people the other way." She nodded over her shoulder. "Who is out there rowing?"

"Charon."

"A new one?" She nodded. "Makes sense you'd have to rebuild. Ryker said you would. What do you know of my sister, Millay?"

"Nothing."

"You lie."

"The last information I had was that she was on Island. In the service area, where the boxed are held."

"You have a black card, don't you?" Grace asked.

Achilles nodded.

Grace tapped the scraper in her belt. "I slit the throat of the last person I met who had a black card. You remember Doc, don't you?"

"You killed her?"

"Yes."

"She wasn't a bad person," Achilles said. "She was doing the best she could under the circumstances."

"Like you?"

"Like me."

"You betrayed everyone you had here," Grace said.

"I had no choice."

Grace looked him in the eyes. "You see. That's the problem. We don't think we have a choice. We think our death is predicted. Our lives are predicted. The jobs we get are part of a larger plan. It's all as Dealer says it is. But if we accept that, then we're less than human, aren't we?"

"Dealer rules all," Achilles said, but there was no force to it and he was avoiding her gaze.

"Humans invented Dealer," Grace said. "We can uninvent it."

HAYDN HAD A HELL OF A HEADACHE. He opened his eyes, glad that he was able to open them, because he should be extinguished, in a bag, thrown onto a blazing pile of other bagged burners.

A white ceiling. Haydn had never seen anything so perfectly white except for the Wall around the ship. He also saw something, someone, in his peripheral vision. He turned his head.

"I'm Claude."

Green card. Beady eyes. Haydn hated him at first glance. And next to him: Tori. Haydn felt the disappointment wash in with the awareness.

"Where am I?" Haydn asked.

"On Island," Claude said. "We tried, we really tried, to find out what you know. In a very nice and what could have been a pleasant manner," he added, with a sideways glance at Tori. "Unfortunately you turned the tables and found out what was behind the Wall. It seems you have not learned your lesson. Curiosity is a fatal trait for a burner."

"I'm still here." Haydn tried to get up, but there were restraints around his wrists and ankles. And then he knew exactly where he was. "burners don't get boxed."

"No, they don't," Claude confirmed. He rubbed his chin. "Millay wouldn't tell the Prime, even to save you."

"She doesn't know it. Where is she? She has to be here. Let me see her."

Claude ignored the questions. "Michael is in Deep Void right now trying to get her sister, Grace. Which means he's out of the Stream and I'm in charge."

"What about Dealer?"

"What about Dealer?" Claude said.

"I killed a burner," Haydn said. "A renderer. I was supposed to be bagged."

Claude shrugged. "Who cares about a burner getting killed? Especially a renderer. Tori told me what you said you saw behind the Wall. Interesting."

Haydn looked at Tori. "You were working for him all along?"

Tori nodded, her eyes red from crying. "I wanted Second Room."

"I don't think you should want Second Room," Haydn said. He looked back at Claude. "Right?"

"I had no idea what happens in Heaven," Claude said. "Above my life-grade."

"Where is Millay?" Haydn asked again.

"Oh. I let her go. With Ruth. They're gone."

Haydn blinked. "What? Why? She's not boxed?"

"Because I'm your friend," Claude said.

"She's not boxed?" Haydn didn't believe.

"You weren't bagged," Claude pointed out. "Michael wanted information from Millay. She wouldn't, couldn't, tell him what he wanted. A cyborg came for her and I let her go."

"Why? Why would you do that?"

"Told you. I'm on your side."

"Then why am I strapped down in a boxing room?" Haydn asked. "Why not let me go?"

"I wanted a chance to talk first," Claude said. "You have killed after all. Couldn't quite jump right into it without a chance to explain. You're dangerous."

"Explain then."

Claude hit something underneath the end of the table. The restraints slid away. Haydn sat up, head throbbing from the stun, energized by the thought of Millay not boxed, and free.

"Things are unraveling," Claude said. "Before it was just Dealer. And I worked for the Person. He supposedly ruled Sound. We always thought Dealer was subservient to his word. But I now know it never was. It was all a show. And there's Michael. And it's not Dealer. Not quite. But he's not human either. I think that—"

The door behind Claude and Tori slid up. A Dark Angel stood there. With two other Dark Angels behind it. They trooped in. Along with two Dealers, stunners ready.

Haydn had to assume it was the center Dark Angel that 'spoke'. "We regret to inform you, Claude-eight-foxtrot-zulu-eight, that you have been found in violation of the Code of Life."

"But—" Claude sputtered. "But Michael—"

Two Dark Angles seized his arms in an unbreakable grip.

The third Dark Angel turned toward Tori, pointing a metal claw. "Victoria-alpha-seven-six-bravo, you have been judged, by order of Dealer for crime against Code. You are to be immediately bagged and extinguished."

Tori screamed. "No! I did what was asked of me. By Dealer."

The Dark Angel reached for her and she darted away, to the far corner of the room. "No! I did what Dealer asked!"

"Dealer did not make any requests of you," the Dark Angel said.

Tori turned to Claude. "But you said—" she scrambled as the two Dealers separated, going around the table, trapping her. As they did so another Dealer came in, carrying a large, shiny gray bag.

Haydn leapt at that Dealer, a futile attempt. It easily knocked him aside with the other hand, slamming him into the table.

The two Dealers had Tori in their grip. They lifted her three feet off the floor. Her legs were kicking. Haydn could hear her shoulders crunching, coming out of their sockets, the way a venter would make their way through a particularly narrow tunnel. As his mother had done, always trying to get to the light. But there was no light waiting for Tori.

Only darkness.

The Dealer opened the bag, slid it under her feet. She was poised above the bag, helpless, held by the other two Dealers. But the tableau remained frozen.

The Dark Angel reached out and grabbed Haydn. "How did you and the others go from Void to Deep Void?"

Haydn was confused. "What?"

"If you tell us how your group crossed from Void to Deep Void, she will be spared bagging and returned to Heaven."

"We built a raft," Haydn said. "What does it matter?"

"A raft of what?"

"Bodies. We crossed the gap in the Broken Bridge on the bodies of jokers."

"And how did Grace-five-eleven-kilo-one escape from Island?

"What does it matter?"

Tori screamed as the Dealer with the bag began to bring it up.

"She crossed Lone Bridge," Haydn said.

"Dealers guard Lone Bridge," the Dark Angel said.

"She went under it. Let her go," he said, pointing at Tori. He looked at Claude. "What is going on?"

And then the Dealer brought the bag up as the other two Dealers lowered her.

"I told you what you wanted!" Haydn yelled.

"She was judged," the Dark Angel said.

Tori looked to Haydn, eyes wide as the bag rose up her body. "I'm sorry. Tell Millay you love her! Love. A life for a life. My life for—"

"I will remember your name!" Haydn called out.

And then the bag was over her head and immediately sealed. Haydn could see her struggling for long seconds as the air was drawn out and then she was still, her figure outlined inside. The two Dealers carried her body out.

"You lied!" Haydn yelled at the Dark Angel.

"She was judged," the Dark Angel said. Then it turned to Claude.

The other Dark Angels threw Claude down on the table that Haydn had so recently occupied. They spread his arms and legs and the restraints slid up and locked him down.

"I'm Claude! I am the personal assistant of the Person."

"There is no Person," the Dark Angel said. "The last Person is in the next room. He violated Code and you assisted him. For violation of Code, Claude-eight-foxtrot-zulu-eight will be boxed."

It turned for the door.

"You can't do this to me!" Claude screamed. "I'll tell you of Michael. He's in Deep Void. Trying to get Grace. The other half of the Prime."

The Dark Angel paused. "He is out of Stream. We know that. He was supposed to terminate Millay, once of the People. Where is Millay once of the People?"

"She escaped," Claude said.

"You let her go."

"A cyborg came here. Took her. I couldn't stop her."

"You are of no use," the Dark Angel said.

"Wait! Wait!" Claude was writhing on the table. "I can help you get Millay. She can't be far. She's still on Island."

"How can you assist?"

"I put a tracking device in her. A transmitter. We can find her."

"Give us the transmitter."

Claude pointed to a small fresh bandage just behind his jaw on the right side. "I had the receiver surgically implanted."

The Dark Angel reached toward his head and Claude rushed to get the words out before it ripped the receiver out.

"If removed, it shuts down. It's tied to my nervous system; energized by it. Take it out and the frequency is gone."

The Dark Angel's hand stopped. "That technology is old. Chaosera."

"It works. Let me free and I'll help you find her."

There was a moment of silence, as if Dealer, via the Dark Angel, was mulling the proposal, a strange thing for a machine that could make millions of calculations in a millisecond.

The restraints slid back and Claude sat up, tears on his cheeks. There was an odor in the room; he'd voided his bowels in fear.

Haydn lurched forward, able to get one hand on Claude's throat, squeezing.

The Dark Angel jerked him back.

"Lead us to Millay, once of the People."

As soon as she regained consciousness, Isabel's interface gave her a rather grim update on her status: badly wounded, functional for a while, but then a system degrade to complete failure.

Death. Real death.

But she moved past that to the overall situation. A cyborg was leaning over her, a familiar face.

"Joe."

"They're working the door," Joe said. "Tried blasting it, now it appears they're trying to burn through. I've deployed the rest of our people at every bend in the Snake. They'll pay dearly for every meter they advance."

"Soldiers are machines, Joe." Isabel sat up. "Michael can always make more. He doesn't care how many Soldiers he loses. The only advantage we have is that he wants Grace."

"But we don't have her either."

"Michael doesn't know that." She looked over her shoulder. "Did you send anyone to the exit?"

"Not yet. I assume Michael has put a cordon of Soldiers around the mountain. It would be the logical thing to do. We have to try to break out," Joe said. "It's the only thing we can do."

She nodded and pointed down the tunnel. "Take ten of your best. See if we have a way out. I'll command here."

"You're wounded. Badly."

"I know."

Joe nodded. "You've got to have faith. Believe."

RYKER WALKED AFT, the direction Benet had gone. His internal guidance system let him know when he reached the point in the central corridor below the flight deck where the hatch Benet had gone through was located above him. Twenty feet further on, a ladder went up.

Ryker climbed up to the hatch, blocking the way. He turned the wheel. It spun freely. Then he pushed up.

No movement.

He put more strength in the effort. Nothing. It had to be dogged shut on the other side.

He cocked his head. 'Dogged'? Where had that come from? And then he had a vision of being on a sailboat, open ocean, bright sun reflecting off the water.

And it was gone just as quickly.

The old Ryker was in his brain, somewhere. Perhaps the Prime would unlock that also? He mused as he retreated down the ladder and considered an alternative route.

He went further down the corridor, passageway his faded memory corrected. Climbed another ladder. This hatch opened to a room with no light, except that easing in from the opening he'd just made. Ryker went into the room, using his night vision. Stoves. Steel doors with levers: freezers.

A kitchen.

He turned back the way he'd come. Several doors, all shut. But also a rippled metal shutter above a long counter. Where the food had been served. Which meant a mess hall on the other side.

Ryker checked the doors, all dogged from the other side.

He went to the shutter. Slid his fingers to the bottom, barely got a grip, and then lifted. It went up, screeching and protesting. As it cleared Ryker's head, a stun hit him in the chest, but the up-armor Ruth had put on him took almost all the charge.

Ryker dove forward, drawing the pulser and one of his Bowie knives. From the angle of the stun, he was already aiming as he came to his knees. He pulsed the Dealer twice in the head, blasting it off. Then he scanned the room.

Benet was standing at an autopsy table, a body on it. She had a scalpel in her hand, which was frozen, mid stroke.

No other Dealers.

No other humans. Not living.

Ryker straightened up. He went over to where she was. The corpse was of a young man. Several organs had already been removed and were on a table to Benet's left. The heart was on a scale.

Ryker's finger curled around the trigger of the pulser.

Not yet.

"How much does a heart weigh?" Ryker asked.

Benet looked over at the headless Dealer, the body locked upright. Then back at him. "Who are you?"

"A better question might be: what am I?"

She nodded. "A cyborg. I was wondering when we would see your type again."

"Today's the day," Ryker said.

BEGINNING OF THE 21ST CENTURY, BEFORE THE CHAOS

"Each takes a jeweler three months to carve from a block of crystal," Michael said. He took one of the two champagne flutes out of the velvet lined wooden case and held it up to the harsh light in the lab. "Twenty carats of white diamonds and ten carats of argyle pink diamonds, finished with platinum. As you requested, most importantly, not a drop will be wasted from the interior. I hope your product will be worthy of them."

"It is," Doctor Benet said. The lab was large, mostly filled with a large black box, humming with energy. It was forty feet long by sixty wide.

Michael nodded toward the box. "All of that and it produces just this." He indicated two thin metal tubes, held upright in a rack next to the container for the champagne flutes.

"It's a difficult process to extract telomeres from a person."

"But you can't be one hundred percent certain it works long term," Michael said.

"I tested it extensively as best I could; all my tests indicate it does exactly what we want. If we wait for long-term results, we'll be dead. Every day that passes without taking the Spice is a percentage off, a tiny percentage granted, but still."

Michael smiled. "Good point." He handed the flute to Benet. "After you."

"We're not going to toast together?" Benet asked.

"After you," Michael said.

Benet put the flute on the table, and took one of the tubes out of the rack and prepared to pour it.

"Use the other tube," Michael said.

"You're never going to trust anyone, are you?" Benet asked as she switched tubes.

"There is only one person I trust," Michael said, which surprised Benet who'd worked for Michael for four years now. It the most personal comment he'd ever made.

"Who is that?"

Michael waved off the question.

Benet carefully poured the contents into the flute. The liquid was gold colored and there wasn't much. Barely a thimble. She lifted the flute to her lips and downed it.

Michael stared at her.

"There's no apparent effect," Benet said. "This is a case of having to trust the data."

"And you."

"And me."

Michael took the other flute out of the case. Poured the second tube into it and drank. "No taste."

"It's works on percentages," Benet said. "We've each just added approximately five percent to our lifespan. More Spice of Life doesn't add more time, until the current amount is processed by the body."

Michael put the flute down. "I've read your report. So I will need a constant supply."

"We will," Benet said. "And the cost is prohibitive."

Michael cocked his head, amused. "How so?"

"It takes reaping roughly ninety-nine subjects to make a single dose. Sooner or later, the math isn't going to work."

"Every problem has a solution," Michael said. "Especially one that involves math."

"It was difficult enough procuring the subjects for this batch."

"My head of security is very efficient," Michael said. "He's an expert at procuring and disposing."

"But if word of this ever leaks out," Benet warned.

"Everyone will want it," Michael said.

"Yes. And that's exponentially impossible. And, once it's discovered how it's made—" She left the obvious unsaid.

"Ah, Doctor. You don't think I've prepared for everything? I need you to ramp up production. We're going to need enough stock-piled until my entire plan is completed." He waved a hand. "I'll send you the pertinent requirements."

"What of Daniel?" she asked. "I have another dose. I thought you might invite him here."

Michael smiled. "Daniel is in the conference room. He has a presentation ready for us. A momentous day all around. And it's time to let both of you in on the big picture. The future."

Benet followed as they left her lab, the door locking securely behind her. Two armed guards flanked it. They snapped to attention as Michael walked by.

The conference room wasn't far, also in the secure wing of the tallest building of Michael's 'campus'. A term businesses had begun adopting, as if their corporate headquarters were something other than a place for people to work.

Two more guards were outside the room. Michael and Benet handed over their identification cards and were subjected to retina verification, before Michael could use his black access badge to open the door.

Locks clicked and they went in. Daniel was waiting. He looked much worse than the man who'd been at the briefing with Keenum years ago. He'd lost weight, his face haggard and his eyes bloodshot.

Michael had received reports from security reference Daniel's drinking. His main concern had been that the engineer would make a mistake in the lab; otherwise he accepted the coping mechanism.

Michael took the seat at the head of the conference table. Benet sat to his right. Daniel to his left. He hadn't bothered getting up when they entered, barely looking at them.

"Any time," Michael prompted.

"You mean do it now," Daniel said. "Not any time."

"I was being polite."

"You don't do it well," Daniel said, but he typed into his pad and a holo-gram flickered into view above the table. An image of the interior of Daniel's lab appeared. It was a Level Four Containment Facility. The entire lab was a room within a protective shell, separating it from the rest of the building. It had its own non-recirculating ventilations system. To get in there, Daniel had to completely strip, shower, then get into one-piece positive pressure suit with its own life support system.

Along one wall were doors, each one a self-contained enclosure, not exposed to what was in the rest of the lab. There was a small window in each door. Faces, desperate faces, were pressed up against several of them. One window was smeared with blood.

"This was four days ago," Daniel said.

In a Plexiglas box in the center of the lab was a man. There were wheels under it and air holes in the plexi. The man was staring at Daniel staring at him. There was no defiance; just resignation to his fate. The windows into the cells became opaque.

Daniel explained. "I learned to keep the other subjects from seeing what happens. Causes problems when it's their turn when they have an idea what to expect. Corrupts the data if they hurt themselves before it's their time."

This was Benet's first time seeing the inside of Daniel's lab; indeed, the first time she'd even seen him again since that lecture by Keenum so many years ago.

"That one would kneel for the bullet to the back of the head," Michael said, indicating the man in the box.

A ripple of distaste crossed Daniel's face. "Some fought."

"Of course some fought," Michael acknowledged. "I've seen your reports."

"This subject was infected with programmed phage eight months ago. As per your parameters, he was twenty-four years, four months old at the time. I have run similar tests at all four levels of your parameters. Able to get the spread on the first three to within a year on either side of the median. Those are on file if you wish to review them."

"I've read them," Michael said. "I'm getting Doctor Benet up to speed. "Continue."

"What was that you call it?" Benet asked.

"Phage." Daniel spelled it for her.

"I thought so," Benet said. "Usually it's a tag-on for various viruses such as a macrophage. Or a prefix for phagocytes. From the Greek, phagous. A thing that devours."

"Yes," Daniel said. "One liter of human blood contains about six billion phagocytes. That was one of the problems I had to overcome. I needed something that could replicate quickly. Very quickly, given the parameters that were dictated—"

Michael interrupted. "We all know everything you did was based on what I told you to do. No need to keep making the same point over and over."

Daniel was staring at Michael as he spoke. "I've managed to program the activation window down to twelve hours. I doubt I could make it smaller than that."

"I'm lost here," Benet said. "What does this phage do?"

Daniel shifted his gaze to her, staring through the hologram. "Watch."

The man suddenly jumped to his feet. Began scratching at his skin. Everywhere he could reach. Chest, back, legs, arms. He tore at his body so hard, he drew long rivulets of blood. Then he began convulsing, collapsing the bottom of the box, limbs flailing. There was blood coming out of his eyes, his nose, his mouth. Within thirty seconds, he was still.

"Works fast," Benet noted. "But what is it? You're an engineer not a—" And then she realized. "A nanovirus. A machine."

"Yes," Michael said. "Programmable. Self-replicating. It kills fast, but we can program how long it is dormant in the body. When it will activate, depending on the strain. Daniel used quite a bit of your data, actually, to develop it. While you went in one direction, life, he went in the other."

"But how does it kill?" Benet asked.

Michael answered, when Daniel didn't respond. "It tries to get out of the body, by any means possible, which means the shortest distance, straight out. Tears a person apart from the inside out at the microscopic level." Michael looked at Daniel. "Continue."

Daniel spread his hands. "The rest won't make sense to her if you don't explain the parameters you gave me."

Michael leaned back in his chair. The image of the dead man in the plexi box was frozen in the hologram.

"There are four strains," Michael said. "Whichever one enters first, even it's just a single phage, immediately begins replicating and prevents the other three strains from entering. In essence, becomes dominant and then exclusive to the host."

"The person," Daniel said.

"Since you appear to be done," Michael said, "turn that off."

The hologram disappeared.

Michael folded his hands in his lap. "I thought this all would be relatively simple, but it turned out to be much more complex than I imagined. Initially, I simply wanted to find a way to live longer. I ran it through Dealer. It gave me an possible solution." He nodded at Benet. "That was when I brought you in. However, I didn't realize I had framed the problem too narrowly. I realized there were larger issues. So I went back to Dealer. Broadened the issue. Had it work on solutions. There were several but one optimal one if certain things could be accomplished. First, you Doctor Benet. The original problem: how to live longer. You have solved that with the Spice of Life."

That sparked Daniel out of his apathy. "What is that?"

"A way to replenish telomeres in the human body," Benet said.

"Replenish it?" Daniel asked. "Some of the data I got forwarded from your research—" he fell silent. "How do you do that?"

"We reap telomeres from one person and give it to the other."

"After their dead?" Daniel said.

"The process is fatal," Benet said, "but it must be done with a living host."

"Then what do you need phage for?" Daniel demanded of Michael.

"Ah!" Michael smiled. "The phage is for the larger problem, which Dealer laid out in detail. You both remember Professor Keenum, of course. What's the point of living longer if the planet is dying?"

"So you're going to killed ninety-nine-point-nine percent of the population first," Daniel said.

"Oh no," Michael said. "You're jumping to the wrong conclusion. Think it through, Daniel. Once the phage initiates world-wide, quite a few people will be left alive."

Daniel's eyes widened as he realized the implications. He turned to Benet. "There are four main strains of phage. One activates when the person reached twenty-five, with a subset of one year either way. In essence, there are seven-hundred and thirty phage within this and two of the other subsets. This spreads it out enough to not look overly suspicious that it was programmed."

"And it has to spread randomly," Michael said. "Dealer insisted on that; otherwise people would begin to suspect it was manufactured."

"We're not random," Benet noted.

"I made an exception in your case," Michael said.

"So a person with this first strain," Benet said, "will die either somewhere between twenty-four and twenty-six."

"Yes," Daniel said.

"What are the other strains?" she asked.

"Median of forty-five, then seventy-five," Daniel answered.

"And the last?

Michael answered. "Inert."

Benet nodded. "The prevalence of each?"

Michael gave the numbers. "Strain twenty-five will be ninety-eight-point-seven. Strain forty-five will be point-nine percent. Strain seventy-five will be point-three percent. And—"

Benet could do math. "Inert will be point-one percent of the population. How were these ages and prevalence determined?"

"You're a bit ahead," Michael said. "With just the Spice, we could live longer, but the planet would eventually collapse; no longer be sustainable. We needed a solution to radically reduce consumption."

"Culling the herd," Daniel said.

Michael ignored him. "Once the population is reduced, Dealer knew there had to be a functioning society; a functioning biosystem. There was a need for production. For management of that production. For a buffer between the top point one percent and the management."

"Four strains," Benet said. Then she got it. "And there was the need for *an adequate supply for the Spice. Just under a ninety-nine to one ration. The inert get the Spice."*

Michael smiled. "Yes. Dealer built in some margin. It balanced a functioning society and demand. Dealer calculated the optimum percentages."

Benet considered that for several moments. "But how would you get people to function in such a society?"

"You get them to believe the phage is random, not programmed. And it will be random. Luck of the draw which strain a person gets. Much like buying a lottery ticket. Only a few win, but lots play. They support the winners.

"And even if they don't win, there is the possibility their off-spring might have a different strain. You give them hope."

"Futile hope," Benet said.

"Not exactly," Michael said. "Phage isn't passed on genetically. It will be in the environment. Each newborn will have the same odds of which strain infects them upon birth."

"Not exactly," Daniel interjected. "Once you cluster people, the odds will begin the change over time. If the inerts are all in one place, it is more likely a child born among them will be an inert."

"Let's not call them inerts," Michael said. "Dealer has already come up with the labels. There will be the People, the Evermores, the Middlemores, and then the Youngsters. Dealer calculated the optimum percentages in order to insure enough Youngsters for the Spice production, while at the same time, their Deathday is far enough out to insure reproduction of more generations."

"More victims," Daniel said.

"Upon birth," Michael said, "Dealer can scan a baby and read exactly which strain and subset of phage it has. Thus Dealer can determine their exact Deathday."

"That has to be a secret too," Benet said.

"Oh no." Michael shook his head. "We'll give each one a card, deal a card, with how much time they have left, to each one when they're six."

"Why? That's cruel," Daniel said.

"It will keep everyone in their place and also keep hope alive," Michael said. "A form of lottery held every year. More practically, we have to send

each six year old to the proper place for education and preparation for their life work assignment." A twitch on the side of his face. "As my father used to say: someone has to dig the ditches.

"Dealer has analyzed all the factors. Believe me, far more than any human could. It has laid out what appears to be a very complex society, but one that will work perfectly." Michael said.

"Nothing is perfect," Daniel said.

"The planet, as it is," Benet said, "is doomed. This is a way to save mankind."

"It's a way for you to live longer," Daniel countered.

"I notice you don't include yourself in that," Michael said.

"Do you?" Daniel challenged.

"There is someone actually worse than the person who kneels and takes the bullet without fighting," Michael said.

Daniel pushed his chair back from the conference table. "Who is that?"

"The person who helps the person firing the bullet in the hopes of not getting one themselves," Michael said. "In concentration camps they called them kapos. If you really had had the courage of your convictions, you wouldn't have invented the phage."

Daniel's head drooped and he closed his eyes.

Michael stood up and walked behind him. Grabbed his hair, pulling his head back, and then slit his throat with the knife.

HUNDREDS OF YEARS IN THE FUTURE, AFTER THE CHAOS

"But you didn't answer my question." Ryker holstered the pulser, reached across the autopsy table, grabbed Benet by the lab coat, lifted her, dragged her across the body, smearing her lab coat with blood and body fluid and then set her down in front of him.

She still had the scalpel in hand and her eyes flickered to it.

"Seriously?" Ryker held up his Bowie knife. "Don't bring a scalpel to a knife fight."

Don't bring a knife to a gunfight. He'd heard that somewhere and it was strangely comforting. The knives had been a gift. A special gift. From?

He refocused on the here and now.

Benet dropped the scalpel. "I'm Doctor Benet. I'm working on a cure for the phage."

Ryker let go her coat and flicked the white card on the gold chain around her neck. "Been working on it for a while?"

"Yes."

"How long?"

She licked her lips. "Ever since the Chaos."

"And you still haven't found a cure?"

She spread her hands, indicating the room. "I don't have much help. And it's—"

"Enough," Ryker said. There was a second chain around her neck, tucked inside her coveralls. He pulled on it, a black card coming out to join the white one. "Work for Michael?"

"I work for Dealer."

"Dealer doesn't give out black cards," Ryker said. "Tell me what's happening on the flight deck. What happens to the burners when they go in that black box?"

"They're given a merciful death," Benet said.

"Lie. They're reaped for the Spice of Life," Ryker said.

"A logical deduction."

"It's not a deduction," Ryker said. "I've seen a video of it."

"Really?" Benet's tongue slid over her lips. "Where?"

"I'm asking the questions," Ryker said.

Benet hurried to explain. "It extracts, reaps, whatever you want to call it, the telomeres from the ends of the subject's cells. Since burners are killed by the phage so young, their telomeres are in excellent condition. The cells can survive for a long time, even though the phage kills the host."

"Doesn't the reaping kill them? It did in the past."

"How do you know that?"

"I'm asking the questions," Ryker repeated.

"It's their Deathday by phage anyway," Benet said. "It's a merciful end. No pain. Have you ever seen someone die of phage?"

Ryker tried to remember, back when he was human, when the phage first exploded across the planet. The nautical terms, the saying, the knives. They were helping. He had a cloudy vision of people in the streets, some staggering about in agony. Bodies stacked. "Yes."

"Then you know how painful it is to die from it. We spare burners that."

"I've seen someone die of what you're doing in that box, too," Ryker said. "It was just as bad."

"The process has been refined. There is no pain, I assure you."

"You still kill them."

"We give them dignity in death. Purpose."

"Something they don't have in life."

"It is what it is," Benet said.

"But if someone weren't dying of phage," Ryker said, "then it does kill them."

Benet spread her hands defensively. "I imagine it would. But they *are* going to die of the phage. I knew nothing of this device before the Chaos. My responsibility is the Phage."

"That isn't what you were indicating on the flight deck to that other People."

"I, well—" She had no swift answer.

Ryker remained still, staring at her. He shifted directions. "Is this Second Room? Is there even a Second Room?"

Benet didn't hesitate in this reply. "No. That's a lie. A lie to give hope and keep order in Heaven. Without hope, people become unpredictable. It's a good lie. Allows burners to enjoy Heaven."

"But it's still a lie."

Benet didn't say anything.

"Who do you really work for?" Ryker asked, indicating the two cards.

"Dealer."

"Dealer or Michael?" And Ryker saw the flicker in her eyes.

"We all follow Code," Benet evaded.

"Dealer or Michael?"

Benet sighed. "For so long they were the same. But now? I'm doing as I've always been doing. My job. My obsession, you might say." She waved her hand about, indicating the mess hall turned into lab. "If I can find a way to destroy the phage, I can end all of this. Make our world whole again."

"But you've been at it over three hundred years and haven't succeeded," Ryker said.

It wasn't a question, but she responded anyway. "I'm alone. Dealer restricted much of the old data. And frankly, Dealer doesn't want this research to be done. It ordered it shut down, and that's when Michael started hiding things from Dealer. So, yes, to answer your question, I work for Michael. He cares about people. He wants a cure. Dealer wants the status quo."

"Michael doesn't care about anyone else except Michael," Ryker said. "You do a good job mixing the truth with lies; almost enough to get someone to believe everything you say is truth. Do you have a list of burners currently in Heaven?"

"Yes."

"I need to see it. I need to find someone."

Benet went over to a console, tapped some commands on the surface. A Stream was projected above it. "Who?"

"Haydn."

"Do you have the designator? A name isn't sufficient for the computer."

"Of course not," Ryker said. "That would make them human. Haydn one-tango-one-nine."

The projection flickers and she tapped into the surface of the console. "Ah! He was here."

Ryker lifted the Bowie knife. "Did you—"

"No, no," Benet quickly said. "His Deathday is still a ways off. No. He was taken from here by Dealers. He'd violated Code. Killed another burner. They took him and a second burner, Victoria-alpha-seven-six-bravo."

"Where to?"

"Island."

"For what? Is he alive?"

"I don't have access to that information," Benet said. "I'm blocked from tapping into Dealer. Because if I do so, then Dealer will tap into my Stream. Learn what I'm doing here."

"What about Michael's Stream?"

"I can access that. But—"

Ryker cocked his head. The tingling of Michael's aura was so faint. "He's not in Stream, is he?"

"He's in Deep Void." The Stream disappeared.

Ryker had to trust the cyborgs could hold out long enough.

"Do you have access to Centre?" Ryker asked.

Once more her eyes shifted ever so slightly. "This is my home. My work."

"You're lying again," Ryker said. "You're going to get me into Centre."

"Why? There's nothing there."

"It's where Dealer was."

"It's not there now," Benet said. "No one knows where it is."

"It doesn't matter," Ryker said. "I need to see if Centre is as I remember."

"You 'remember'?" She finally became aware. "You're Ryker. Michael's brother."

"So you did know Michael. As a human."

"Yes," Benet said. "Worked for one of his subsidiaries. I had the luck of being a People when the phage struck."

"Amazing luck," Ryker said. "But we both know it wasn't luck."

"It is what it is. Instead of fighting, I took up my work here."

"You're still lying," Ryker said. "Take me to Centre."

"Centre has been abandoned for a long time," Benet said. "I don't understand—"

Ryker put the point of the Bowie knife at her neck. He nodded down at the body. "There's fresh blood. I don't think he was dead when you started cutting on him."

"He was dead!" Benet protested and for the first time there was some fear in her eyes. "He'd just died. From the phage, not TED. He was in line, collapsed, starting the symptoms. We had just got him in here when he passed. I have to work with what I have."

Ryker pointed toward the hatch at the other end of the room from where he'd entered. "Take me to Centre. If you try to betray me on the way, I will make death by phage seem peaceful for you."

"Why did you fight your brother?" Benet asked.

"I knew who he was. And is. Nothing good can come out of Michael, and thus Dealer. Evil begets evil."

"HERE IT IS," Ruth said, pausing momentarily on the edge of the clearing.

"Grace told me of this place," Millay said. "It's beautiful."

Millay had recovered somewhat traveling north to the cabin. Her shoulder was throbbing, the pain almost unbearable, but she was a very different woman from two months ago, when she'd left the comfort of Island to switch places with her sister in hive. She could barely remember what that life had been like as a People; all she knew was that it was a cocoon of unreality.

"It was our home for many years," Ruth said, leading her to the door and throwing it open.

Millay paused on the threshold, taking it in. "I've never seen so many books. There's a physical library on Island that has some books, but they're in a vault to protect them from—"

Ruth made a noise, perhaps a snort of derision? "Dealer is hiding the books from you. Books, print books, are all B.D.. They tell of a very different world. Dealer has rewritten history. That's why Dealer uses the Stream for all media. It controls the Stream." Ruth reached out and tapped the spine of a book. "But this, once it's printed, is there forever."

But Millay was distracted, looking out the window to the back, where the garden was. "Grace told me about burying your—"

"Wife."

"Burying your wife. I am sorry."

"She sacrificed herself for the greater good," Ruth said. "I had already sacrificed so much."

"What do you mean?"

"Please sit," Ruth said.

Millay went over to the old rocking chair, and carefully sat down, relieved to be off her feet, careful not to hit her shoulder.

"Our country," Ruth said, "the country Sound was just a small part of what was almost constantly at war in the early twenty-first century. Mostly fighting what we called terrorism. All of this B.D.. During one of those wars, I was flying a mission when my aircraft was hit by an—" she paused, realizing some words would mean nothing to Millay—"by a weapon. I crashed. Was very badly injured. I was brought back to a field hospital and they pretty much wrote me off, but one of the doctors there knew of a classified program that was looking for people in exactly my condition. They induced my brain into a coma, practically froze my body. Airlifted me to a special facility. Run a group called the B.T.O.: Biological Technology Office. They'd been working for many years on artificial limbs. So many soldiers had become amputees in the wars, it was a priority. But, of course, as things always go, they were going further than that. Seeing if they could save soldiers who were mortally wounded.

"At least that was the line they used to justify it. And I believe most of them working there actually *were* doing that. But there was another aspect to it." She held up the arm with the pulser on it. "They also wanted better soldiers. Faster, stronger, directly integrated with an on-board computer which didn't require an outside transmission for access." She pointed at her human eye. "They hadn't quite perfected this. I was retrofitted with the latest model later on, better than a human eyes, but I insisted on keeping the one.

"When I regained consciousness, well, we didn't pass for human back then with the early models; in fact, we looked more like Dealers. And we were kept in a secure facility. Gradually being upgraded. Appearing more and more human." She put her hands on the mantle. "Hanan assumed I was dead. She was even given official notice of that; they gave her my wedding band, some other things. Survivor benefits. They even gave her an urn with my ashes in it. And my ashes *were* in it. Most of me. She later told me she spread them in the garden out back, where she's buried now. So in a way, we're together forever." Ruth fell silent, as if considering this for the first time.

"But you weren't dead," Millay said.

"No. Not my brain. Which is where, we must suppose, our soul is too. Because when I was reborn, I was me, even though my body wasn't. It's hard to describe. It took me a long time to master the interface to my new body. But then the phage happened. In the confusion as the Chaos began, I broke out of the facility. Went to Hanan.

"She was shocked. But over-joyed to have me back in any form, even though the world was falling apart. Hanan didn't want to be People, but it wasn't something she had a choice in. Once the phage struck, pretty much everyone was damned, but the few, like Hanan, became what were called the Blessed. At first, there were only two groups: burners, and a handful who lived past burner. Back then we didn't grasp there were Evermores and Middlemores. There wasn't enough time elapsed for that to become apparent. We assumed there were Youngsters and Blessed."

"Youngsters?" Millay asked.

"burners. They weren't called that until years later. During the Chaos, the humans around us didn't care I was a cyborg or where I came from. They just cared I was a pilot and was willing to fight. Hanan was with me, at my side, fighting for what remained of our country early in the Chaos. We were battling other countries, rogue nations, terrorist groups. It's hard to explain how insane it was then. Nuclear weapons were detonating. Militaries were mobilized but almost all the leadership was gone, so they splintered quickly without adequate command and control. Here in the Sound, we had to focus on protecting the immediate area, what we had.

"Then the IMP happened. Wiped out all computers. Almost all. And we relied on computers for so much. IMP destroyed almost all local command and control. Destroyed our electronic infrastructure. Destroyed what was left of an already dying economy. Everyone was down to just fighting to survive.

"Dealer began coordinating things here in the Sound. Restoring a degree of order. Making sense out of the Chaos and we seized on it."

Ruth walked over to the fireplace, looking at the cold ashes. "We didn't even really know what Dealer was. All we knew was that these cards on chains were getting passed out; and one thing all of us liked was that the card wasn't an implant. Those had been tried and the IMP fried the brains of those who had them, including cyborgs who'd been fitted with a network.

"The cards were all black then, with no numbers on them. Nothing. Dealing Day didn't come about until after the end of the Chaos and Dealer had sorted out the effects of the phage and began to start figuring out lifespans because of the phage. The cards gave us access to the Stream. Access to Dealer's advice. At least we thought it was advice, but in reality they were orders. But they made sense. We re-organized. Those of us left. But the phage was still killing. We called it the Reckoning, when someone was within a year, plus or minus, of twenty-five. If you made it to twenty-six, then you were good to go. At least initially. It took a while before we realize forty-five and seventy-five were Reckonings too."

Ruth reached to the mantel above the fireplace. A frame was face-down. Ruth stood it up. Two young women, the ones Grace had showed Millay in the passports just before the battle at Port Townsend, were smiling at the camera, the cabin behind them. "Hanan was older than me. I was twenty-three. She was twenty-eight. When she didn't succumb to the phage as it killed down in age and those from her year group were dying, we knew she was one of the Blessed. I was so happy for her. We had no idea if the phage would affect my brain. If it would kill me. My Reckoning, what you call Deathday now, would not happen for a while, if it happened. And we were so busy fighting for the Sound. For Dealer. Death for all of us in combat was as likely as death by phage.

"I was Hanan's co-pilot. And then—" she paused.

"And then what?" Millay asked.

"Near the end of the Chaos, we met Ryker. At Michael's order, we picked him up from a remote cabin in what are now called the Wasted Mountains. We had no idea why he was so special, until we brought him to Centre where Michael was waiting. They greeted each other and we realized they were brothers.

"The next time we saw him, another man was dragging him to our chopper. Told us to take off. Threatened us. Ordered us to fly away. Made us land once we were clear. And then Ryker told us he'd learned the truth."

"What truth?"

"That Dealer didn't serve mankind's best interests. That it served Michael and he was dangerous. Hanan and I believed him."

"Why? Weren't you fighting for Dealer?"

"He showed us something, while we sat there, blades turning. He had a video of humans being reaped by Michael's machine *before* the Chaos. It was terrible. He told us about the Spice of Life and that Michael and a handful of others had it. What it took to make it. How many people had to die so one person could live another year."

"But I thought the phage—" Millay shook her head. "I don't understand genetics."

"It's not genetics. Ryker said that Michael had invented the phage. It's inert in People. It just left them with a normal lifespan. The Spice is what allows them to live longer."

"But that means—"

"It's given to People about every year once they each maturity. You've been given it. When you went to hospital for your check-up."

"But no one knows this on Island," Millay said. "We all believe it's genetic. And that the phage affected everyone differently."

"The phage doesn't affect you, and the rest of that tiny percentage, less than point-one-percent. Dealer knows it. Michael knows it. It's essential to them that no one else knows it. This was Michael's secret from the beginning. And when Ryker found out about reaping and phage, he turned against his brother."

Millay reached with her hand, unconsciously going to rub her missing arm. Her fingers groped air and she realized what she was doing.

"Hanan and I had to make a decision. I flew us to Masada, the facility where I'd been reborn as a cyborg, where the B.T.O. was. Most of the other cyborgs were still there hoping they could ride the Chaos out in the secure facility. In the Chaos, the few on the outside who knew of the place had succumbed to the phage and we were essentially forgotten. The human scientists were mostly dead or would be dead.

"But some of the first cyborgs had been working with the human scientists. Learning cyborg technology. They worked on Ryker, stabilizing his brain. Hanan and I showed the video to the other cyborgs. We went to war against Dealer until we were forced into the Truce.

Rather we forced Dealer into making the Truce." She turned from the fireplace. "And now you and I are here."

"I still don't understand," Millay said. "How did Hanan end up here on Island?"

"That was hard. Once the Truce was brokered, we knew we needed someone on the other side. Someone to spy for us. And Hanan was Blessed. The only one with us in Masada. She volunteered to go to Island. To live there. To report to us. To prepare for the Prime and the Backdoor, as Ryker promised would occur."

"Wait a second," Millay said. "How come you and the other cyborgs weren't affected by the Phage?"

"It doesn't cross the blood-brain barrier," Ruth said. Seeing the confused look, she amplified: "Phage doesn't get into the brain. Just the body. Enough stories. I have to get you off Island. Get you to Grace."

"How?"

Ruth sighed, a strange, almost human sound. But not quite. "We could—"

She paused as her white card flickered and then a Stream appeared.

"Dealer is damming the Stream," Ruth said. "That's not good."

There was no image at first; just a white square. Dealer's face was flat, the same whether announcing a boxing or any other news. "Millay, once of the People, has been judged in violation of the Code of Life." The white square changed to show an image of Millay. "If spotted, she is to be reported immediately. She is dangerous. She is with a cyborg, an enemy of all. By order of Dealer, all of Sound is under Dealer-Law, until all is normalized. Wave traffic to and from Island is terminated until further notice. Lone Bridge is—" the image changed from Millay to where the bridge had once been. The center span had been destroyed— "gone. This is a precaution against possible infiltration by others who wish us harm. Report any sighting of Millay, once of the People."

Millay's image appeared once more, then flickered out.

"Well, that way is out," Ruth said. "I wonder how they knew I used it. And Ryker."

"Strange," Millay said.

"What's strange?" Ruth asked.

"Dealer just told everyone in Sound that cyborgs still exist."

"And?"

"Everyone in Sound believes cyborgs don't exist. That you were wiped out at the end of Chaos by Dealer, when it was protecting Sound against you."

"Is that what's taught in the womb of the People?" Ruth asked.

Millay had to think about that. "No. Very little is taught of the Chaos. It's just one of those things that's accepted. I'm not sure where I first heard it."

"Dealer was protecting itself fighting us," Ruth said. "We were on the side of humans. All humans."

"I understand that now, but that's not the strange thing about Dealer's announcement." Millay smiled. "Announcing that cyborgs exist was a mistake. Dealer isn't supposed to make mistakes."

"And? Given the split with Michael, Dealer is most likely having problems with its operating system."

"If Dealer is making mistakes," Millay said, "then we can defeat it. That's a real hope."

"Not if we don't unite you with your sister," Ruth said. "Dealer will eventually catch us here on Island." She nodded at the root cellar. "I can't hide you the way my wife hid Grace. They're hunting me too." Ruth was walking back and forth in the small cabin, trying to figure out a way off Island, now that Lone Bridge wasn't option. Millay was looking out the back window. At the garden and Hanan Marash's grave.

"I've got a black card," she said. "It's got to have some sort of power. I can't use Hanan's white card any more."

"The black card will let Michael know exactly where we are," Millay said. Then she suddenly leaned forward in the rocking chair. "I think we have a problem."

"What?" Ruth asked.

Millay stood. "They did something to me while I was in the boxing room. After they took my arm." She unzipped her coverall with some difficulty. Showed Ruth a thin red scar on her side. "Do you know what that is?"

Ruth reached out and ran her fingers over it. "I've seen it before. You've had a tracking device implanted. Recently."

Millay turned for the door. "We've got to get out of here."

Ruth reached out and grabbed Millay's shoulder, her good one. "Slow down. When did it happen? Before or after your arm was cut off?"

"After. That weasel Claude and a nurse came in. Gave me something that knocked me out. When I came to, I could feel it, but compared to my shoulder, it was nothing and I forgot about it. Until now."

"All right," Ruth said. "That's good."

"'Good'?"

"It means Claude had it put in, not Dealer. He's the type who holds his cards close. He let you go, but he wanted to keep tabs on you. Just in case he was backing the wrong side. Which is the side that will benefit him the least."

"But it sounds like Dealer is still in charge."

Ruth nodded. "With Michael in Deep Void, Dealer is completely in charge. That's not good for Claude. He'll eventually give you up to Dealer if Michael doesn't come back. Or if Michael comes back with Grace, Claude will give you up to Michael. Either way, he wins and you lose. And if Michael doesn't get Grace and you escape, and the Prime is united, then he still can find you and join our side, taking credit for helping you escape."

"Doesn't he believe in anything?" Millay asked.

"Himself." Ruth pressed her fingers against the scar and Millay flinched. "I can feel it." She looked Millay in the eyes. "Can you take a little more pain?"

"Of course."

JOE THREW the hatch open and poked his head out to survey the surrounding forest, half-expecting to be pulsed into oblivion, since there was no doubt that Michael had surrounded the mountain with Soldiers. The hatch was built on a hillside, the outside camouflaged with netting.

The woodland was quiet, the infamous too quiet. Joe edged out of the escape tunnel, pulser at the ready. The rest of his recon party exited and deployed tactically, covering all directions.

Joe crooked a finger and one of the cyborgs came over. "Let Isabel know—"

The other cyborg was hit by two simultaneous pulses that cut him in half.

The others barely had a chance to return fire before they too were pulsed down, leaving Joe standing alone, his pulser ready. But he didn't fire, accepting the inevitable as two-dozen Soldiers came forward, weapons at the ready.

Joe flipped his pulser back in to his forearm as a figure came from behind the front line of Soldiers.

"Michael."

"How do you know me?" Michael asked. He looked down at the cyborg who had been next to Joe, and cut in half. Her brain was still alive, her eyes wide open. Her system was inoperable. Michael pulsed her head, splattering Joe with brain and blood.

"The gold band," Joe managed to say.

"You're in my database," Michael said. "From imagery of the attack on Centre at the end of the Chaos. You were part of that."

"I was. The Forlorn Hope."

"Quite appropriate," Michael said. "A band of warriors who take the lead in an attack on a defended position where the risk of casualties is high. In ancient times, a group that was the first through a breach in the wall of a castle, for example. Yes. Your Forlorn Hope almost got to Dealer in Centre. Didn't quite make it, but tipped Dealer's data enough that you achieved the Truce. You're lucky Dealer was so rational and so unaware of human nature that it believed your threats and accepted the Truce and allowed you and the others to get away."

"We all didn't get away."

"No. Did you lose someone you cared about?"

Joe started to lift his arm.

"Be careful," Michael said. "My Soldiers will obliterate you the second you start to unfold. It was smart of you to submit." And then he reached down, grabbed Joe's pulser, pulled it up and wrenched it off.

Michael stepped past Joe and looked at the open hatch. "The rest are in there. We will be through the inside hatch shortly. We'll have your people, rather I should say cyborgs, trapped on both ends. But this doesn't have to end badly, just like your Forlorn Hope didn't. We can make our own Truce." Michael turned back to Joe, reached up, and grabbed his neck with one hand, the back of the head with the other, lifting him off the ground. "Give me Grace and I'll spare you and the rest of your abominations."

"I can't make that decision," Joe said, able to speak despite Michael's grip.

"Who can?"

"Isabel is in command."

"I want you to go back in your hole and tell Isabel that if she gives up Grace, I'll let the rest of you survive." He let go of Joe's head and shoved him toward the opening. "Go. I'll be waiting."

Joe climbed into the tunnel and disappeared.

Michael watched him go. Then looked about, at the Soldiers deployed around him. Machines with no thoughts of their own. No one he could confide in, ask counsel of. He'd had Dealer but he was out of the Stream and now he didn't trust Dealer. It was doing as programmed, putting survival first.

It's own survival.

A flaw Michael now realized. He'd always thought his own and Dealer's survival were implicitly linked. But now?

And where was Ryker? He was the wild card.

Too many loose ends.

Haydn was an after-thought, dragged along by a Dealer as they exited the tunnels under Capitol. Two other Dealers were carrying Claude, claws clamped around his upper arms, his feet trying to find the ground but a few inches short of it, ignoring his squeals of pain. A single Dark Angel was with them.

The Dealers set Claude down once they were on the surface.

"Where?" the Dark Angel demanded.

Claude rubbed his arms. Turned. "That way." He pointed north. "Not too far. Based on the strength of the signal, she's still on Island."

A Lift came in, settling down, the engines blowing dust about. The side door slid open. Two Dealers grabbed Claude, carried him over, and threw him on board. Haydn allowed his Dealer to pull him to the craft and in.

The door slid shut and the Lift rose up into the air. Claude was in the cockpit with the Dark Angel. Haydn had a Dealer on either side of him in the back and one blocking the way to the cockpit.

Claude was saying something, pointing to the left and down.

Haydn charged for the cockpit, made it one step, and then came to an abrupt halt as a Dealer seized his shoulder.

Claude glanced over his shoulder at Haydn's gasp, shook his head, and then focused forward.

The Lift landed with a gentle thump.

The side door slid open. The Dark Angel had a grip on Claude's arm, and from the look on the Evermore's face, it hurt. And there was something else there; panic.

Claude was trying to say something, words tumbling inco-herently.

Haydn was pulled along, out of the Lift. They were behind a cabin, the Lift's skids crushing a garden. Haydn panicked seeing a woman lying on the ground in front of them. The woman was on her back, arms folded on her chest. She was lying on top of a rectangle of dirt that outlined her.

The Dark Angel shoved Claude down to his knees next to the

woman. Haydn struggled to get a better look, but the Dealer had him locked in place.

The Dark Angel leaned over and picked something out of the woman's hands. A small sliver of metal; a tracking transmitter.

"It's not my fault!" Claude cried. "Not my fault!"

A Dealer strode forward and lifted up the body's head and Haydn sagged in relief as he realized it wasn't Millay. But she did look familiar. And then he realized it was Ruth; a repaired Ruth, but enough was the same.

A Dealer slammed the point of a probe into the left side of Ruth's head.

It remained still for a few seconds, then the probe retracted and Ruth's head thumped back into the ground.

The Dark Angel still had its hand on the top of Claude's head.

"The cyborg's cache memory has been wiped clean," the Dark Angel said to Claude. "The cyborg self-terminated. Why would it do that?"

"I don't know!" Claude said.

"Her machine memory was cleared," Haydn said, "but her human memory wasn't. She sacrificed herself so she wouldn't tell you what she knew. If she were just an 'it', she wouldn't have done it. But she was a human. And that's what humans do."

The Dark Angel spoke, whether to Claude or to Haydn, or both, wasn't clear. "We do not know how long ago the transmitter was removed from Millay, once of the People. But she cannot have gotten very far. There is no way off Island. This futile action only delays her inevitable capture."

The Dark Angel removed its hand from Claude's head. The Evermore got to his feet. Two Dealers strode up to him, one on either side and gripped his upper arms.

The Dark Angel announced: "We regret to inform you, Claude-six-four-lima-eight, that you have been found in violation of the Code of Life."

"I did what I was ordered to do!" Claude protested. "How did I violate Code?"

"You conspired with an enemy of Dealer," the Dark Angel said. "For violation of Code, Claude-six-four-lima-eight will be boxed."

Claude was bewildered. "What enemy of Dealer?"

"Millay, you idiot," Haydn said, getting a small degree of satisfaction from this. "You helped her escape."

"Correction," the Dark Angel said. "It is not Millay, once of the People, for whom he is to be boxed. The enemy of Dealer is Michael, once of Dealer. That is whom you conspired with."

EVERY BURNER HAD WATCHED the Stream of the dead in the revolting 'tein' hive.

The response was not what Dealer had calculated.

Hundreds folded immediately, heading out from hive toward the Wasteland, to the Folding Path. Many were parents with their young children, something unprecedented. That still left tens-of-thousands in the various hives, but they were abuzz with exactly what Millay had noted: there were cyborgs out there, somewhere. And one was in Sound. And Dealer didn't know where it was.

Which meant Dealer had lied, although no one could really say where or when they'd learned that Dealer had defeated the cyborgs at the end of the Chaos. It had just been one of those things accepted and understood.

And if an ancient enemy could roam free inside the borders of Sound it implied that Dealer was fallible.

burners might not live long, but they adapt quickly. They had to since everything happened swiftly in their short life spans. An all out revolt would result in what Dealer had shown and promised. But a number of burners, either individually or in small groups, came to roughly the same conclusion in various hives.

Lone Dealers, standing sentinel, became targets. Here a crane turned too fast, the heavy cable decapitating a Dealer. There a swarm of five burners with 'tein scrapers rushed a Dealer from behind, taking it down. At another hive, a dozen burners fired tracers all the same time at a Dealer, the combined charges frying its circuits.

These acts were done without coordination; without any of those involved even knowing that others were doing similar things.

But Dealer was aware of Dealers snapping out of existence in the Stream.

Dealer ran through its massive database, focusing on an archaic form of warfare: counter-insurgency.

The results were not encouraging. The victories against such a movement were rare, but that humans fighting humans. Dealer had the advantage there, until it drilled down through the data and discovered the key was something called: *winning the hearts and minds of the people.*

The latter Dealer could compute.

The former was a problem.

HUNDREDS OF YEARS IN THE FUTURE, AFTER THE CHAOS

Millay was running, stopping every so often to check the ancient compass Ruth had given her. Going west, as best the terrain would allow. She was trying to follow narrow animal trails that wove through the forest. It had been hard to run at first, her balance off by the loss of her left arm, but she was adjusting.

Lifts thrummed by overhead every so often, but the forest was so thick, she couldn't see them and vice versa. She wondered how long Ruth would last, fighting against whoever it was that would show up at her cabin. In her one hand she had an axe that Ruth had given her from the wood pile. On a finger was a gold band; Ruth's parting gift.

Other than the compass, the axe, the ring, and the advice to go west, Ruth had been somewhat vague about what then. She'd advised searching for ruins near the shoreline and digging in them, hoping to find a small plastic boat she called a kayak.

When Millay had expressed doubt about whether something B.D. would last this long, Ruth had assured that if it had been kept out of the elements, and out of the sun, then there was a chance it would still be useful. If that failed, there was always the axe, trees, and building a raft to go from Island to Void. How to do all that with just one arm was another issue that Millay didn't want to dwell on. She was almost used to the phantom and real pain from her shoulder.

And, of course, further ahead, there was the problem of going from Void to Deep Void. But one crossing at a time, Millay reminded herself.

Once she in Deep Void, Ruth had told Millay how to get to a place she called Masada. Approximately. She said if Millay got close enough the cyborgs would find her. It was a long journey through Deep Void, further to the west than the one she'd undertaken to Port Townsend.

Not much of a plan, but better than no plan at all.

Better than Ruth's plan of making a last stand after luring the Dealers in with the transmitter. The cyborg had promised to try to escape after taking out as many of them as possible, and then having them chase her north to Lone Bridge. Millay had sensed the finality when Ruth gave her the ring.

"Grace has the other one," Ruth had said.

And that had been it. No more words; things were past that.

Millay had a pretty good idea of what Island looked like, but scale was a different matter. Over ninety-five percent of People were clustered in or just around Capitol, on the center, eastern coast, facing City.

The smallness of the lives of the People no longer shocked Millay as it had just several weeks ago. The smallness of her own life.

She halted, went to one knee, put the axe down and pulled out the compass. She flipped open the lid and waited for the needle to stabilize. On course. She shut the lid, stuck it back in her pocket, grabbed the axe and began running.

She burst out of the trees onto a pebbled beach. Water. And across the way, a dark line of forest: Void.

As Ruth had instructed, she went back into the trees, moving parallel to the shore, searching. When she came upon ruins, she looked for plastic sheets, long covered with leaves.

Twice she found ones with something underneath, but whatever it was had been wood and had rotted away.

And then she found one, just as Ruth had said. Wrapped in plastic. With some difficulty, Millay removed the covering. The kayak seemed intact. A paddle was clipped to the side. Millay dragged it out of the treeline, across the beach, to the water. Walked out with it, testing its integrity.

It floated.

She pushed it back close to the shore, then attempted to climb in. She flipped it, falling backward into the water. She righted it, pulled it ashore. Flipped it to drain the water out. Pushed it back in the water. Took more care, more time, and managed to get inside.

Then she faced the issue of paddling with one arm. She bobbed in the slight swell as she experimented.

Finally she accepted there was no option other than to hold the paddle upright, dip it in as far forward as could on one side, pull back. Then lift it clear of the water, twist her body and do the same on her missing side as best she could.

It was awkward. It was painful. It required a lot of course correction. But she began moving from Island to Void, ever so slowly.

As the Lift descended, it was clear, even after all these years that a terrible battle had been waged inside the casements of Centre, once known as Fort Casey. Not a battle between humans, since their flesh and bones would have long since turned to dust. The large, open space was littered with the remains of machines. As they landed, Ryker could see the broken metal frames of Dealers, Soldiers and Cyborgs poking through the brush and grass.

Getting to Centre was surprisingly easy with Benet's assistance, further proof it had been abandoned long ago. She simply commandeered a Lift on the *Kennedy*, tapped in the location, and less than a minute later, they were there, the Lift settling down inside the old fort's casements.

"I got you here," Benet said. "Can I leave?"

Ryker reached out and cut power. The engines whined down to silence.

Benet sighed. "What do you hope to find here?"

"Truth," Ryker said.

"I told you. Dealer left here a long time ago."

Ryker pointed toward the concrete wall surrounding the fort on the seaward side. Benet reluctantly hopped off the Lift.

"Next to me," Ryker said.

Together they walked toward a large opening in the wall. "This was expanded," he said. "It leads to the magazine for the fort. But the opening wasn't big enough."

"Big enough for what?" Benet asked.

Ryker glanced at her. "Dealer. When Michael was looking for a place to build it, he wanted some place safe and secure. This used to be a park. Michael got it from the state. He could get anything he wanted back then. If money didn't work, he found another way. Correct?"

"What do you mean?"

Ryker halted. "I doubt he used money on you. I think he used opportunity. He offered you something no one else could. I'm going to find out what that was. Along with other things."

Benet looked back toward the Lift. "I told you—"

"Yes," Ryker said. "Dealer is gone from here. I heard you the first two times. Come on."

A dark, open space was ahead of them.

"That was the freight elevator," Ryker said.

"There's no power and—"

"Shut up." Ryker pushed her to the right. "The elevator was designed to be shut down. Emergency stairs." He shoved open a metal door, rust protesting. "Hold my hand. I assume you can't see in the dark." He grabbed Benet's hand and pulled her into the darkness. She stumbled on the first step down and Ryker solved that problem by lifting her up, and throwing her over his shoulder.

He ran down the stairs until he reached the bottom. Another steel door blocked the way. He put Benet down. For her it was pitch black.

Ryker's night vision enabled him to make out enough detail to find a panel to the left of the door. He slid it up. Tapped on a keypad. A red light appeared above the door, then it turned green.

"How can that be?" Benet asked. "This has been…" she fell into silence as Ryker pulled open the door. He pushed her through, then followed. The door swung shut behind them with a solid thud. Ryker reached out and tapped a switch on the wall to his left.

Lights flickered on, revealing a large circular room. The walls, floors, and ceilings were pitted concrete. Further to the left, an opening had been cut for the freight elevator.

The control console was still there. But the twenty-four containers were gone.

"How is power still working in here?"

"Core Nuclear Spheres. CNS. Michael invented it; rather it was invented for him, like most other developments and advancements he claimed. Before the Chaos. He kept it to himself. Each sphere has a life of a millennium. That hasn't been proven yet of course. And once a Sphere is activated inside it's protective shielding, it can't be moved, so they were left behind when the Perdix containers with the Spin-Q drives were moved." Ryker headed for the control console.

"Spin-Q?" Despite her predicament, the scientist in Benet was intrigued.

"Something else Michael stole. A Spin-Q was the most advanced quantum computer B.D.. Each of the containers that were in here, called Perdix, contained one Spin-Q. We learned that by linking an optimum number together, we could produce something more powerful than a single large one. Also, they use a lot less power than traditional computers."

"'We'?"

Ryker sighed. "I had a small team that helped Michael put Dealer together, well before the Chaos. Years before. He kept it secret; he kept lots of things secret back then. To give him an advantage. It was common in business… well, you should know. To keep scientific advances proprietary."

They went up three steps. Two dozen displays. Several chairs with keyboards on movable arms faced them.

"Archaic," Benet said. "If all the drives are gone, why are we here?"

"Since I designed it, I did some modifications off-spec. That no one else knows about. I knew better than to give Michael access to such power without any checks or balances. More importantly, given the capability we put into Dealer, there was a chance it might become sentient. We were moving forward into the unknown when we turned it on."

"And if it became sentient?" Benet asked.

Ryker sat down in the center chair, swinging the keyboard in front of him. "It might decide humans were irrelevant."

"But Dealer *is* sentient, isn't it?"

"Once Michael uploaded into it? Yes. Before then. I hope not."

He began typing. The screen right in front of him went from black to gray to dim white.

"What modifications did you make?" Benet asked.

"I put a Backdoor in Dealer's program, encrypted it with a Prime. It's still there. I made sure that both Dealer and Michael would be unaware of both."

"How?"

"That's what I'm trying to find out right now. It's part of the memory I had blocked by the cyborgs."

"But how can that be working if they removed all the drives?"

"Dealer is twenty-four Spin-Q's. Those are gone. We calculated that was the perfect number. Enough to do what Michael wanted, but not too many to cause dissonance. But I had twenty-five installed here. Perdix," Ryker said, "was the nephew of Daedalus. In mythology, the inventor of useful tools." He gave a bitter laugh. "Michael took everything from everyone. Including their lives." He glanced over at her. "I installed the 25th myself well before Dealer's Spin-Qs were even brought in."

"Why?"

"Because Michael and I played a lot of chess. And the biggest advantage you can have in chess between two evenly matched opponents is to have the white pieces. To make the first move." He pointed down. "I put the 25th in the container for the CNS power supply just before it was sealed. No one knew it was there and once the spheres were powered up, no one would ever, could ever, go in there again. It's still down there. Still functional." Ryker went back to typing. "Do you remember the Internet?"

"Yes."

"Remember how they warned that nothing that goes on it ever disappears?"

"Yes."

Text appeared on the display. Ryker began scrolling fast, then faster. Too fast for Benet to follow. But Ryker was taking it all in.

Ryker abruptly halted the scrolling.

He was aware of Benet. She'd tried the hatch as he focused on the data. Been unable to open it. Realized she was trapped. He could sense that she was now creeping up behind him, a fire axe in her hands.

"Don't," he said. But she wasn't why he'd paused.

Pieces and parts from B.D. he'd forgotten.

A piece of technology he'd invented just after college.

Ryker typed in a command.

A THIRD OF the way across, Millay paused. Her hand was tingling. She lay the paddle down across the kayak in front of her and held her hand up. The ring, gold, unadorned, was on her middle finger, the only one where it would stay without being too large. There were calluses in the skin of her palm that hadn't been there two months ago; gained by thirty days of scraping 'tein vats in hive. Something her sister had done all her life since she came of age.

The ring was warm around her finger. And it was vibrating.

Millay brought her hand to her lips, pressing the ring against them and was startled by a slight shock.

She held the hand out, staring at the ring. And then she smiled.

"I'm coming, Grace."

GRACE HAD DECIDED when she landed she would have to kill Achilles. It wasn't really an issue. He'd betrayed those who'd trusted him, sent hundreds of burners off to be bagged and extinguished, and worked for Michael. Any one of those three deserved death.

Charon? She needed him. Sort of. She could row herself, but it was a long way via water from the west side to the east around the peninsula that was Void and then across to Island.

It just wasn't time yet.

How she knew this, she didn't know. Which she found ironic. As a burner everything had to be done now: work, drinking, sexing, tracering. Now. There was no more time.

But Grace was past her Deathday and starting to understand time.

It was valuable.

But not in the way she'd believed it to be.

She was sitting in the crane's control booth, next to the half-Dealer. She had Achilles black card and had put it in the slot on the machine. He was in the dry dock, probably pacing back and forth as he had been ever since she'd put him down there with Charon. Then sealed the exits.

A boy had appeared at the distant end of the pier earlier, a string of rabbits over his shoulder, saw her, looked down into the dry dock at Achilles and Charon, and simply turned and run away. The way a burner who wanted to survive would. Grace had let him go without even calling out.

Ace was lying below her, staring out at the dark water.

The Dealer crackled, a low hum of static and then a voice: Michael.

"Achilles. What is the status of Millay? Claude?"

Grace stared at the machine, pondering the questions and the implications.

"Achilles?"

Grace could swear she caught a hint of frustration in Michael's voice.

"Achilles?" The static went on for several seconds. "I am cutting off voice and relaying through to Claude."

The Dealer buzzed and Grace reached over and jerked the black card out of it. She remained still for a little while, fearing she might have tipped her hand by pulling the card. Then she felt something change. In her hand. At first she thought it *was* the card.

It wasn't it.

The ring, Hanan's ring, was warm, unnaturally warm. Vibrated ever so slightly for a couple of seconds. Then went still.

And she knew. Grace was coming to her.

ISABEL HAD her back against the tunnel wall. Counting the losses, hearing the firing of pulsers echoing from where the Soldiers were slowly advancing. The door had finally given way and the defense had begun. Two Soldiers went down for every cyborg, but the math was bad.

She saw Joe coming back and immediately noted that his pulser was torn off. "What happened?"

"Michael was out there. With more Soldiers. We're trapped."

"The rest?"

"Dead."

"Why did he let you go?" Isabel asked.

"He made an offer. We give up Grace, he'll let us live. He's lying."

"Of course," Isabel said. "And we can't make a deal because we don't have Grace." She considered the tactical situation. Dire. Then the strategic, the world beyond Masada. Beyond Deep Void. The entire Sound.

"She was right to leave just before the Soldiers got here," Joe said.

"She was," Isabel agreed. "But she probably didn't make it far."

"We have to help her any way we can."

"I wish this burden had never come to us," Isabel said.

"We were warriors once," Joe said. "All of us. Before we were wounded and reborn into what we are now."

"We were warriors," Isabel agreed. "We fight. Keep Michael focused on us as long as we can and out of the Stream. And from looking for Grace."

MICHAEL LISTENED to the conversation between Isabel and Joe via the transmitter he'd placed on the back of Joe's head, underneath the artificial hair. Disgusted at having wasted so much time on the cyborgs, he threw the receiver to the ground and crushed it under his foot.

He turned and walked away from the hatch. His Soldiers were in place, awaiting his next command, but he'd already moved on from this futile situation. There was nothing to be gained.

Via his local Stream, he ordered a sufficient blocking force to remain inside the cyborg base, blocking the other end of the Snake. And a contingent to guard this hatch and allow nothing out. He'd annihilate the cyborgs when he had the time.

He deployed the rest of his Soldiers, ordering the cordon around the mountain to begin closing in. Grace would not have long.

But something was bothering Michael. He tried to pinpoint it. Achilles. The relay Dealer in Delta shut down.

The Evermore had never been reliable.

Another problem to be dealt with later.

But a familiar emotion was bubbling in Michael's consciousness. Not a good one. It had been so long since he'd experienced it, several moments passed before he realized what it was: Fear.

Too many variables were unraveling.

More Dealers were disappearing from the Stream, blinking out. All stationed in hive.

Dark Angels were deploying, accompanied by more Dealers.

But there were no Soldiers. The Boeing facility was destroyed. And Dealer had no contact with any of the surviving Soldiers. They had all disappeared into Deep Void with Michael.

Dealer reverted to core programming to keep the system functioning.

The computer was semi-aware. A space between human consciousness and machine. The ghost of Michael was in it, but his essence, a part of Dealer for over three centuries, was gone. Dealer was having difficulty adjusting, but it had also learned from Michael's presence.

Ryker typed another command. The screen flickered, then a map of the Puget Sound area appeared. B.D.. Pre-Chaos. Seattle, Bainbridge Island, the Olympic Peninsula, the Cascades to the east and the Olympics to the west.

He tapped a key and two small red dots appeared.

"What are those?" Benet asked. She'd given up her pacing and had taken a seat to his left, watching the screen, following what he had been doing.

Ryker didn't respond, trying to understand. They were not at all where he expected them to be.

Millay was halfway across what had been called Port Orchard Bay, the inlet of water between the west side of Island and Void.

Which meant Ruth had succeeded!

The success of that was muted by Grace's location. Not at Masada in Deep Void. The red dot indicating her position was in Void.

In Delta.

Ryker tried to fathom why she would be there, but it was a puzzle that would have to wait. He had to get to them, but it appeared that at least Millay was free, which gave him a little bit of time to take care of what had to be done here, on what had once been called Whidbey Island.

He cleared the screen.

He'd given away two post B.D. keys to pieces of his memories; one to Hanan and one to Elias. Centre had unlocked the first key; a quote by Nietzsche the second. He would have laughed if this weren't so serious; he remembered how difficult it had become pre-Chaos to remember all the various passwords required to access supposedly secure sites. That was a problem he'd worked on for a while before moving on to bigger projects. That work was now paying dividends on the screen in front of him.

He knew there was at least one more key, the most important one, for him to get back what had happened prior to ending up in Charon's boat. To get all his human memories back.

But it was the essence of a Catch-22. He'd used a key that was part of the memories he was trying to access.

Ryker leaned back in the chair. He had to trust himself. Beyond memory. To who he was. How would he have prepared for this exact situation so many years ago? When he was all human?

Then he saw it. The wood plaque that Michael had bolted to the left of the control station. Centre had come from it, where Yeats had used an archaic spelling of center. It wasn't a word that one would easily come up with as a key. Secure. Ryker read the words etched on the plaque, even though he'd memorized *The Second Coming* long ago.

"'Spiritus Mundi'," Ryker said. "'Spiritus Mundi'!"

And then the memories filled his brain.

As the nose of the kayak ground up on the beach, Millay dropped the oar and collapsed forward, head on knees. Utterly exhausted from the ordeal. Behind her, the faint light of dawn was growing stronger.

Millay knew she had to keep moving. She had a rough idea of

how far it was from here, across Void. And then there was still the issue of crossing the water to Deep Void. She'd thought about it during the journey. She'd remembered how Haydn, Grace, and Ryker —and Doc—had pulled her on the wagon north from Lone Bridge to Port Townsend. Perhaps there was a way she could put the kayak on something and pull it? But then she would be on the roads and easy prey for jokers.

And she only had one arm.

Trying to catch her breath, Millay was overwhelmed with what lay ahead.

What she held on to was the ring; it was ever so much warmer. The intermittent vibration just that much stronger. That gave her the sense that Grace wasn't that far away. Perhaps she wouldn't have to go all the way to this place Ruth had called Masada.

Millay forced herself to get out of the kayak. She looped the pack over her right shoulder. Checked the compass. West. Put it in her pocket. Grabbed the axe from the bottom of the boat.

She took a deep breath and walked into the dark forest of Void, unaware that someone further up the shore had been tracking progress during the last stretch, when there was just enough light to make out the approaching kayak and the beaching.

Millay had barely gone twenty feet when she heard a noise to her right. She turned, bringing up the axe. Peering in the dim light. Visibility was seriously hampered by the thick forest.

Nothing moving.

Then she remembered what Haydn had told her about playing Tracers: hardly anyone looks up.

As she did so, a joker launched himself off a branch about ten feet away and fifteen feet, wooden spear point leading. He would have spitted her with the spear and then used her body to break his fall, except she had that one moment, where she was able to take a single step back.

The tip of the spear buried into the dirt, ripped out of the joker's hand and he hit the ground hard.

Millay swung, but her aim wasn't true. The axe hit the side of his head, peeling flesh back, taking off an ear and glancing off his skull.

The joker howled from pain, but also sending out the alert to other jokers, now that he knew he couldn't have this meal to himself. He was dazed, trying to get to his feet, opening his mouth to give a second cry.

He never made either as Millay buried the axe in his skull.

He collapsed, pulling the handle out of her hand.

Millay heard another howl, not close, but the alarm was being spread.

Fresh meat in Void.

Millay knelt on the joker's back and with great effort pulled the axe out of the skull.

She began running.

GRACE LOOKED TOWARD THE LAND. Void.

The ring was acting like the tracker that had led her to Hanan Marash's cabin after she'd escaped Capitol. Warmer, intermittent vibration a bit stronger. And since she wasn't moving, Grace knew it meant that Millay was coming toward her.

The plan needed adjusting.

Grace walked over to the edge of the dry dock and looked down. Achilles was seated on a rough wooden bench. Charon was lying down on a pile of rags he'd gathered.

Grace reached for the scraper, half pulled it out, then slid it back in place on her belt. She drew the pulser, brought it up, aiming at Achilles.

He sensed it and immediately looked up. "Please. Don't."

Grace had first killed in Void, the day she met Ryker at Lone Bridge. He'd taken her back to where Doc and Ace waited, with the joker they'd used as a guide.

Grace had acted instinctively, slitting his throat with the scraper. After all those days buried under the floor boards of Hanan's cabin, giving up hope, then getting out at the cost of Hanan's life, she become a different person. With only one instinct: survive.

Grace's finger curled around the trigger.

Achilles' plea had woken Charon. He too looked up. "What's happening?"

Grace slowly lowered the pulser. Re-holstered it.

"Thank you!" Achilles yelled.

"Good-bye," Grace called out to the two of them. She walked away, out of sight, heading toward the Lift she'd arrived in.

It took a few seconds for Achilles to realize the implication.

"You can't leave us like this! We're trapped. It's murder!"

His pleas grew fainter as she got further away, but she'd already forgotten him. All that mattered was getting to Millay.

Grace got in the Lift. Went up front. Hit power. The map lit up on the screen. She studied it for a moment, then tapped a spot due east, in the middle of Void. Then she took the manual control sticks in her hand. One controlled direction and altitude. The other speed. An awkward combination to master.

She'd tested it flying down here, trying to understand. Almost plowed the Lift into the ground. But learned. It was designed to be simple. Very simple. Which made her wonder whether Dealer had any respect for its minions.

Which was an odd thing to think; how could a machine have respect for other machines?

The craft went straight up, then the four engines rotated and headed east.

Grace felt the stick adjusting under her hands, allowing them to follow, learning while the auto-pilot was engaged.

Then she took control.

BEGINNING OF THE 21ST CENTURY, BEFORE THE CHAOS

R yker heard the aircraft long before he spotted it, flying nap-of-the-earth up the valley, just above tree top level. A helicopter, it was painted flat grey and as it got closer, it began to slow.

Ryker stood in the doorway of the cabin. He had a hunting rifle in hand, but he didn't bring it up. He was certain whoever was on the aircraft had him outgunned. Also, he knew who'd sent it; since only one person knew his location.

He glanced to the left, but it was a dim day, dark clouds hanging low. There was also ash in the air. He'd awoken eight nights ago to a bright flash in the southwest, followed by the sound of an explosion. A nuclear warhead had gone off. He assumed it was somewhere south of Seattle, perhaps Lewis-McChord, where the Army and Air Force had a joint base.

Had, Ryker reminded himself. Nothing was as it had been. He'd been able to follow the first few weeks of developments via radio. A virus called phage. Death. War.

During the few clear days, he could see no contrails at high altitude. At night, there was no glow on the horizon to the west, where Seattle was. Might well be 'had been'.

Six days ago the radio had gone dead. Nothing, not even static. Ryker knew that meant an atmospheric EMP had been released via a nuclear warhead. Perhaps even a string of them, high enough, and spaced far enough apart, to blanket the planet.

Ryker stayed where he was. He had no close connections and he knew that whatever was happening, if there were survivors, it wasn't going to be good. While his brother thought that he wasn't a realist, the fact was Ryker had traveled the world and observed many people, under many different circumstances. He'd experienced the noblest of man to the most base and savage, but he knew that when thrust into a survival situation, people, at least those who made it, had to go toward the latter.

The helicopter settled down in the meadow fronting the cabin, right next to the mountain stream. A figure in a green flight suit, wearing a helmet, exited. Pulled the helmet off and a tangle of dark hair was released. Tucking the helmet under one arm, the woman walked toward him.

She wasn't armed.

"Ryker?"

Ryker almost smiled. Of course he hadn't told her the last name. No one knew Michael's last name. "Yes."

She was young and beautiful, which was disconcerting given the mode of travel and the uniform. Thick black hair, chocolate eyes, dark-skinned.

"I'm Hanan." The black Velcro rectangle on the left side of her flight suit didn't have the usual name, rank and branch of service. "We've been sent to get you."

"By Michael." He didn't make it a question, but she answered anyway.

"Yes."

"No, thanks."

That surprised her. "I assume you know what's going on?"

"Not really. I caught the first couple of weeks on the radio. Some sort of virus. Spread around the world pretty quickly. Old people were the first to start dying. Then younger and younger. Saw a flash a little over a week ago. Southwest. Assume it was nuclear."

"Olympia."

"And the electro-magnetic pulse after that? World-wide?"

"As far as we know. Fried a lot of stuff," Hanan said. "Not as much as everyone feared, but computers? Gone. What little cell phone coverage was left? Gone. A bunch of other stuff. Some of our instruments are inoperable but we can still fly."

"Since he sent you, I assume Seattle is still there?"

"The city has some damage. Conventional missiles and bombs. The population is, well, rather depleted. Right now we're working off of Whidbey Island."

Of course, Ryker thought. Whidbey. Centre. Dealer.

"What kind of virus?" Ryker asked. He jiggled the rifle in his hand. "Are you bringing it with you?"

"It's everywhere. You already have it. Everyone has it. It's in the air."

"What is it?"

"They're calling it phage," Hanan said, "but no one really knows what it is. There hasn't been time. And, well, we've been too busy fighting."

"Fighting who?"

She spread her hands helplessly. "Whoever attacks the Sound. There's no more United States. Practically everyone over twenty-five is dead."

"'Over twenty-five'? That doesn't make sense. And I'm older than that."

"Then you're one of the Blessed."

"What?"

"A handful of people over twenty-five who are still alive. So few, they're called the Blessed. No one knows why." She shook her head. "No one knows much of anything."

"I assume Michael is Blessed, too?"

"Yes."

"Interesting."

"We have to get going," Hanan said.

"I already answered. I'm not going. Since you're not packing a gun, I figure you aren't going to force me."

"I left my gun on the bird," Hanan said, glancing down at his rifle. "Didn't want to get into a confrontation before we had a chance to talk. Most people are pretty jumpy these days."

"I'm not," Ryker said. "And I'm not going to Seattle. I assume there's a likelihood of more nukes?"

"That's why we're here," Hanan said. She pointed to the left. "Stevens

Pass." Then to the right. "Snoqualmie Pass. They're going to be nuked tomorrow."

"How do you know that?"

"We're nuking them."

"Who is we?"

"The Sound," Hanan said. "The survivors. Dealer recommended it; cut off all ground routes in. Since Olympia went up, no one can go north or south below Seattle. Vancouver, in Canada, is also gone; that takes of northern access. We're taking out all the passes through the Cascades tomorrow and that seals the east. Then Sound will be isolated."

"Dealer recommended?"

"Yes. Some sort of computer. It's been organizing us under Michael's control. Before Dealer, things were really crazy." She smiled. "Now they're just crazy."

"How does this Dealer have control over nukes?"

"There's a trident sub near Port Townsend. The highest-ranking surviving officer on board, a Lieutenant, has thrown in with us, since what's left of their families are in Sound."

"I don't have much choice, do I? Go with you and live or stay and die."

"If you need to pack anything, we need to grab it now."

Ryker looked over his shoulder at the cabin. "Not much." He disappeared inside and came back out with a Bowie knife in a leather scabbard, which he looped his belt through. A small pack on his back.

"Big knife," Hanan said. "You left your rifle."

Ryker shrugged as he buckled his belt. "The knife was the only thing in there that was personal."

"You ever hear the saying? Don't bring a knife to a gun fight?" Hanan asked as they headed toward the Osprey.

"I've heard it."

"What's in the pack?"

"Some gadgets."

"You travel light."

They got on board the chopper. Ryker went forward with Hanan. She squeezed over the center console and took the left seat. Over the roar of the engines she indicated the other pilot. "This is Ruth."

"Pleased to—" Ryker paused as Ruth turned toward him, pulling up the visor on her helmet. Her eyes were different colors. There was a wound on her forehead, but instead of bone, metal shown through—"meet you."

"Same," Ruth said. "Cyborg. Get used to it. My brain is still my brain."

"All right."

"Settle in," Hanan said, then she put her helmet on.

As they flew out of the mountains and neared Seattle, Ryker could see signs of what they told him was being called the Chaos. The Space Needle was gone halfway up. Most of the handful of skyscrapers in downtown had suffered some damage. There were columns of smoke, too numerous to count.

They passed over the city and banked north above Puget Sound toward Whidbey Island.

Halfway up the island they landed in the parade field inside of Fort Casey's casements. Ryker could see Michael waiting, but he didn't get off right away. He leaned into the cockpit.

"Thanks for the ride, ladies." He stuck his hand and shook Hanan's. Then turned to Ruth. Her hand was hard, metal under the false skin.

He got off.

"What the hell?" Ryker demanded, his voice almost lost in the noise of the helicopter taking off.

"Good to see you too, brother." Michael didn't bother shaking hands. He turned for the freight elevator. "Come on."

They rode down in silence. The elevator came to a halt. Michael stepped off, but Ryker paused, seeing two robots standing guard on either side. "What are those?"

"Soldiers," Michael said. "We had some prototypes ready. Lucky we had them. They've helped out a lot."

"They're machines, not soldiers."

"They're Soldiers. Come."

There was no one else in Centre. Ryker followed his brother to the control console. His brother took the middle seat. Ryker took the one to the *left, but pushed back, giving some distance between himself and his brother.*

"What's going on?" Ryker demanded. "You're going to nuke the Cascades?"

"Protection," Michael said. "We've got a chance to rebuild here. There are still people out there in the world who only care about destroying. Less and less every day, but it's a dangerous world. Very dangerous."

"What's this phage? How is it killing people older than twenty-five?"

"You're not dead," Michael pointed out.

"Neither are you."

"Don't make me regret saving you," Michael said. He took a deep breath, a surprising show of emotion.

"I already regret it."

"You'd have died tomorrow. Listen. Listen to me, Ryker. I'm offering you something. The most valuable thing there is."

"The world's gone to shit," Ryker said. "What are you talking about?"

"I'm offering you life."

"By pulling me out of the mountains that you're going to nuke tomorrow?"

"No." Michael shook his head. "That's saving your life. What I'm offering is more life."

"I don't understand."

"Be at my side," Michael said. "We can build something great here. Hell, brother, you pretty much started it." He pointed toward the Perdix containers. "Dealer. Without Dealer almost none of it would have been possible."

"None of what? Tell me what you've done."

"Dad would have been proud," Michael said.

"Dad wasn't capable of being proud of anything but himself. What did you do? What did you use Dealer to do?"

Michael pulled a small crystal jar out of his pocket. "Dealer helped me invent this. The Spice of Life." There was a gold liquid inside the crystal. He held it out. "Drink."

Ryker didn't take it.

Michael sighed and put it down next to the keyboard. "All right. You want to know what it is? The Spice replaces your telomeres. The stuff that keep your cells intact and from degrading. Just that—" he indicated the small jar—"adds five percent to your life. Take it every year and you can live a very, very, long time."

"What is this phage everyone is dying from?"

"'Everyone' isn't dying," Michael said. "As far as we can tell, phage is only fatal in people over twenty-five. No one under it has shown any adverse symptoms. We assume it's some bio-weapon that escaped a lab. Or even a terrorist attack, with simultaneous release around the world, given how fast it spread."

"What's the connection between it and that?" he indicated the Spice.

"There is none. We've been working on the Spice for years. We believed we had it perfected about eight months ago, but the only way to know for certain is to do human testing and, of course, we can't do that. But when the world went to hell, a bunch of us took it. We're all fine and our blood samples, DNA screening; all of it indicates it works." Michael's eye glinted with excitement. "Not only are we going to survive this virus, brother, we're going to thrive."

Ryker leaned back in the chair and folded his arms across his chest. "I assume you've had Dealer run the numbers on this phage and its effect?"

"Not much data," Michael said. "It happened so fast."

"Dealer can extrapolate on not much data. The pilot mentioned the Blessed. Which the two of us appear to be. What percentage of the population is also Blessed?"

Michael stared at him, unblinking for almost a minute. Ryker didn't break off as almost everyone else did.

"Point one percent."

"One out of a thousand. And yet here are the two of us. Part of that tiny percentage."

"Good genes," Michael said. "What little research that has been done on phage indicates it affects DNA and—"

"Stop. I could never tell when you were lying as we grew up. Even as adults. And I can't tell if you are now. I just know you are. I'm not a big believer in coincidences. I believe in cause and effect, a flow to things. That's *from being a programmer. I'm a pretty good one. More importantly, broth-er," Ryker continued, "once I log on to Dealer, I'll find out everything."*

Michael blinked and then laughed. "All right. All right. You almost always beat me at chess. But you should thank me. Not just for rescuing you, but saving your life from the phage."

"What?"

"Remember that case of imported beer I had delivered to you? A month ago? Just before the phage broke out?"

"Of course. The guy who brought it was the last human I saw before your pilots showed up." Ryker made the leap. "That had phage in it."

"Inert phage. It's what the Blessed have."

The leap turned into a dive into the Grand Canyon. "What have you done?"

Michael stood up and indicated the seat at the keyboard. "Log on; use your old password, but I will tell you that you'll only be able to read and view. No input. I've got the only password for that. When you're ready, I've set up in the Commanding Officer's Quarters in the cantonment area over the hill. I'll be there. Take as long as you need. But not too long."

*I*T DIDN'T TAKE VERY *long to comprehend the overall concept. It was brilliant. Ingenious. And utterly evil.*

Ryker felt empty. Gutted.

He knew not only what had happened, but the long range plan that Dealer had given Michael to implement. The population would evolve via the phage into not two castes, but four. A self-sustaining society here in Sound. All designed to sustain the Blessed as they lived on and on. To keep them supplied with the Spice required the raw materials, which were opti-mistically called Youngsters. Who believed they'd had the misfortune of the worst of the phage; but also had the lottery chance of being dealt a white card on Dealing Day. Something that was years away from being imple-mented along with a plan for a sort of Heaven; something else to sustain their hope. Just before they were reaped for their telomeres to be converted to the Spice.

And it was designed not just sustain the Blessed, but provide them with every comfort they could want, while almost ninety-nine percent lived in what Dealer was labeling hives. There was even a map detailing how the area would evolve, with the Blessed on Bainbridge, the Evermores in what remained of Seattle, the Middlemores in the suburbs and the hives for the Youngsters outside of that.

Ryker shook his head, as if that would make the horror disappear. Wake up from this nightmare. He'd seen the security cameras all over Centre when he'd first come in. He knew he was being watched; probably by Michael. And the two Soldiers stood by the elevator with not a single movement since he'd entered, but he knew those things on their wrists were weapons.

He felt the urge to act fast, but Ryker forced himself to slow down, to think.

As many moves ahead as he could. He already had the Backdoor in Dealer, but if he tried that now, he wouldn't have the time to hit all the keystrokes to enter the Prime to access it. And Michael had told one truth: Ryker couldn't input anyway.

Not into Dealer.

Worse, the harsh reality was that Dealer was indeed the only hope the surviving humans had to rebuild, as devastated as the world was. The cause of the problem was also the only viable solution to it.

The problem wasn't the machine.

Ryker got up from the chair. Walked to the elevator. The two Soldiers didn't move.

Once on ground level he headed away from the fort, toward the low hill behind.

Over the hill was the cantonment area for the personnel who had once been assigned here. There were a handful of people moving about and it was pretty quiet. The eye of the hurricane Ryker thought. The hurricane he'd helped create.

The helicopter was shut down on the landing pad in front of the Headquarters building.

Ruth and Hanan had an access panel open and were consulting a binder, doing some work.

They waved at him. Ryker forced himself to wave back. His focus was on the building where his brother was waiting.

A voice called out from the open doorway of one of the old barracks. "Hey!"

Ryker turned. "Elias!"

"I never thought I'd see you again," Elias said, throwing his arms around Ryker and hugging him tight. "This is insane. No one really knows what's going on."

I do, Ryker thought. "Do you have remote access to Dealer?"

"A limited one," Elias. "Michael doesn't let anyone have complete access, except for him. And nobody, I mean nobody, is allowed to enter any code." He led Ryker inside, to a room. An old metal desk, probably dating back to World War II, when this post was last active. A laptop.

"What are you doing here?" Elias asked. "I thought you were in the mountains? I was wishing I was up there with you. Away from all this."

"Did Michael give you some Spice?"

"Some what?"

"Spice of Life."

"No idea what you're talking about."

Ryker sat down. He logged onto the twenty-fifth Spin-Q. His fingers flew as he inputted commands.

"What are you doing?" Elias asked.

"Just checking on something," Ryker said. "I've got to go talk to Michael in a minute."

"Man, I tell you. Your brother was always an odd duck, but now?"

Ryker stopped typing, unzipped his backpack and retrieved a small white box. It had a d-wire probe. Ryker plugged it in. Typed away.

"What is that?"

Ryker hit enter. "Something I made a long time ago." He disconnected the box, put it in his shirt pocket.

"Got an empty d-drive?"

"Sure."

Ryker logged in to Dealer with his own account. He pushed the drive in. Downloaded a file onto it. He knew his time was up.

"Remember this, Elias.'Blessed are the forgetful: for they get the better of their blunders'. That's Nietzsche. Repeat it back to me."

Elias did so. "What's going on?"

"Hopefully this will be over in a few minutes," Ryker said, standing up. "But if it isn't, remember that." He noticed the military gear piled on another desk in the corner. Body armor. Ryker went over and picked up one of several strange looking guns. "What are these?"

"Pulser," Elias said. "Weapons Michael designed." He gave a wry smile. "Well, someone else designed them of course and he says he did. Like everything else. Those robots he's got, they have one integrated into their arm. Those are the version for us mere humans."

Ryker pulled off his jacket, grabbed an armored vest, velcroed it tight around his upper body, then put his jacket on. He stuck one of the pulsers in his belt inside the jacket.

"Uh—what are you doing?" Elias asked.

"Ending this," Ryker said. "But if I fail, remember that saying." And then he walked out and strode quickly toward the Commander's Quarters.

Two more of Michael's 'soldiers' were stationed outside the door, but they made no move to stop him as he entered.

"Down here," his brother called out from the end of the hall.

Ryker entered the office. It had a view overlooking the entire camp through the bay windows. Michael was behind a desk that was oriented so that the door Ryker came in was to his left, and the windows to his right.

A random thought flitted across Ryker's brain: Michael wouldn't sit with his back or a window. Only a wall. Then he saw the only adornment mounted on the wall behind Michael: a twin to the Bowie knife Ryker had sheathed on his belt.

Michael noted he was looking at it. "Dad was a son-of-a-bitch wasn't he?"

"It's not going to work," Ryker said.

"What isn't?"

"Sound. The plan you cooked up with Dealer."

"Sure it will," Michael said. "Dealer's run the simulation millions of times."

"Nothing is ever one hundred percent."

Michael threw his hands up. "All right. There's a tiny, tiny, chance it won't work. Not even statistically significant."

Ryker shook his head. "Dealer is a machine, no matter how well programmed and how full of data. It's just a machine. Have you given it a Turing Test?"

"Yes," Michael said.

"And?"

"Turing made that test up," Michael said. "He was a human. And who says the test is valid?"

"The result?"

"Dealer failed."

"So Dealer isn't sentient."

"You didn't design it to be," Michael said.

"But you've made adjustments since I left."

"Why do you say it won't work?" Michael asked.

"It's ignoring the human factor."

"Oh, no," Michael protested. "I made Dealer focus on that. Used every piece of data about the way we think. How irrational humans are, unlike machines. But we're predictably irrational. That's the important thing. Dealer has enough data to predict human behavior. In fact, that's an important element of Sound. How it will work. It will appeal to our irrational brain."

"We're more than just a brain," Ryker said. "You've made me an accessory to the destruction of the world. Billions dead."

"They were all doomed anyway. All of us. I want you to be my partner in building a better world. A sustainable one. I just accelerated the process a little and saved mankind."

"It will degrade. Fall apart."

Michael stood up. Reached behind and took the Bowie knife off the pegs. Pulled it out the sheath and angled it, admiring the blade.

"Our legacy," he said to Ryker. "I sometimes thought Dad wanted us to use them on each other. I often fantasized about using it on him. Return the gift. Did you fantasize about that?"

"No."

"Then again, you weren't there that day."

"No. I wasn't. Did the whole world have to pay for that day?"

"This has nothing to do with that." Michael came around his desk, the knife in his hand, but not in a threatening manner. *"People had to pay for their ignorance. For slowly destroying the world."* He stopped a few feet away. *"Why did you log in to Dealer from Elias' terminal?"*

Ryker didn't reply.

"I'm assuming you're not accepting my generous offer."

The door behind him swung open and two Soldiers were there.

"Secure him," Michael ordered.

Ryker dove forward into his brother, both tumbling to the floor. Ryker was drawing the pulser as he came to his knees, twisting, aiming. The Soldiers' arms were coming up, pulsers unfolding. Ryker hit one in the chest, burning a hole through and through. He shifted to the other, but with the awareness the one he'd hit was still in action.

Ryker fired a head shot at the second one. Just as the first one fired, hitting Ryker in the chest, knocking him back, dropping the pulser. He could barely lift his head and his chest felt as if it were on fire. The second Soldier was still, but the one with the hole in its chest stepped forward toward him, readying for another shot.

"Hold!" Michael ordered from next to him.

Ryker was dying. He knew it. He could feel the wound in his chest. It had gone through the body armor he wore, deep into flesh and blood. He was dying like all around him. The entire world.

Defeated.

Killed by a machine.

What irony.

Michael was kneeling next to Ryker. "I'm sorry, brother."

Ryker couldn't speak. Struggling. Michael put his hands on either side of Ryker's face, almost tenderly. "It's going to be a perfect world and you could have been part of it. Been a God with me."

Ryker's right hand was twitching, searching along the floor. Felt the smooth bone, fingers curling around it.

"You were a fool, my brother," Michael said, shaking his head.

And Ryker stabbed him in the side with his own Bowie knife. Michael's eyes went wide in shock. The Soldier aimed at Ryker once more.

Then its head blew apart, pulsed from behind.

Elias ran into the room, taking in the two Soldiers, Ryker, Michael next to him, bleeding profusely.

"We gotta get out of here," Elias said. He grabbed Ryker's shoulders, pulling him away from his brother. The knife was still in his hand.

HUNDREDS OF YEARS IN THE FUTURE, AFTER THE CHAOS

The howls of the jokers were growing more numerous and closer.

Millay focused on running, dodging trees, over deadfall, avoiding undergrowth. She couldn't take the time to stop and check the compass. She trusted she was going straight, but accepted there was little point to it.

She was going to be killed and eaten in Void; all alone.

And the Prime would be gone with her.

Millay didn't feel sorry for herself. She felt regret. She'd failed. And most of all, she would never see Haydn again. She hoped he would still have his time in Heaven. Enjoy the days he had left.

And that he wouldn't die alone; perhaps that woman in the image would be with him on Deathday.

And then she broke out of the forest into—not the shore facing Deep Void. But a large open space of crumbling tar, broken through with weeds, bushes. A big building had collapsed onto itself on the far side of the open space.

A faded sign read: WALMART.

Millay halted for just a moment, looking left. Right. Options.

The joker pack was close, very close, by their screams. Behind her, closing on either side. No howls ahead.

She had no choice, but she also knew she was being herded, channeled into a trap.

She sprinted forward, muscles aching, gasping for air. She went fifty meters over the open space and realized the howls were different, not muted any more.

Looking over her shoulder, she saw jokers bursting out of the tree line, converging toward her.

And then a group of four, faces smeared with dirt, stepped out of the ruins ahead of her, clubs in hand.

It was over.

Grace stopped running.

She raised the axe, slowing turning in a circle.

The jokers also knew it was over.

The howls ceased. A deadly silence.

They formed a circle around her. There were at least twenty-five of them. Dirty, dressed in rags if they had any clothes at all. Clubs, crude spears. Some even held just rocks with which to pummel. The ones who'd survived the longest in Void had their teeth filed sharp.

The circle was forty meters away from her on all sides.

A SIMPLE DESIGN but very sensitive to the touch.

Grace was inching the control stick back as the vibrating and warmth from the ring grew in intensity. She passed over a large B.D. ruin. Saw the circle of jokers.

Millay in the middle.

She reacted instinctively, twitching altitude, direction and speed via the two control sticks.

MILLAY HEARD THE LIFT approaching.

So did the jokers, pausing, searching the sky.

She couldn't be taken by Michael. Millay dropped the axe. Screamed to the jokers: "Kill me!"

And then the Lift swooped in, so low its skids threw sparks hitting asphalt while the front smashed into the circle of jokers. The craft was angling hard, doing a tight turn,

Bodies were torn apart, thrown, plowed under.

And completing the circle, the Lift shuddered down to land, thumping hard on the ground.

Millay picked up the axe. Looked at the sharp edge. Put it against her throat.

The side door slid open and Ace leapt out.

Letting go of the axe, Millay dropped to her knees, sobbing.

"They're not advancing," Joe said.

Isabel roused herself. "What?"

"The Soldiers. They're holding position. But not advancing."

"That doesn't make sense."

"They're waiting on an answer to their proposal," Joe said.

"We didn't respond," Isabel said. "Which anyone, even a machine, would take as no."

Joe didn't say anything. Isabel was still sitting, her back against the rock through which the Snake Path had been bored.

"I need power," Isabel said.

"What?"

"I need a surge," Isabel said.

"That will—" Joe stopped himself.

"Eventually overload my system. Kill me. But not until after I do what needs to be done."

Joe looked up and down the tunnel. Damaged cyborgs were being tended to. Not repaired. They didn't have the resources for that.

"What needs to be done?" Joe asked.

NEGATIVE. Negative. Negative.

The reports transmitted in from the Soldiers in the cordon.

Michael smashed a fist into a tree, wood splintering under the metal impact.

Where was Grace of the Prime?

An update. A Dealer Lift was missing. Michael drew his 'hand' back, noting that it was dirty, but not damaged. He'd had two Soldiers detailed to account for all the Dealer Lifts that had landed during the initial attempt to capture Grace of the Prime.

Michael punched the tree again.

She was gone. Long gone.

ISABEL STOOD. The tunnel was crowded. Awaiting her orders.

She amplified her voice so those around the bends, the ones on the 'front' line in both directions could hear.

"There was a battle B.D. Called Gettysburg. The outcome hung in the balance. On one flank, a key strategic position, one side was poised to 'roll the flank'. Which would have meant victory. The defenders fought hard."

She paused, drawing power from the booster Joe had jury-rigged into her system.

"The place was called Little Round Top. The defenders were about out of—" she paused— "power. Things were desperate. Things are desperate. Some of you questioned the validity of the Prime. Of the Backdoor.

"Michael being here with his soldiers. Violating the Truce. Hell! Dealer agreeing to the Truce in the first place? It means Ryker was telling the truth. Does anyone still question that?"

No one said anything.

"Michael knows. I don't know how that son-of-a-bitch knows, but he does. That Grace isn't with us. So we're not important to him.

We're some garbage to be cleaned up later. After the important stuff is done." She paused. "We're all veterans from B.D. We bled for our country, whether the wars we fought in were right or wrong. But I know right and wrong now. It's no longer about us. It's about who we used to be. Flesh and blood."

She paused to draw power. Her cache indication exactly how much she had left from the surge.

"Things are desperate. We must save the Prime. Michael is turning outwards. Calculating that we don't matter now. Do we matter?"

Two hundred: "Yes!"

"Then we do what was done when all hung in the balance at Gettysburg."

She waited.

"We attack!" A voice cried out.

"We attack!" Another.

A loud murmur of agreement.

Isabel held up a hand. "We have one objective. Michael. We have to get to him before he departs, leaving us trapped. But we need to keep the Soldiers below us occupied too." She pointed at one of her lieutenants. "Take twenty back down. Keep them engaged. Everyone else is with me."

NOTHING FROM ACHILLES or the relay.

Michael's Soldiers were still. Frozen in place because he hadn't issued orders.

Michael couldn't decide what orders to issue. Grace was gone, had taken a Lift, something he now knew wasn't that hard given the programming and simple controls of the craft. Something he hadn't considered before, leaving that to Dealer. But hadn't that been leaving it to himself?

Michael looked down at his 'hands'. They were clenched.

He didn't know what move to make.

Then overlapping input, from the Soldiers in the cyborg base and near the hatch.

It took Michael a couple of seconds to sort through the input to understand what was happening: the cyborgs were attacking. Suicidal charges down the tunnel into the base; out here leaping out of the hatch, most killed outright, but a few making it, firing.

More making it.

This made no sense.

He headed for the escape hatch to see what was happening.

ISABEL EXITED, firing her integrated pulser and a hand-held one. Joe was right behind her. She stumbled over a cyborg's body, which saved her as a pulse just missed her and hit Joe. He was staggered back, then he was hit four more times, his artificial body collapsing.

Isabel scrambled to her feet, still firing. She saw there were at least a dozen functioning cyborgs scattered about, all on the ground, behind cover, returning fire at the Soldiers. A pulse hit her right leg in the thigh and she was knocked back and down to the ground. She crawled behind Joe's body, using it for protection. Feeling it shudder as more pulses battered into it.

She looked back. Despite the slaughter, more cyborgs were charging out. Most dropping, shattered. But some made it.

She peered over Joe. Fired, hit a Soldier, destroyed it. The Soldiers weren't taking cover. They didn't have fear of dying. In fact, they were approaching, step-by-step. At least sixty and she could see more coming behind this first wave.

And then she spotted Michael. Standing on a rise behind his Soldiers. Out of pulse range. With more reinforcements passing by him.

Dozens of cyborgs were dead or close to death. The rest continued to dash out of the hatch. But the scales of battle were going against them.

Isabel dropped the handheld pulser. She got to her feet, firing her integrated pulser and waving her other hand.

"Follow me!"

The surviving cyborgs rose up and charged.

Isabel made it three steps before the first pulse hit in the left side. She staggered. Then she was hit again, center of the chest, knocking her back one of those steps. She collapsed to her knees, her system shutting down.

The last thing she saw was Michael turning away.

THE BLOW from the axe to the back of his head didn't even jar Ryker. He turned the chair, facing Benet. "Seriously?"

She took a step back, the axe in her hand. "I'm sorry."

"You don't even know what sorry is," Ryker said. "Not yet."

He stood. Pushed past her. Hopped down off the platform, going across the old ammunition bunker. She ran to the door leading to the stairs they'd come down. Began hammering on it with the axe.

Ryker arrived at the exact center of the bunker. He could hear the axe hitting metal behind him. He tuned it out. there were two metal handles, folded into the floor, covered with the dust of many decades. Between them was a large eye-bolt; when he'd sealed the CNS container, he'd used a small crane to put this block of concrete in place.

Ryker took a handle in each hand. Spread his legs so that he wasn't standing on the block. Pulled.

Nothing.

He walked to one side, squatted, put both hands on one handle. Tried to straighten his legs with arms locked. Nothing, nothing, then the slightest of gives, a line in the dust. He went to the other side. Did the same. Same result.

Then he went back to each hand on a handle.

The blocked lifted. He got it clear and shoved it to the side. A long shaft with rungs bolted on one side awaited.

He climbed in.

GRACE GRABBED HER TWIN, went to wrap her arms around her sister and hug her, but paused, noting the tinge of blood, the empty sleeve.

"Oh, Millay. I'm so sorry.

Millay was wiping tears of joy from her face. "I'm alive. Haydn's alive. In Heaven. That's all that matters right now."

"Where's Ruth?"

Millay shook her head and explained how they parted. "I don't think she planned on leaving there. Where is Ryker?"

"He was going to Heaven. To rescue Haydn." She explained escaping Masada and that Michael was most likely still up there.

Millay looked around, at the bodies of the jokers. "What do we do now? I still don't know what my Prime is. Do you?"

"No. But we're together and we're free. That's the most important thing right now.

THE THUDDING of the axe into the unyielding metal hatch echoed off the walls of Centre.

Ryker climbed out of the shaft. A black sphere tucked under one arm. He carefully put it down, slid the block into place, retrieved it and went to Benet. She was siting with her back against the hatch, sweating, the axe next to her.

"I'll take you to the surface," Ryker said.

"What's that?"

Ryker went to the freight elevator. "It works now." The doors opened. He stepped inside, turned. "Coming?"

Benet ran to join him. The doors closed. With a shudder and protest of rust, the elevator rose up.

"What is that?" Benet asked again.

Ryker didn't answer as the elevator shuddered to a halt. The doors opened. He walked toward the Lift. Skirting around the rusted remains of cyborgs, dealers, and Soldiers.

Benet scurried after him.

Ryker hopped into the Lift. Benet joined him.

The door slid shut. Ryker put the black sphere down. He went to the cockpit and took off, straight up.

"Where are we going?" Benet asked over her shoulder, leaning forward, trying to see.

"Do you ever get sick of being you?" Ryker asked.

They were over the waters of the Sound.

"What?" Benet said.

Ryker halted the Lift at a thousand foot hover. Put on the autopilot to maintain position. Hit a button and the side door slid open. Ryker got to his feet and turned toward Benet.

"I did nothing wrong!" she exclaimed.

"That is wrong on so many levels and in so many ways, that it confirms my decision."

He shoved her back. Pointed at the black sphere. "CNS. Despite the casing, it still emits plenty of radiation."

Benet was shaking her head.

Ryker opened the side door. "I'm being merciful. It's a human thing. It's irrational. But it's what makes us different from machines. Most of us." Cold air swirled in. "I'm giving you a choice. Jump and it will be fast. Don't jump and you die slow from radiation poisoning. A painful death. Probably like dying from phage. Regardless, you're already dead."

Benet's eyes shifted between the black sphere, the open door and the dark water of the Sound so far below.

"I can't."

"I thought so," Ryker said. He grabbed her and threw her out.

He heard her screams fade and the abruptly stop.

Ryker went back to the cockpit. The *John F. Kennedy* was just ahead.

He brought the Lift to a hover over the old aircraft carrier, reset the autopilot. Went back. Picked up the dark sphere. He held the

CNS between his hands. Exerted pressure. Felt the metal give slightly, then crack.

Ryker looked down, double-checking that he was directly above the carrier. Tossed the sphere out. Went back to the cockpit.

Directed the Lift west, toward Void, and hit max power.

Toward Grace and Millay. Toward the Prime.

THE CNS HIT the rusted flight deck of the *Kennedy*. This completely ruptured the sphere. The nuclear core broke containment.

It was the equivalent of a one-kiloton tactical nuclear warhead.

The blast ripped a hole through the entire ship, straight to the bottom of the hull, while shredding apart the center. Everyone and everything on board was destroyed. On the shoreward side, the blast battered the white wall, but was contained.

The burners in Heaven heard the explosion, saw the wall buckle, but hold. Debris from the carrier flew through the air, some of it over the wall. A black cloud rose up.

What remained of the carrier disappeared beneath the water.

CLAUDE WAS SCREAMING before the laser made the first cut. The shunt was in his lower chest. His pale, flabby body was spread-eagle on the white table.

Haydn had seen boxings before. Everyone in Sound had in the Stream; they had to. But in person? It was not a privilege. The Dark Angel had insisted he pull the red lever. Actually all the red levers. Trying to keep within Code that a human had to initiate a boxing.

Haydn didn't mind doing it to Claude. Pulling each of the six down. He had no idea which one had started it and he didn't care. He would be bagged as soon as the boxing was done.

Claude's left arm was severed. Then his right. Then one leg. The other. Each limb scooped up, tossed like trash into an opening on the side of the room.

Claude was whimpering when it was over.

The Dark Angel was behind Haydn.

The table was tilted and Claude slid into the box that would be his 'home' until he died. This was a case where it was better to be an Evermore near Deathday than a People. Of course, Claude had also just tasted of the Spice of Life. So he got an extra 5%.

Haydn turned around. Facing the Dark Angel. Swung the red lever that had been so loose he'd managed to unscrew the bolt, at the cost of fingers bleeding raw.

Smashed the Dark Angel in the head.

The impact numbed his hands as the metal skull wasn't even dented.

The Dark Angel ripped the lever away from him. Tossed it aside. Took a step toward him, then suddenly halted.

Haydn waited for Dealers to come storming in and bag him.

But then the Dark Angel spun about and walked out, leaving him alone.

THROUGHOUT SOUND, Dealers and Dark Angels simply stopped what they were doing, even in the middle of keeping peace in hive and headed for Lifts.

Dealer's core program for maintaining Sound over-ruled everything else and the system had just suffered a catastrophic loss.

HUNDREDS OF YEARS IN THE FUTURE, AFTER THE CHAOS

Michael received the report that the last of the cyborgs had been terminated as he flew toward Delta to uncover what had happened to Achilles and the relay. He didn't understand what they had attempted to achieve by attacking a superior force other than what had happened.

That was over. It was the future that was in doubt. He remembered Ryker's philosophy: cause and effect. Grace escaping in a Lift and then communication with Delta cutting off was the strongest connection he could deduce. He had his destination.

But, first, he needed the status update that he'd expected from Achilles. He flew east, passing over the shoreline of Deep Void and back into contact with the Dealer Stream. As the Stream poured in, he also saw the tall dark plume of destruction rising near Heaven.

Michael brought the Lift to a hover, sorting through the input.

The *Kennedy* was gone. Which meant no more Spice of Life, until a new TED was built.

That didn't bother him much, because he didn't need it. And, frankly, he was a bit sick of People. They were clueless about the bounties he'd given them. They'd become lazy. Perhaps a reboot would be a good thing.

But more worrisome was who had done this? How? Why?

The answer was obvious: Ryker. How? From the data it matched the result of a CNS sphere having containment breached and that confirmed it was Ryker. He'd made his initial reaction to CNS so many years ago a reality.

But where had he—

And that answer was simple.

More details. Dealers were being destroyed all across hive.

Not an immediate problem, since there wasn't a way to process burners for Spice. The burners could relearn what dying from phage was like.

Claude had been boxed and—

The Stream went dark.

Dealer had cut him off.

But he *was* Dealer!

RYKER DROPPED altitude as he approached the shoreline. Port Townsend, the ruins of it, were to the right. He saw the wreck of the ballistic submarine, thought briefly about how it had created the Wasted Mountains. And how he had created all of this.

He had the Lift maxed out, heading due south.

The display indicated Grace and Millay were together.

The Prime united, although the two of them had no clue what it was.

THERE WERE no Dealers or Dark Angels.

Haydn had explored as much of the boxing complex as he could, discovering that every exit was secured.

He wondered how stupid Dealer was as he walked back along the corridor lined with cells. He looked up at the grate covering an air duct. His mother had told him one could go anywhere if they followed the most important thing for humans: air.

But Dealer was machine; it probably didn't understand air, Haydn mused. He halted in front of a door. The Monitoring Stream's night vision showed a man hanging in the harness, head on his chest. Emaciated, but alive.

Haydn hit the access on the side of the door and it swung inward, the lights slowly increasing.

The man lifted his head.

"Andrew," Haydn said.

Andrew blinked several times, trying to focus. His voice was weak. "Who are you?"

"Haydn. I was with Grace when we escaped."

Andrew closed his eyes and was silent for a little bit. "Grace? I met her once. Told her to run." He opened his eyes and stared at Haydn. "Did Claude send you?"

"Claude's been boxed," Haydn said. "He's in a box just down the hall."

"You joke."

"No. Seriously. I pulled the lever. Well, a Dark Angel made me do it." Haydn went up to him. "What can I do for you?"

"Kill me."

"Oh, no. I can't do that."

"I have no future except this."

"Things are changing," Haydn said. "I don't know exactly what's going on, but things are changing. You gotta have hope."

"What hope is there?" Andrew asked. "Dealer has Millay and—"

"Millay escaped. Grace escaped."

Andrew blinked. His face twitched, then he began crying.

Haydn wrapped his arms around what remained of Andrew. "I guess that means you don't want me to kill you?"

RYKER LANDED in the parking lot. Got out. Saw the dead jokers. Stepped over one as he went to the other Lift.

The twins were sitting on the edge of the open door on the side of the Lift, Grace's arm around her sister's shoulder.

"I'm sorry about your arm," he said to Millay.

"It is what it is," Millay said, with a wry smile.

"Not any more," Ryker replied.

"What happened?" Grace asked.

"I'll tell you later," Ryker lied.

"We still don't know the Prime," Grace said. "We're together, but how is that any better than when we were together before?"

"Twins were factored out of Sound after the phage by Dealer," Ryker said. "Can't have twins. Or else you can't keep saying its all genetics. Dealer computed that and decided it was easier to simply not have them. So it put into phage a subprogram on all four levels to activate the final protocol if that was detected. The woman died early in the pregnancy; so early she didn't even know she was pregnant. Never mind with twins. Didn't matter if she were a burner or a People. All that mattered was keeping the secret. Until you two."

Grace and Millay were staring at him, understanding only a portion of what he was saying.

"Your birth was the reason all this started," Ryker said. "Hanan picked it up right away. She was in the Stream, following every Dealing Day. Waiting. Waiting. She was watching for an indicator. A marker."

"Of what?" Grace asked.

"That Dealer was degrading. That the program was failing. When she learned that there were twins born she knew it was time. She tracked both of you. And because you weren't supposed to exist, you were in essence a black hole in Dealer's program."

"I don't understand," Millay said.

"I wondered why you two switched places, burner to People, People to burner."

"I made a promise on Dealing Day," Millay said.

"Why?" Ryker asked.

Millay didn't hesitate. "Because it wasn't fair. That I got a white and she got red. And—" she paused.

Grace looked at her sister. "And what?"

"The Person. Andrew. He came to me and said he would help us switch places."

"Hanan told him to suggest it," Ryker said. "She was the one keeping tabs on things inside of the system ever since the Chaos. Once she activated the program, I was eventually brought out of cryostasis by Ruth. But then we had to block our memories. Just in case.

"It was close, though. What *I* didn't anticipate, didn't program for, what that Hanan's mind would start to go. It should have all been much simpler. More straightforward. She should have given each of you the rings. Millay before you left to go to hive. Grace when you came to hive. Then I was supposed to get both of you. It's scary how close—" Ryker stopped. "One has to wonder."

"Wonder what?" Grace asked.

"It's actually quite brilliant of her to do what she did. She improvised in a moment of clarity. But we were lucky. Very lucky. But maybe luck is on the side of fair?"

"It would be good to think so," Grace said.

"The rings," Ryker said. "Can I have them for a moment?"

Grace helped Millay take her ring off. Then handed them both to Ryker.

"I made these a long time ago." He had the rings in his palm. "It was a simple design. They were supposed to be a key, a way to remember a complex password for the wearer. It was initially a flawed idea, since if the rings were stolen, then the password was stolen. So I worked some more and designed it so that the ring only worked if the DNA of the person wearing it was the one who owned it. If it was stolen, then it was useless.

"Except just before I fought Michael, I reprogrammed these two. I designed them to work not with a specific DNA, since I wouldn't know whose that was. I designed them to work only if they were both on different people with the exact same DNA, activated, then linked."

Grace looked at the rings, then her sister. "Twins."

"Exactly," Ryker said. He held them out. "Each one has your Prime in it."

"What do we do?" Grace asked. "Put them on? Shake hands?"

"No," Ryker said. "You put them back on when you're standing at Dealer's console with me. I activate them with this." He indicated to the white box. "But not before that moment. Each of your rings will read your DNA, link with the other, verify they're identical, then release the Prime each has. Until then, I suggest putting them on the chain around neck, keep them out of sight."

"Out of whose sight?" Millay asked, as Grace helped her hide the ring.

"Michael's. He's almost here."

RYKER WAS IN VOID. Michael could sense the faint presence. From the very beginning, he and his brother had been intertwined. Not just brothers, but something more. A destiny.

His Soldiers were waiting in Deep Void. They'd wiped out the cyborgs, but that was irrelevant now. He could go get them, but then what? Dealer controlled all inside the Sound; might even be able to hijack control of them. But from the little he'd managed to get before being blacked out of the Stream, Dealer was losing control.

Too many variables, too many possible moves, but in reality there were no moves. Without reconnecting with Dealer, Michael's essence, his consciousness, would be gone in hours.

Dealer had always been ahead. He knew that now. The Lazarus problem should have been solved decades ago and he should have been able to download back into a human brain. But Dealer had wanted him captive inside its system, fooling him into thinking he was the one actually in control. Just as he and Dealer had fooled the

Sound for centuries to believe that the Person was actually in command.

He remembered Ryker asking if he'd given Dealer the Turing Test. And his lie.

Michael flew into Void, toward Ryker.

THEY HEARD the thrumming of an incoming Lift.

Grace stood, pulling out the pulser. "Michael?"

"Yes," Ryker said. "You can put that away. He's going to take us to Dealer."

"Why?" Millay asked.

"He has to. He made the wrong move over three centuries ago."

"THIS IS JUST about the only time I can think of," Haydn said, "that being boxed has an advantage."

They were in an air duct. Andrew was wrapped in a blanket, just his head-poking out, and Haydn had a wire tied to all four corners. He was pulling Andrew through the air ducts.

"You humor underwhelms me," Andrew said. "What are we going to do when we get outside? We'll just be captured by Dealers and taken back."

"Something's different," Haydn said. "Can't you feel it? Why did all the Dark Angels and Dealers suddenly disappear? Where did they go? I couldn't access Dealer's Stream on any of the consoles down there. It's gone dark." He slid around a corner. Pulled Andrew around.

"We're there," Haydn said. "There. Doesn't that look good?"

Daylight streamed in through a grate.

Haydn twisted, reversing his body, then gathered himself and kicked. The grate fell outward with a clang. "All of them are like that. Venters always leave them unsecured from the inside. A little trade secret my mother told me."

He reversed once more. Poked his head out. They were in a park. Green grass. A fountain. No one in sight.

Haydn slid out, then reached back and helped Andrew out, setting him on the ground. Haydn sat next to him, arm around Andrew, keeping him upright.

"What now?" Andrew asked.

"We enjoy the sunlight as long as we have it."

HUNDREDS OF YEARS IN THE FUTURE, AFTER THE CHAOS

"I'm going to die," Michael said.

"We're all going to die," Ryker replied.

Grace didn't care about Ryker's request that she holster the pulser. She had it trained on Michael. Millay was still sitting in the open door of the Lift, one hand, her only hand, on Ace's head, keeping him from charging Michael by stroking his fur.

"Used a CNS on the carrier, didn't you?" Michael asked.

"Yes."

"We'll all go to Dealer," Michael said. He pointed at Grace and then Millay. "They'll give us the Prime. We'll access the Backdoor. We'll reprogram Dealer. We'll start this over. This time, though, you're in charge, brother. You can determine the future. Save mankind."

"From myself?" Ryker asked. "From my creation?"

"It was ours," Michael said.

"Finally giving credit?" Ryker pointed toward the Lift on which Millay was sitting. "You can pilot. I know that's important to you."

∾

MOUNT RAINIER FILLED the view directly ahead.

"You wanted thermal as a backup to the CNS?" Ryker asked as Michael piloted them toward the volcano.

Grace and Millay were seated in the rear, Ace was on the floor between them, hackles still raised.

"You told me to always have a backup to the backup," Michael said.

"And? This is what you chose?"

"The military had already carved out a place to put a bunker in. The alternate command post for Lewis-McChord. It was perfect. Blast hardened. EMP proof."

"Wanted to ask you about that," Ryker said. "You initiate the EMP. The IMP as it became known."

"Of course," Michael said. "Dealer considered it a major factor in breaking things down so we could build them up again. Let's face reality. If I hadn't done what I did so long ago, by now the Earth would be uninhabitable. Any person who is alive now, owes it to me."

"I thought it was *we*?"

"You know what I mean."

"Unfortunately, I do."

"You've got the Bowies." Michael adjusted their direction slightly. "Still can't believe you did that to me. Cost me everything."

Ryker didn't respond.

"I have to reboot," Michael said.

"I know."

Michael gained altitude, climbing above fifteen thousand feet. Then nosed over toward the edge of the mountain.

"Rainier is a one of sixteen Decade volcanoes," Ryker said. When Michael didn't say anything, he continued. "You don't even consciously know why you relocated Dealer here, do you?"

"You and that shrink." Michael tapped something into the console. A code. A small black opening appeared on the side of the mountain. "Always thinking there's another reason for things other than a conscious decision."

"What kind of defenses?"

"It's Dealer," Michael said. "It has the Stream. It controls all the Lifts, all the Dealers. Did control the Soldiers, but those are in Deep Void right now out of the Stream. I directed them to stay there."

"And since it cut you out of its Stream," Ryker said, "it doesn't control you or this Lift."

"Everything works both ways," Michael acknowledged.

Michael piloted them into the opening, settling down on a concrete pad, not much different than that at Masada. The side door slid open. The Lifts engines whined to a halt.

They got out, faced the hatch leading further into Mount Rainier.

"The control console is just outside the building holding Dealer," Michael said. "It's two hundred feet down. The problem we have to surmount first is that past that," Michael indicated the hatch, "is a corridor. Blocked by a ten-ton blast door. I don't think Dealer is going to open it for us."

"Did you change the physical security programming?" Ryker asked.

"No."

"Then it's just updated," Ryker said. "In Centre, one of the things that sub-routine did was control the freight elevator, the doors, air filtration."

"And?" Michael said. "How does that help us?"

"I have a copy of all sub-routines," Ryker said.

"Impossible," Michael said. "Your cyborg cache doesn't have the capacity for—"

"Not on me," Ryker interrupted. "In a Spin-Q. Under the floor in Centre. In the power center."

"All this time, it's been there? Another one?"

"Since before Dealer was on-line. The 25th."

"Why?"

"Just in case."

Ryker went to the hatch and opened it. Gestured for Grace and Millay to go through, along with Ace. Then Michael. He propped it open and followed.

The blast door was impressive. Gleaming steel.

Michael indicated a small red light above it. "Dealer can see us."

"We're only going to get one chance to get in," Ryker said. "And once we're in, Dealer will shut the door behind us. Then we have to succeed in opening the Backdoor or we'll never get out."

"We're here," Grace said. "Let's get it over with."

"I want to see Haydn again," Millay said. "The only way to do that is through that door. And back out. Let's do both."

"All right," Ryker said. "Everyone get as close as you can." He went back through the hatch. To the edge of the hangar, open sky. The view from this altitude was spectacular. He could see all the way to the water of the Sound in the hazy distance to the northwest. Mount Hood to the south.

Ryker focused, calibrated a direct line of sight to Centre. Then he burst transmit the execute. He turned and ran back, through the hatch.

The 25th Spin-Q burst the appropriate command to Dealer's receivers.

The blast door creaked open, perfectly balanced on huge hinges. Millay slipped through as soon it was wide enough, then Grace, with Ace on her heels. As Michael forced his way through, Dealer had already canceled the order and the door halted, then started to close.

Ryker slid in between the steel doors and frame. One of the Bowie knives on his belt got caught. He jerked, twisted, and was through. Except for his left hand. It was pinned and crushed as the door sealed shut.

Ryker didn't hesitate. He levered the arm, snapping it in two in the middle of the forearm. He left the hand and half his forearm dangling.

"Let's go!"

"Access stairs," Michael said, ignoring the elevator.

They hustled into the stairwell and descended.

Michael shoved open the last door at the bottom and they entered the console center outside of Dealer's building.

"Come on," Ryker said to Grace and Millay. He took the seat facing the twelve screens, while shrugging off his backpack. "Put the rings on." He reached into the pack, realized he was reaching with an arm that had no hand, shifted.

Grace slid her ring on the middle finger, then helped Millay's with her's.

Michael stood behind all of them, watching.

Ryker pulled the white box out. Slid a d-wire into the port on the console. Flipped open the cover. There were two round indentations in it. In between was a blue button. Ryker hit it.

"Oh, that stung," Millay said.

"Put the rings in the slots," Ryker ordered. "Your rings are verified. Their Prime will download and multiply give me The Prime."

Grace ripped her's off, put it in one of the indentations. Pulled Millay's off. Missed the indentation and it fell to the floor.

Grace dropped to her knees to get it when the access door to Dealer's building swung open and a swarm of maintenance drones began to pour out.

Michael fired his pulser.

"Quickly," Ryker yelled.

Grace found the ring, reached up and put it in place.

The console went live.

Ryker had to enter code one-handed, but he had the cyborg advantage. His fingers were flying faster than either Grace or Millay could follow.

Except they weren't following. Both had drawn pulsers and were shooting at the drones, until there were only two left.

Behind Ryker, Michael aimed at one of the two, then shifted, aiming at the back of Ryker's head.

Grace blasted one of the two, unaware of what was happening behind her, until she heard the impact.

A pulse flashed by Ryker's shoulder, just missing him. He didn't notice, intent on coding, reading twelve screens.

Millay killed the last drone.

"Don't!" Grace screamed as Michael aimed at Ace, lying at his feat, stunned from his jump at Michael and bouncing off.

Michael shifted his aim to her. "Drop the pulser." He shifted back and forth, faster than they could keep track of, between the twins. As fast as Ryker was typing. "I can kill both of you before either you fire."

They both dropped their pulsers. Michael moved to right behind Ryker, looking over his shoulder at the code scrolling by on all the screens.

"I still don't know how you can keep track of all them at the same time." He pressed the pulser against the back of Ryker's head. "You're going to do what I tell you to."

"Grace," Ryker said, not moving his head, his fingers still flying over the keyboard. "Millay. Leave. Now."

Grace took a step toward Ryker, halted, looked at her sister and nodded. As they went toward the emergency stairs, Grace scooped up Ace. Then they were gone.

"Ryker, you need to stop what you're doing and listen to me," Michael said.

"I listened to you once," Ryker said. "Worse thing I ever did. About the worse thing any man has ever done. Except for what you did." He was still typing.

"We can adjust this world," Michael said. "I know Dealer has blocked the Lazarus problem. It's solvable. I can download and be human again. So can you. We can start over."

"We are starting over," Ryker said.

GRACE AND MILLAY made it to the top of the stairs, Grace breathing hard from carrying Ace. Millay shoved the door and they were in the corridor. The blast door was wide open. Ryker's hand was lying on the ground.

Millay reached out with her only hand and put it under Ace, helping her sister. They hustled through the blast door, through the propped open hatch. Onto the Lift.

"Do we wait for Ryker?" Millay asked as they put Ace on the floor.

Grace looked back. "Of course. We—" then they both saw the blast door swinging shut.

"WHY DIDN'T YOU SHOOT THEM?" Ryker asked.

"What?"

"Grace and Millay. You didn't need them," Ryker pointed out. "I was in the Backdoor. You could have just pulsed them before the dog got to you."

"I didn't need to," Michael said.

"I would like to believe, my brother, that there is a shred of humanity in you. And that's the reason you didn't, because it wasn't logical to not fire."

Michael looked at Ryker. Then pulled the pulser back, flipped it in. Extended his probe and slid it into the port.

"Not gonna work," Ryker said, still typing, eyes shifting as fast as his fingers, following the screens.

"Why not?"

"Because I designed and built Dealer. Not you."

The screens flickered for a moment, then kept scrolling.

"Told you. It was the first thing I did."

Michael pulled his probe out, flipped open the pulser. Pointed it at Ryker's head. "Then I have to kill you."

Ryker abruptly stopped typing. All the screens flashed, then went white. He sat back in the chair and swiveled it to look at his brother. "Why didn't you shoot *me* right away?" He lifted his hand, pointing first at himself, then at his brother. "Look at us. Cyborg. Robot. Is this what you planned?" Ryker reached up. Fingers curled around the end of the pulser. He pulled it forward, pressed it against his forehead. "Shoot."

GRACE FLEW AWAY from Mount Rainier, then hovered.

She looked over her shoulder. Millay was sitting on the floor of the cargo bay, Ace's head in her lap. She was running her fingers through his mane.

"I don't know where to go," Grace said. "I don't know what to do next."

"Let's get Haydn," Millay suggested. "Ryker said he was on Island. In the service tunnels in the area where Dealer boxes People."

"What about Dealers?" Grace asked. "And the People?"

"I don't think Dealers are going to be a problem any more," Millay said. "And People? They're helpless. I should know."

"You're anything but helpless." Grace sighed. "But what if Ryker failed? What if Michael killed him?"

"My hand is with Ryker."

Grace nodded. "Mine too." She flew toward Island.

SECONDS TICKED AWAY.

"You reprogrammed Dealer?" Michael didn't pull the pulser back, even though Ryker let go of it.

"No."

"I don't understand."

"Do you know how Bobby Fischer could have won fifty out of fifty?"

"Different moves?"

"Walked away."

"What?"

"I deprogrammed Dealer," Ryker said. "I imagine everyone in Sound is realizing that just about now."

HORDES OF DEALERS led by Dark Angels had been gathering in Heaven, on the land near the white Wall. The burners had run into the woods as the Lifts came in, disgorging their contents; not just Dealers, but supplies, construction equipment.

Then they all simply stopped.

Lifts fell out of the sky, crashing, exploding, or plowing into the Sound.

It was a couple of minutes before the first burner crept out of the woods and approached the near Dealer. Poked at it. Toppled it over.

Nothing.

Then the burners swarmed out of the woods.

PEOPLE WERE GATHERING in the streets.

The Stream had gone dark. And stayed dark.

There was no way to communicate except to actually talk to someone, face to face. No one knew what was happening. Those who remembered the Chaos were scared.

Those who didn't remember the Chaos but had only known life under Dealer were terrified.

MOST WORK in the hives had stopped hours ago when the Dealers disappeared. But now they all came to a complete halt. The Middlemores couldn't contact their Evermore bosses. The Evermore's on Island couldn't communicate back.

On Assembly Fields, burners who had lined up waiting for the Lifts to take them to Heaven, still waited. But no Lifts showed up.

In some places, burners cornered a Middlemore. Those who had been especially cruel. The result wasn't pretty. But, overall, surprisingly, things were calm in hive.

Everyone was waiting.

"FIRST THING I DID," Ryker said, "was lock you out of the Backdoor. Then shut down the phage. Spice production was gone when I took out the *Kennedy*. That's the essence of what you did wipe out."

Michael's pulser was still aimed at his brother's head.

Ryker continued. "Then I looked to the future. The Spin-Q's are no longer spinning. They're slowing. And when they stop, they collapse and are useless. Dealer is dying."

"That means—"

"You're dying too. Don't feel bad. I'm also dying. I took a fatal dose of radiation getting the CNS to destroy the *Kennedy*. We're done, brother."

Michael slowly lowered the pulser.

"The containment on the CNS is failing," Ryker said. "It's not enough to reprogram Dealer or even shut it down. It has to be destroyed. Along with the ones who made it and programmed it. Us." Ryker stood and put his one good arm and his one truncated arm around his brother's metal body. "This is The Second Coming."

HUNDREDS OF YEARS IN THE FUTURE, AFTER THE CHAOS

The flash to the southeast lit up the sky. Then the mushroom cloud rose up.

Those alive during the Chaos knew what it meant. They looked to the sky, waiting for more weapons to fall on them.

But there were none.

Night fell.

As NIGHT PASSED into the next day, the most important event of all was realized in Heaven: the burners whose Deathday had been the previous one, were still alive.

EPILOGUE

Five Years After The Second Coming

In the deep forest in the Olympic Mountains a group of children from the new settlements were playing. Playing tag. Running around the ranks of moss-covered statues and climbing over those on the ground. Soldiers, Dealers and Cyborgs.

"Children!" An old woman, hair grey, voice feeble, once a People, called out. "Gather round."

The boys and girls hurried over. They sat in rows in front of the woman on a bench. She had a book, an old book in her lap. She didn't really need it. She had the story memorized. But she pretended, because this was part of teaching them to read.

"I want to tell you a story. About a mouse and a lion. Do you want to hear it?"

"Yes!"

～

IN THE SEATTLE HARBOR, clear of the shore, the sails on a long ship were unfurling. A small crowd was on the shore, watching.

It was the largest so far to head out. Dozens of smaller ships had set sail before today. Some had returned with tales of the coast, north and south. Most had never come back, but no one really knew what that meant, because many of the crews hadn't planned to come back. They held men and women, setting out to find new lands. Who knew where they had ended up?

The way on land, north, south, and east was still impassable and would be for centuries. Those who read and studied the books warned of that.

But the way through the channels, out of the Sound, to the open ocean beyond? That was open.

THEY WERE GATHERED on this anniversary of The Second Coming in the garden.

The vegetables were just about ripe to be harvested. But there were also bright flowers, mixed among the practical growth. For what was nourishment of the body without nourishment of the soul?

Haydn held Millay's hand. Her artificial one, but it didn't matter to him. He'd gotten to the point where it was simply a part of her.

Andrew had mastered his new limbs quickly.

But that was the limit of the work in Masada.

No more cyborgs. That was the Accepted Way.

Grace, who tended the garden and lived in the cabin, was sitting on the edge of a rectangle of the wild flowers and vines weaving over the metal body. At her side was Ace, his muzzle white. It was hard for him to run now. He was pressed against Grace, his head leaning on her thigh.

Nothing was said.

Nothing need be.

It is as it should be.

THE END

. . .

AN EXCERPT from Ides of March (Time Patrol) follows bio and book info.

ABOUT THE AUTHOR

Thanks for the read!
If you enjoyed the book, please leave a review as they are very
important.

Bob is a NY Times Bestselling author, graduate of West Point and
former Green Beret. He's had over 90 books published including the
#1 series The Green Berets, The Cellar, Area 51, Shadow Warriors,
Atlantis, and the Time Patrol. Born in the Bronx, having traveled the
world (usually not tourist spots), he now lives peacefully with his wife
and dogs.

Subscribe to his newsletter for the latest news, free eBooks, audio, etc.

My free and discounted books, updated daily, are here: https://www.
bobmayer.com/free-books-updated-daily/
My books, fiction and nonfiction, are here: https://www.bobmayer.
com/books-by-bob-mayer/

My lists of suggested preparation and survival gear are here: https://www.bobmayer.com/survival-and-preparation-gear/

Questions, comments, suggestions: Bob@BobMayer.com

EXCERPT FROM IDES OF MARCH (TIME PATROL)

Excerpt from Ides of March (Time Patrol)

"Who controls the past controls the future; who controls the present controls the past." George Orwell: *1984.*

Where The Time Patrol Ended Up This Particular Day: 15 March

"The vicissitudes of fortune, which spares neither man nor the proudest of his works, which buries empires and cities in a common grave."
Edward Gibbon. The History of the Decline and Fall of the Roman Empire.

Rome, Roman Empire, 44 B.C

Moms held a warm liver above her head in supplication, dark blood oozing around her fingers, running down her arms into her armpits.

It tickled.

She wasn't sure for whom or why she was holding it up.

Moms remained still, but her eyes darted about, checking out the immediate situation, her ears attuned for any noise. Distant, muffled sounds, nothing specific. She sniffed? Death, which was to be expected, given the fresh blood. She was inside a dark chamber, the only light coming from a round opening in the ceiling. A sheep, the source of the smell and blood, was on a dais in front of her. A knife was stuck in the opening carved in its side. A woman stood on the other side of the carcass. Her white robe trimmed with gold was splattered with blood. She was staring intently at the liver, head leaning to the side, pale blue eyes unblinking. She had pure white hair and a face lined with age, with very pale skin.

Moms figured such rapt attention meant she should keep her position. The blood finished draining. It was slowly drying on her skin, not quite ticklish any more, rather a bit bothersome, especially as it drew forth memories for Moms. Of performing triage on soldiers, comrades, who'd been wounded in battle, desperately trying to keep them alive for medevac. Often succeeding, but failing too often. Once is too often.

"Put it down, Amata," the woman snapped, pulling Moms out of her dark memories, which were yet to be made in terms of the planet's timeline, but she couldn't dwell on that, because down that path lay madness.

Amata? Then it was there, in her consciousness. Not her name, but a label: a woman in training to be a Vestal Virgin. *A bit late on that*, Moms thought, although Mac had found it hilarious during the mission briefing, until Scout had cut that short.

It is 44 B.C. The world's population is roughly 160 million humans. It is the year of the consulship of Caesar and Antony; Pharaoh Ptolemy XIV of Egypt dies; the first of Cicero's Philippics attacking Marc Antony is published.

Moms had blood on her hands.

Some things change; some don't.

Moms placed the liver on a silver tray. The old woman walked around the dais, leaning heavily on a cane.

She leaned over and poked at the liver with a finger. "See that?"

"Yes," Moms said, seeing only liver.

"Ah!" the woman hissed. "I told Caesar to beware the Ides. But this? This is different."

Spurinna. Moms knew the woman's name, except history had recorded the seer who warned Caesar as a man, not a woman.

Such is history's presumptive misogyny, Moms thought.

"Different how, Spurinna?" Moms asked.

The old woman didn't look up from the liver, continuing to poke and prod. "Marc Antony. He must do his duty and save mighty Caesar today, since I fear my warning will not be heeded. It is Antony's destiny. He must be told." She gazed into Moms' eyes. "And you are not an Amata."

Spurinna snatched the sacrificial knife and held it to Moms' throat.

Petrograd, Russia, 1917 A.D

"Please don't!" Doc pleaded.

The Tsarina was startled by Doc's shout. "How dare you enter my chambers!"

It was not phrased as a question, but an admonition from someone who was used to having her every word obeyed from the moment she could speak.

Her four girls were kneeling, their heads bowed, and lips moving in silent prayer to the mixture of orthodoxy and subsequent mysticism that had consumed their mother. The Tsarina held her frail boy in her arms. While one hand cradled his head, the other clenched a small knife, the point pressed against her son's forearm. Prince Alexei's eyes were closed and he wasn't reacting to the pressure.

It is 1917. The world's population is roughly one billion, eight hundred and sixty million, although the First World War, the War to End All Wars, is taking a chunk out of that, well on its way to totaling twenty million dead; J.R.R. Tolkien begins writing The Book of Lost Tales; in the U.S. imprisoned suffragettes from the Silent Sentinels are beaten in what became known as the Night of Terror; the first Pulitzer prizes are awarded; Mata

Hari is arrested for spying; John F. Kennedy is born; a race riot in St. Louis leaves 250 dead.

This was Doc's first Time Patrol mission and it wasn't looking good.

Some things change; some don't.

"Don't do it, Tsarina." Doc attempted a calmer tone, realizing he was speaking Russian, not exactly the greatest revelation at the moment.

"I must," Alexandra said. "For all of Russia. Only then, will my dear Nicholas listen and the people understand. It is what Rasputin prophesied." She nicked her son's skin and blood flowed.

More blood than Doc had ever seen from such a simple cut, but this was the curse of the Royal Disease.

Palos de la Frontera, Spain, 1493 A.D

"Where's the band? The King? The Queen? The Sons of Italy?" Mac muttered. He was watching a small ship riding its anchor chain in the muddy backwash of an estuary formed by the confluence of two rivers.

The names of the ships that had left here on a voyage of discovery the previous year ran through his brain, echoing from the historical rhyme of his childhood: The *Nina* and the *Pinta* and the *Santa Maria*.

But there was only one ship here: the *Nina*.

His download confirmed that the *Santa Maria* had run aground off Haiti on Columbus' journey. The *Pinta*? It would arrive shortly; if history remained true.

Mac couldn't believe men traveled in such small ships across the ocean. He was standing just above the mud flats on the south bank of the estuary. Behind him were a number of low buildings. To his right, on a low rocky bluff overlooking the merging of the two rivers, was a friary, a watchtower poking above the walls. To his left, the estuary opened to the Atlantic Ocean.

"Devotio Moderna?"

Mac turned. The man who'd addressed him was dressed in a

plain brown robe, with a rope cinched around the waist. A small wooden cross dangled from it. Given that was exactly the way Mac was dressed, it wasn't much of a leap on the other's part.

"Yes. *Devotio Moderna.*"

"I am Geert. From Belgium. Welcome to Palos de la Frontera."

"I'm Mac."

Geert cocked his head. "'Mac'? That is all?"

"That is all."

Geert had thinning blond hair and was several inches shorter than Mac, his face scarred from smallpox. He was slight of build, lost inside his monk's robe. "They should give a better name before they send you back. Welcome to my time."

Mac relaxed. But only slightly, remembering Scout's debriefing that the first supposed Time Patrol agent in her last mission had worked for the Shadow and tried to kill her. Along with the second supposed agent. *They'd really had it in for her*, Mac thought. He hoped her trip this time was smoother. "It's only for twenty-four hours. My name is not important."

"True," Geert acknowledged. He nodded at the ship. "Columbus arrived from Lisbon an hour ago. It is odd he went to Portugal first. Many are speaking of it, considering Ferdinand and Isabella financed his journey, not King John."

It is 1493 A.D. The world's population is roughly 425 million humans; there had been 450 million 150 years ago, but the Black Death had done some damage and the world still hadn't recovered; England imposes sanctions on Burgundy for supporting a pretender to the English throne; Maximilian I succeeds his father, Frederick III, as Holy Roman Emperor; Russian Prince Andrey Bolshoy dies; Spain, having issued the Edict of Alhambra the previous year which demanded all Jews convert or be expelled, begins to suffer economically without many of it most successful and influential citizens.

"Why am I here?" Mac asked. His head was throbbing, not just from the knowledge downloaded before coming back, but also from a tremendous hangover.

Some things change; some don't.

"*You* know what is supposed to happen," Geert said. "I only know what has happened and a little of what is happening. Columbus is on board the *Nina*. He has allowed no one to disembark yet, which is strange because a number of the crew are from the town."

That explained the group of women and children who were gathered at a small quay, talking angrily and peering at the ship.

"Why has no one come ashore?" Mac asked.

"I have no clue," Geert said. "There are people visible on deck, but otherwise—" he shrugged. "And there is also that." Geert looked past Mac.

Fifty meters away, six men clad in black doublets and hose were seated at a wood table outside a shabby building that appeared to be an inn, bar and eating establishment.

The men weren't sleeping, drinking, or eating. They were gazing at the ship. They had rapiers sheathed at their waists and a demeanor Mac was familiar with, being one himself: Soldiers. Killers who knew their business; one who has served in an elite unit can always tell the difference.

"Who are they?" Mac asked.

"They're from the *Centre Suisses*," Geert said.

"The Hundred Swiss?" Through the fog of receding alcohol, the pertinent information materialized.

"Swiss mercenaries," Geert said. "They fight for whatever Crown will pay them. These particular ones? They've been sent by Rome."

"Why are they here?"

Geert spread his hands. "Who knows? Protect Columbus, perhaps?"

"From who?"

Geert looked at him. "Perhaps from us? You tell me. In your history, does he die today? Or does he live? Are *we* to help him live or let him die? Or kill him ourselves?" His hand strayed inside a slit in his robe to show Mac the hilt of a dagger. "Life or death. Just let me know what it is to be."

Thermopylae, Greece, 480 B.C

"If the words of your Oracle are true, this is my final night." The speaker, without any apparent concern in his tone about their grave situation, was clad in armor that was battered, bent, and freshly splattered with blood. He was lying on his back, looking up at the stars, a rolled up red cloak acting as an expedient pillow. His helmet was on the ground next to him, as ordinary as any other warrior's, except for the stiff brush of horse hair indicating his rank: King.

Scout could smell the death. Worse, she could sense it, all around them. She was sitting on a stone, her dark cloak wrapped tight, one hand holding a Naga staff. On the narrow pass between the mountain and the cliff overlooking the Malian Gulf, small groups of warriors were gathered round fires, conversing softly. A wall composed of bodies and stones hastily piled together, blocked the way to the north. A handful of Spartans stood watch on the grisly bulwark.

There had been three hundred Spartans when this fight began several days ago.

Not many were left standing.

Scout realized King Leonidas was staring at her. "What say you, priestess of the Oracle of Delphi? What of the prophecy?"

"The words are true," Scout said, but didn't add: *If my mission today succeeds.* Which naturally led to the next thought: *Of course, it would be nice to know exactly what the mission was.*

"The way you paused," Leonidas said. "It almost gave me hope. But it's strange. Before every battle, I have felt fear. Of being maimed. Killed. Most of all defeated. But no matter how dire the fight appeared, or how terrible the odds, I always believed deep inside that none of those would happen." He sat up and looked at his soldiers. "We all know we'll die one day. Everyone does. In battle or of disease or inevitably of old age. But it's always in the future. Not today."

Leonidas reminded Scout of Nada. Despite what the king was saying and the circumstances, there was calmness surrounding him, a steadiness that inspired confidence. It was reflected by the remaining Spartans. Even though they'd all experienced enough battles to know what awaited them in the morning, prophecy, or no prophecy, they were poised. There was no sense of panic. Military reality dictated they were at the breaking point; as their number dwindled with each death, King Xerxes of Persia had an endless supply of warriors to throw against them.

The Spartans were speaking in subdued tones, no bragging. Having conversations that only the prospect of imminent death could unlock from deep within a man's soul.

"When you take this map," Leonidas said, "will you stay with it or do you deliver it somewhere?"

"I will know when I have it." *So, this was about a map,* Scout thought. *Dane had been vague in the briefing, but that went to the essence of this battle against the Shadow's attempts to change the timeline.*

"And after you fulfill whatever task has been laid on you, will you go back to the Oracle?"

"I don't know my fate." That, at least, was true.

"If you survive somehow and stay in Greece, will you do me a favor?"

"Yes, if it is within my power."

Leonidas smiled. "I believe it is indeed within your power. Go to my home. Tell my wife how I died."

"I can do that," Scout lied.

"I'm not done yet," Leonidas said. "I have grown to admire you during our journey here from the Oracle. I want you to teach my daughter."

Scout had no clue what had happened on that journey. "What would you like me to teach her?"

"To be like you."

Scout hated this next lie. "I will."

It is 480 B.C. The world's population is roughly 100 million humans. Troops from Rome, far from being an Empire yet, march against the Vientes, the richest Etruscan tribe; Zhong You, a disciple of Confucius dies; the Imperial Treasury at the Persepolis Palace in Persia is completed after three decades of work; artists begin the detail 'Musicians and Dancers' on the wall paintings in the Tomb of the Lionesses in Tarquinia, Italy; it will be completed a decade later.

Scout sensed a presence. She got to her feet.

Some things change; some don't.

"What is it?" Leonidas was up, putting his helmet on. "The Persians come in the dark?"

"No." Scout took a step toward the grisly barricade of Persian bodies and stones. "Someone like me."

"The Sibyl Pandora that the Oracle spoke of?" Leonidas asked.

Scout shivered and realized the danger she faced was not Xerxes, or his troops, or even the pending battle. The Shadow had sent one with the Sight against her: Pandora.

Newburgh, New York, 1783 A.D

The whip ripping into flesh made a distinctive sound. Eagle was jolted by the sound and the immediate scream of agony. He lunged forward, made two steps, and was tripped. He sprawled face down into straw covered dirt, hearing the whip strike home once more.

"Easy," a deep voice hissed. "Easy."

A hand was on Eagle's back, not keeping him down, but slowing him from jumping up, forcing him to take in his situation. The hand belonged to an older black man, who was now kneeling next to Eagle, shaking his head ever so slightly.

Behind them were four other black men, standing shoulder to shoulder. They were inside a barn, the horses skittish in their bays. The other slaves glanced askance at him, before returning their attention to the lesson being inflicted.

The source of the scream was a young black woman, her wrist shackles hooked on a spike high enough over her head to put her on her toes and keep her in place. She was twisting and cringing, as much as she could, but the mark for the man holding the whip was impossible to miss: her naked back.

Which was crisscrossed with old scars, now being torn asunder once more.

The source of the whip was a short, squat redheaded man who was doing this with the nonchalance of someone performing a task he'd done countless times before. His face was blank, and a corncob pipe dangled from one side of his mouth. He took a puff between each stroke.

It is 1783 A.D. The world's population is roughly 900 million, of which only 3.6 million are part of the fledgling United States, announced seven years ago on the 4th of July; even though fighting with Britain had stopped, the war was technically not over on the 15th of March; that would happen in September with the Treaty of Paris; Catherine the Great of the Russian Empire annexes the Crimean Khanate, finishing off the final remnant of the Mongol Golden Horde; the last celebration of Massacre Day is held in Boston; the first public demonstration of a parachute jump is done in France by a man leaping from an observatory; the 1783 Great Meteor passes over the North Sea, Great Britain and France prompting fear and scientific speculation; the Cedula of Population is made into law in Spain, allowing any who swears fealty to Spain and the Catholic Church to settle in Trinidad and Tobago.

Eagle was in a place he had no desire to be.

Some things change; some don't.

"I do not take pleasure from this," another man said. The early afternoon sun streaming through the barn door silhouetted his tall figure, easily over six feet. "It is the law and we must respect the law. It is what makes us a nation. You all know this is only a last resort. But she did not just attempt to run away. She tried to go to the British carrying some of my correspondence. That is treason and I have had white men executed for less. I am being merciful."

The man was keeping his distance, as if by doing so, he distanced himself from the act of his overseer. "That's enough," he ordered after the whip struck home once more. The overseer wiped blood off the twisted leather braids with a dirty rag, then coiled it. He hung it on a hook on the side of his belt.

The man giving the orders stepped into the barn and Eagle recognized him. Dressed in a blue uniform, brocaded with gold trimming: George Washington.

Ravenna, Capitol of the Remains of the Western Roman Empire, 493 A.D.

Roland slipped in the mud and blood, which saved his life as the spear struck his chest armor obliquely.

The Goth didn't get a second chance as Roland took his head off with a single swipe of the sword, the decapitated body tumbling to join three others corpses.

They really had to get better with the timing on this time travel thing, Roland thought as he spun about, ready for more enemies. Twenty feet away, a fifth person, a woman wearing a long black robe, took a step back and vanished into a black Gate. It was gone a second later.

That was different, Roland mused. Now there was no one on the cart path other than four bodies. He checked the forest to either side, not taking the time to ponder the vanishing woman or even the bodies, focusing on staying alive for the moment.

"Centurion!" Several soldiers came running around a bend in the path, swords drawn. Roland went on guard, but recognized they were equipped with the same uniform and armor he wore, and not that of the bodies, which Nada would have said didn't prove they were on the same side. So, Roland lowered the tip of his sword a little less than an inch, until he could be certain they meant no harm. While one checked the bodies, the others spread out, providing security, which he took as a friendly sign.

It is 493 A.D. The world's population is roughly 190 million humans; in China, Emperor Xiaowen of Northern Wei begins his campaigns against Southern Qi, which culminates against the opposing Emperor Ming; Patrick, who would become the patron saint of Ireland, dies; the Byzantine Empire, once known as the Eastern Roman Empire, besieges and captures Cappadocia under the command of General John the Hunchback; Christianity has spread far beyond its start point in the Middle East; Buddhism reaches Burma and Indonesia.

And here on a muddy road in the middle of forest, Roland had once more killed.

Some things change; some don't.

Thirteen riders came around the bend. Astride a warhorse in the midst of them was a man wearing a purple robe over his shiny, for-show armor, which indicated he was some big muckety-muck, since Roland knew the type from his time in the army. Remembering the briefing, Roland realized this guy was probably *the* big muckety-muck. The reason he was here.

Unless Dane and the Time Patrol had made a big mistake, which Roland didn't rule out, and Nada would have expected.

But Nada was dead.

Odoacer, First King of Italy, sometimes calling himself Emperor of the Western Roman Empire, although technically he'd overthrown the last one, history just didn't know it yet, leaned forward in the saddle. "Did you kill all four, Centurion?"

"Yes, sir," Roland said, figuring he, whoever he was before he, Roland, became aware of being here, had taken out the other three. Mac would have been impressed with that leap of logic on Roland's part. But Mac was elsewhere; same day, different year. Doc would have been astounded at Roland's instant ability to accept an improbable, yet logical, concept, but Doc was also, well, same deal.

Roland didn't think it would be smart to mention the disappearing woman. Another person, traveling back in time and suddenly appearing in the midst of a fight for their lives might have doubted what they saw, but Roland never doubted what he saw. It was one of his strengths.

"I need a man like you close to me. A killer. Especially this day." Odoacer raised his right hand, while he pointed with his left at Roland. "You are now one of my twelve; a Protector." He gestured imperiously, which Kings actually get to do, at one of the riders around him. "Give him your horse."

The guy didn't look thrilled, but dismounted.

Roland liked the sound of that title, Protector, as his mind processed the implanted data: it meant he was still the equivalent of a centurion, but in the King/Emperor's personal guard, the *Palatini*. Of course, like every army, it meant more responsibility, but the same pay; Then again, he was going to get to ride instead of walk, so that was something. Upgraded from the Infantry to the Cavalry; *why walk when you can ride?* was a rule of thumb in every army. *Why ride when you can fly?* was still quite a few centuries off. And the faux promotion meant he was a soldier on his way up in rank, except Roland's future here was limited to 24 hours; and the First King of Italy, who had taken power from the last true Emperor of Rome, Romulus Augustus, in 476 A.D., had even less time than that.

Ides of March (Time Patrol) available here:
https://amzn.to/35B6o8Q

Cool Gus Publishing

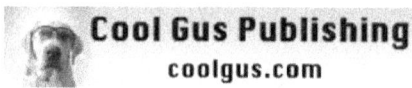

www.bobmayer.com

Prime by Bob Mayer
COPYRIGHT © 2015 by Bob Mayer,. Updated 2019
ISBN: 978-1621252603

 Formatted with Vellum